WITHDRAWN

SEVEN
SORCERERS

SEVEN SORCERERS

CARO KING

ALADDIN

New York London Toronto Sydney

ALADDIN

An imprint of Simon & Schuster Children's Publishing Division
1230 Avenue of the Americas, New York, NY 10020
Copyright © 2011 by Caro King
Originally published in Great Britain in 2009 by Quercus UK
Published by arrangement with Quercus UK.
First Aladdin hardcover edition May 2011
All rights reserved, including the right of reproduction
in whole or in part in any form.
ALADDIN is a trademark of Simon & Schuster, Inc., and
related logo is a registered trademark of Simon & Schuster, Inc.
For information about special discounts for bulk purchases, please contact
Simon & Schuster Special Sales at 1-866-506-1949
or business@simonandschuster.com.
The Simon & Schuster Speakers Bureau can bring authors to your
live event. For more information or to book an event contact the Simon
& Schuster Speakers Bureau at 1-866-248-3049 or visit
our website at www.simonspeakers.com.
Designed by Lisa Vega and Tom Daly
The text of this book was set in ITC Esprit.
Manufactured in the United States of America 0411 FFG
2 4 6 8 10 9 7 5 3 1
Library of Congress Cataloging-in-Publication Data
King, Caro.
Seven sorcerers / by Caro King. — 1st US ed.
p. cm.
Summary: When eleven-year-old Nin Redfern wakes up one rainy Wednesday
morning to discover that her younger brother has ceased to exist, she must venture
into a magical land called the Drift where she grapples with bogeymen, tombfolk,
mudmen, and the spirits of sorcerers to try and rescue him.
ISBN 978-1-4424-2042-7 (hc)
[1. Brothers and sisters—Fiction. 2. Missing children—Fiction. 3. Adventure and
adventurers—Fiction. 4. Fantasy.] I. Title.
PZ7.K5743Se 2011
[Fic]—dc22
2011001432
ISBN 978-1-4424-2044-1 (eBook)

For Kevin

SEVEN
SORCERERS

PART
1

THE THIEF
OF YOU

The Boy Who Never Was

Nin had never liked Wednesdays, but this one took the cake. On this Wednesday she woke up to find that it was pouring rain and that her little brother had ceased to exist.

The first thing to hit her was the rain. As she had forgotten to close her window the night before, the heavy drops bouncing off the windowsill got her right in the face. It wasn't the nicest way to wake up.

With a yell, Nin sat up and glared at the window. Then she scrambled onto her knees and leaned over to struggle with the drenched curtain and the stiff catch. It took ages to slam the window shut, with the storm on the outside where it was supposed to be.

She rubbed her wet face with the sleeve of her pajama top and then peered out of the window at the mass of gray clouds, or at least what she could see of them through the water pouring down the windowpane.

"Great!" she muttered. "Just brilliant. It's got to be Wednesday!"

She looked at her big, purple clock, which told her that it was just less than half an hour until breakfast, then flopped back into bed.

And then the second thing hit her. She frowned into her pillow.

Toby should be up by now. He was always up first, even though he didn't have to go to school as early as Nin. She would hear him every morning, padding to the bathroom and then back again to play with his toy of the moment.

She rolled over again and scowled at the clock. It didn't make any difference. Toby should be up and he wasn't. Nin sighed and replayed the Sacks in the Cellar incident in her head.

She had been sitting in the sun the evening before, reading her favorite book, when Toby had appeared at the door of the conservatory with his tattered monkey tucked under one arm as usual. He stood there for a while before he plucked up the courage to come in and hover by the arm of her chair.

"There's something in the cellar," he said.

With a groan, Nin looked up from her book. "What?"

"In the cellar," Toby whispered. "Something horrid."

"It's horrible not horrid," snapped Nin. "Horrid is a baby word." She didn't think it was really, but he was being annoying so she made it up.

Toby just stood and looked at her in that way he had when he wanted her to sort something out for him.

"Tell Mum then." Nin turned over a page in her book. She had just got to a good bit, the one where the heroine finds her way into another world.

Toby went on looking at her. He had fair hair and eyes that were so blue they were almost purple. Nin on the other hand had ordinary brown hair and ordinary blue eyes. She felt a stab of irritation.

"Look, I'm busy, okay? Tell Mum about it."

"She's at the store."

Tuesday was her mother's shopping day. Nin rolled her eyes.

"Tell Granny about it then. Or Grandad."

"Granny's in the garden and Grandad's . . ." he paused ". . . asleep." What he meant was that he was scared of Grandad.

Nin threw her book down on the table and stood up. "Okay!" she said savagely. "But it'd better be really REALLY worth it."

It wasn't. There was nothing in the cellar but an old table covered in dusty tools, Grandad's collection of wine bottles, some empty paint cans and a couple of lumpy-looking sacks crouching in the corner.

"So," snapped Nin, "where's this *horrid* thing then?" She could feel herself getting into a bad mood. The sort of mood that her grandmother called a "pet" and her mother called "growing grumbles." Personally Nin didn't see why being eleven should make her any more bad-tempered than being ten.

Toby pointed at the sacks. Nin sighed.

"They're sacks, moron-baby. Just empty, dirty old sacks."

Nin noticed that she didn't feel at all like going over there into the dark corner to shake the sacks and show him just how empty they really were.

"Go on," she said, "get back upstairs and stop bothering me." And that had been the end of that.

Now, lying in bed with the rain pouring down the window, Nin sighed. Perhaps Toby had been having bad dreams all night. Or hadn't been able to go to sleep at all because he was scared of the bogeyman. Or something. Suddenly she was feeling guilty about the beastly Sacks in the Cellar incident. Great. Wonderful.

"I should have been nicer," groaned Nin out loud.

"I should have thrown the rotten sacks away and gone around the cellar to show him it was empty."

She got out of bed, pulled on the green dressing gown that she hated and padded up the hall in her bare feet. Toby's room was at the end of the house, past the box room where they kept all of Daddy's old things. She pushed the door open as quietly as she could. She stared.

The room was tidy. In fact it was more than tidy, it was bare.

She stared at the expanse of floor, which wasn't covered in toys and yesterday's socks. Then she stared at the chest of drawers, which didn't have Toby's giant-sized panda clock, his Winnie-the-Pooh drawing pad and crayons or any number of picture books on it. Next she looked over at the bed. It was empty. On top of that it looked like it had been empty *all night*. The duvet was stretched smoothly over the unrumpled sheets and the undented pillows. Nin frowned. The duvet didn't have Toby's Spiderman cover on it either.

She ran across the room and pounced on the wardrobe, yanking it open. There were clothes inside, which was what she had expected. But they were Grandad's old jackets, which wasn't.

Her insides did a flip-flop and she felt herself go cold all over. She took a deep breath and looked around, half thinking she would see Toby giggling in a corner. She didn't.

There was nothing for it. Nin pushed the wardrobe door shut again and headed for downstairs.

She hated downstairs before breakfast. She normally didn't go anywhere near it until her mother had got up and started the toast. Before toast, downstairs was empty and dark and smelled of old nighttime. After toast it was warm and cheery and smelled of . . . well . . . of toast.

Today, Wednesday (of course), everything was different. Her mum, Lena, wasn't up yet. She wouldn't be up for at least another twenty minutes.

Nin stood at the head of the staircase and looked into the darkness below. She could already see that Toby wasn't in the living room because the door, which was at the foot of the stairs, was standing open onto even more darkness.

She pressed the switch, flooding the hall with light. Then she hurried downstairs, doing a U-turn for the kitchen and taking care not to look at the space under the stairs.

When she was as small as Toby, Nin used to think that THINGS lurked in the space under the stairs, hiding beneath the coats. It looked like the sort of place where THINGS would lurk. It was something to do with the way shadows hung around even after the light went on. She hardly ever thought about it now, but this morning she was feeling edgy, and the memory came back to her so strongly that she felt her skin prickle. She hurried past and burst into the kitchen.

In the dim, rainy-morning light, Nin could just make out the humps of the toaster and the kettle on the work surface, and the blank faces of the cupboards. No Toby.

"You're up early," Lena said, appearing in the doorway behind Nin and clicking on the light.

Nin jumped and spun around. "So're you."

Lena shook her head and pushed a hand through her tangled hair. She wasn't dressed yet.

"Didn't sleep well." She sighed. "You?"

"Rain woke me," said Nin, which was true.

Lena went over to the work surface, "Since we're both here, how about I start breakfast?"

Without waiting for an answer she filled the kettle and put it on, then popped four slices of bread in the toaster and went into the cupboard for the teabags. Over her mother's shoulder Nin saw that even the big box of Toby's favorite cereal had disappeared.

"Mum, is Toby okay?" she asked anxiously.

Wednesdays were always bad, but this one was making a bid for the All-Time Most Horrible Day Ever.

"Who?" asked Lena.

After denying all knowledge of her second child, Lena sat at the breakfast table to wait for the kettle to boil.

"You know," said Nin, wishing her stomach would stop turning somersaults on her. "Toby? Your son. About so big." She felt like she had taken a wrong turn into somebody else's life. Bewildered didn't begin to cover it.

Lena laughed. "I'm hardly in the frame for any more offspring. I've got my hands full enough with you! And in case you hadn't noticed, I'm still single. Is this your way of telling your old mum to go out and get a life?"

Nin winced. Her father had been killed in a horrible accident involving a bull and the Park Road underpass three years ago. It was still hard to think about.

"No, Mum," she said sympathetically. "I just . . ."

The moment was broken by the click of the kettle as it boiled itself to a standstill. Lena got up to make the tea just as the toast pinged up in the toaster. Nin hurried to get the marmalade and made a fuss about buttering the toast so that Lena would forget what they were talking about.

By the time Nin was washed and dressed, there was still no sign of Toby. She kept waiting for him to appear from some hiding place and carry on as if nothing had happened. After all, four-year-old kids didn't just cease to exist!

Once she was at school, her brain was so taken up with the problem of Toby that she paid no attention at all in English, which was usually her favorite lesson, and got scolded twice for not listening in geography.

Everything Nin thought of didn't work. He wouldn't be upstairs in the second-floor flat where Granny and Grandad Covey lived because he would have come back down again by breakfast time. He couldn't be with Granny Redstone, who had a house by the sea at Sandy Bay. Toby never stayed at Granny Redstone's on his own. Not to mention that her mother would simply have said, "He's at Granny's, dear, don't you remember," instead of wondering who Nin was talking about. And anyway, none of it would explain why all his belongings had vanished. Even his breakfast cereal.

The bogeyman must've run off with him, she thought, and laughed to herself. It was a grim laugh.

By mid-morning break the rain had finally stopped, so she dragged Linette over to a quiet corner of the school grounds. Linette was moaning on about her dad and how he wouldn't let her do anything fun these days. Nin cut across a story about how he had made Linette eat nothing but cabbage for a week because she had spent her lunch money on chips.

"Never mind that," Nin said impatiently, "the weirdest thing happened this morning."

Linette scowled at her. "Do you mind?" she snapped. "I was talking!"

"This is important," said Nin firmly.

"Oh yeah? And my being starved to death isn't?"

Nin shook her head. "Will you listen! Toby's disappeared!"

Linette stared at her as if she'd gone off her head. There was a long pause.

And then it happened all over again.

"Who?" snapped Linette. "Am I supposed to know who you're talking about?"

"Yes!" Nin wailed. "He's my brother!"

Linette gave an impatient snort. "Honestly, Ninevah Redstone," she said over her shoulder as she stomped off, "sometimes I think you're soft in the head."

Nin got through the afternoon somehow. When the bell finally rang for the end of the day she snatched up her things and ran. She kept going, out of the school and past the bus stop. She didn't think she could face hanging about with the others; she just wanted to go home. And she knew that, on foot, the quickest way home was to walk across the park and through the underpass.

Normally, Nin avoided the underpass like the plague. But today she was going to take the risk.

Someone shouted at her as she charged through the fifth graders hanging about at the park entrance, but she ignored them. She ran on through the park, over the ornamental bridge and the ducks, past the Juniper Café and around the flowerbeds.

Then, suddenly, the underpass was there. It loomed like a great dark hole ready to swallow her up. She slammed to a halt, nearly stumbling because she was going so fast the rest of her tried to carry on after her legs had stopped. For a moment she thought she was going to be horribly sick in the geraniums.

Taking huge gulps of fresh air, she looked it over.

On the one hand it was a dark hole that ran on forever and hid such dreadful ghosts that she felt her eyes sting with tears of fright.

On the other hand it was a concrete tunnel under the road that would get her home quickly.

"Okay, Toby Redstone," she said out loud. "If you're home when I get there and I have gone through this for nothing, I'll put that monkey of yours in the washing machine and make you eat cereal without sugar for a week."

The underpass didn't get any less awful, but the firm sound of her voice did make her feel less sick. She balled up her fists, unstuck her feet from the path and stepped into the tunnel.

It was nearly as bad as she had imagined.

For a start it was darker inside and smelled far worse than it should, an animal smell, almost like the zoo. And it seemed bigger too, but Nin knew that this was only because she was afraid. The echo made the sound of her own feet follow her and up ahead she could see the corner.

A few yards along, the underpass turned sharply to the right making a blank wall that looked like a dead end. This meant that you never knew exactly what was around the corner. It wouldn't bother most people, but it bothered Nin because it was the corner her father had died around.

Nin knew that what had happened to him was so strange it would probably never happen again to anyone else. Which made the chances of the same thing happening to *her*—his daughter—very slim indeed.

She knew that around the corner was just another stretch of underpass and some steps up to the road. It was just that in her head, the long stretch was extra long and extra dark, and almost anything—like a mad bull for example—could be lurking there.

Today there was nothing but a horrible-looking boy dressed like a tramp with a ragged black coat and a frayed red scarf. He was a few years older than Nin and she had seen him hanging around the town a lot lately. She strode past him, making sure she didn't catch his eye.

At last she was at the steps and then she was out in the street again. Her spirits lifted and she hurried on up Dunforth Hill as fast as she could. It wasn't easy.

To say that Dunforth Hill was steep was like saying that water was damp. On the plus side, the view was amazing. It had turned into a bright, sunny afternoon and if Nin had been in the mood to look she would have been able to see all the way across the patchwork of fields and the spangly strip of the river to Midtown.

The house loomed into view, sitting under the shade of the Christmas tree that Dad had planted when Nin was five and that had grown to be enormous. It all looked very ordinary and peaceful. For a moment she almost forgot that anything was wrong.

She let herself in with her key and stood in the doorway listening anxiously. Normally her mother would be there with Toby. Today the house was silent. They weren't back yet, was all, she told herself. And then her heart plunged as the truth hit her like a falling brick.

Her mother wasn't there because she was still at work.

And she was still at work because she didn't have to leave early to pick up Toby anymore.

And she didn't have to pick up Toby anymore because Toby had ceased to exist.

Monkey

The evening had all the usual things in it except one. There was homework, which was supposed to be an essay on an historical figure of her choice, but which turned out to be the name "Toby" doodled over and over again on the page. Then there was dinner, which Nin ate but barely noticed. And TV, where she got to choose what they watched and had absolutely no interruptions while she watched it.

It was quiet and peaceful and very, very empty. It was amazing how much she missed him. Far more than she would have guessed, considering the kid was mostly just a nuisance.

By bedtime Nin was numb with helplessness and worry, and on Thursday morning she told her mother that she felt sick. She had a plan and school didn't come into it. Fortunately, having spent the night going round and round things in her head until she felt dizzy, she looked pale and drawn and Lena sent her straight back to bed. As soon as she heard the front door bang shut behind her mother, Nin got up. She reckoned that Grandad and Granny would be down at intervals to check on her, but she could work around that. Then, apart from pauses to have a drink (brought by Grandad), eat lunch (brought by Granny), go to the bathroom and so on, she searched the house from top to bottom.

Still in her pajamas she even searched her grandparents' flat, watched over by Grandad with his usual strong cup of tea and a newspaper. Fortunately Granny had gone to the store, which was good because she would have asked too many questions. Grandad rarely asked questions, although when he did they were often difficult ones. He might be more ancient than the ark, but Nin had figured out long ago that Grandad wasn't daft. His pale eyes watched her from behind bushy, gray eyebrows.

"Looking for anything particular, kid?"

"Just something I thought I had." Nin hesitated. "Do you think that you can be absolutely sure of something and yet . . ." She stopped, not sure how to go on.

"The brain's a funny thing," said Grandad after a moment, when he could see she wasn't going to finish her sentence. "People think that memory is a fact," he went on, tapping his head with his finger, "that a thing is unchangeable once it's in there. If they remember it then it must be right. But that's just people wanting to feel safe."

Kneeling by the cupboard she had been rooting through, Nin stared at him thoughtfully. She didn't know what Grandad was going on about half the time, but if you listened long enough it usually made sense.

"Truth is, kid, memory is something you can shape any way you want. Tell yourself a lie often enough and you'll end up believing it, just you keep that in mind."

Nin sighed, giving up any idea of telling him more. When you got right down to it, Grandad was saying the same as Linette. Ninevah Redstone was bonkers. It was all in her head.

Grandad watched for a moment or so longer. "Still looking, then?"

"Yep."

He nodded. "That's the spirit. Give up and you're certainly done for, I say."

Nin looked up at him. Her ordinary blue eyes met his watery gray ones.

"I thought you said . . ."

"You don't *have* to do things my way, kid." He smiled at her sadly and went back to his paper.

When she had done the house, Nin pulled on her robe to go outside.

Right at the bottom of the garden, past the lawn and the flowerbeds and down a couple of broken brick steps, was the patch her mother called "the Rough." The Rough was all long, coarse grass over lumpy ground. At the end was a wild, overgrown wall of shrubs and trees. And at the farthest point of the Rough, under the farthest tree just before the garden ran out altogether, Nin finally found what she was looking for.

Evidence of Toby.

In the conservatory, Nin dropped Monkey onto the floor, sat down next to it and began to look it over. Monkey had been fluffy once, but years of being hugged, washed and dragged about had worn him half-bald. Because he had been out in the rain, lost all night in the ragged grass, what was left of his ginger fur had turned a murky mud-color. If she had any doubts about her sanity, they vanished instantly. It was Toby's, all right, she would know it anywhere. And it proved without a doubt that Toby was real.

He had been there. Now he was gone. Something had stolen her brother.

Nin put the grubby toy in the washing machine. She was going to keep it so that she wouldn't lose sight of the truth. With everyone around her acting like nothing had happened she was afraid that somehow their forgetfulness would infect her, make her forget too. Rub Toby out in her head so that he faded slowly into nothing.

Watching Monkey spin around in the machine, Nin wondered what on earth could sneak a kid away in the middle of the night, without a sound. Then remove all trace of him from his home and wipe all memory of him from the minds of his family and friends. The thought that there might be a person . . . no . . . a *creature* out there that could do all that made her shiver.

Except of course that the whatever-it-was had made a mistake.

Not Monkey, that wasn't a mistake. An old toy lying about in the garden would not have been a problem if Nin's memory had been stolen too. After all, it could have been dropped there by a fox or just flung in by some passer-by.

Nin was the mistake. Nin had remembered.

She sat there, thinking about it, until the wash cycle was finished. Then she fished out Monkey, still damp but a whole lot cleaner, and headed up to her room. As she hurried down the hall and turned to go up the stairs she realized with a horrible lurch that there was something under the stairs, pretending to be one of the dark shadows that always lingered there.

Nin kept going without so much as a false step. She wasn't going to let the beastly thing know that she was scared.

Because she *was* scared. Bone-deep, jelly-legged petrified.

The thing that had stolen Toby had come back for her.

Over the next week life went on as normal, but Nin scarcely noticed. The THING became a constant presence. It watched her, with eyes that she could feel rather than see, from anywhere dark and shadowy. Like the back of the wardrobe when she went to get a fresh shirt for school. Or the big cupboard in the hall where the umbrellas were kept. Nobody noticed, although Lena kept feeling her forehead and talking in a worried way about the doctor.

There was nothing the doctor or anybody else could do about it though. Nin was sure that her fate was sealed. At least she would find out what had happened to Toby, all she had to do was wait. She just hoped it wouldn't be too long.

The turning point came on Tuesday, nearly a whole week after Toby had been vanished. Funnily enough, the person who shared the moment with her was the school nerd, Dunk the Chunk.

Normally, Nin would rather have smooched a tarantula than spend longer than a nanosecond within speaking range of Dunk the Chunk, even though he was always trying to be friendly. But when the THING followed her to school and groaned at her from out of the drain in the home economics sink, she made an exception. Compared to that, talking to Dunk the Chunk was small beans.

"Are you okay?" he asked.

Nin swallowed. She was staring blankly at the sink. Dunk's voice dragged her back from the brink of hysteria and made her blink and manage a half-smile.

She was vaguely conscious of her ex-friend Linette sniggering and whispering about her to one of the other girls.

"I'm fine, thanks," said Nin. "Just, my brother's been stolen and something horrible is stalking me."

"Right," said Dunk. "I did notice you hadn't been yourself lately."

"It's all over the place," she grumbled to him on the bus on the way home. "Mostly it hangs out under the stairs, but not always."

Dunk was staring at her, his eyes wide.

"Once," Nin went on, "it was *under the bed*."

"What!" Dunk's voice came out in a squeak. "*Your* bed!"

"Course, idiot. Wouldn't be anyone else's, would it!"

"What did you do?"

Nin shrugged. "Ignored it and went to sleep," she lied, trying to forget about the fit of screaming. "Next morning, I got a broom, like, in case I had to hit it. Only it was gone. Turned up under the stairs again." She shrugged.

Dunk stared at her in humble amazement.

"Sometimes," she said, "it sniggers when I go past." She looked away, out of the bus window. "Thing is, there's nothing I can do. No way I can fight. I wish it would just get on with it and steal me away like Toby. Then everyone would just forget me too and it would be all over."

"No," said Dunk quietly. "I won't forget you. I'll make sure somehow."

Barely hearing him, Nin stared at the rain-wet street trundling past outside the bus, a feeling growing inside her. Anger. The bus jolted to a halt.

"I just thought," she said as realization dawned, "it

doesn't know it's forgotten to make me forget! It doesn't know that *I* know what it's up to." The anger was growing. She clenched her fists. "So I *have* got something, haven't I? Something to fight with! If I only knew when it was going to come for me, I could be READY."

"But you don't know," said Dunk anxiously, following her off the bus. "Do you?"

"I dunno," she said, "it's Wednesday tomorrow, isn't it? It's bound to be tonight then."

And she was right.

Mum Will Fix It

Skerridge was only doing his job. It was just that his job happened to be stealing kids for Mr. Strood.

Peering out from behind a musty-smelling duffel coat, Skerridge watched as the front door opened. He didn't have a shape at the moment and was just being a sinister patch of extra-dark shadow with eyes. It was his favorite disguise. Excellent for scaring kids, and restful too. Much better than mad-faced clown or bug-eyed monster. All that maniacal laughter and slobbering really got him down.

The mother walked in through the door, carrying four bulging carrier bags. She was followed by Right Madam. Skerridge never bothered with the kids' names. He just gave them a description and left it at that. For example, the one before this had been Mangy Monkey because of the state of the toy he carried around. Before that it had been Droopy Socks and before that it had been Snotty.

He sighed. Gently. Just enough to make the girl pull up and send a sharp glance in his direction. She shivered. Skerridge grinned to himself.

"You start putting this lot away, while I sort out

the freezer," said the mother, "then we'll think about dinner."

Skerridge didn't often notice people other than the kid he was after, but there was something about this woman that made him look at her more closely. She was sad, he could see that at a glance. He wondered where Right Madam's father was. Dead, perhaps? Some horrible tragedy?

Not for the first time in his long and tattered life Skerridge felt the stirrings of curiosity. He crushed them at once. It didn't do to get curious about the Quick.

He could hear sounds from the kitchen. The creak and slam of cupboard doors, the clink of tins and the rustle of bags.

"You're quiet today?"

"Just tired is all," said Right Madam.

It was probably true. Skerridge knew she hadn't been sleeping well because he had been giving her the frights.

He chuckled to himself. He hadn't taken to this one at all, not like Mangy Monkey who had been quite a cute kid really. Mangy Monkey had just stared at Skerridge with those deep blue eyes and hung on to his tatty toy. Skerridge had almost felt a twinge of regret when he stuffed the kid into the sack. Almost. But he *had* tied the top especially loose to let in a little light and made sure to keep the kid turned the right way up.

On the other hand, this one would be a nuisance. Skerridge felt it in his bones. And since, when he was in his own shape, he was mostly made of bones feeling something in them really meant it.

"Made up with Linette yet?" asked Sad Mum, sympathetically. The unpacking sounds stopped and Skerridge wondered what they were doing now. Then he heard the clunk of a saucepan.

"Nope. No point anyway, she's such a bore!"

Sad Mum laughed. Skerridge thought it was a nice laugh.

Although Right Madam was up at the older end of the age range, nearly too old to see him in fact, it wasn't her age that bothered Skerridge. The ones that thought they were as good as grown-up often turned into complete jellies once they got a look at him.

It wasn't that she was a bright girl and might try to escape either. Skerridge was faster than any Quick and liked to give them a head start when they made a run for it—let them think they might get away—before scurrying after them. He liked to run over the walls and ceiling and then drop down in front of them just when they thought they had nearly made it.

Doors weren't any kind of a problem either. Turning up behind kids when they'd shut themselves in a cupboard for safety and whispering "Boo" ever so quietly in their ear was another good one.

No, the problem with Right Madam was that she looked like a right madam. The sort who would argue. Skerridge couldn't bear the sort who argued. He was especially nasty to them and had once delivered one to Mr. Strood half-eaten, which didn't go down too well. Skerridge shuddered at the memory.

There were more sounds from the kitchen.

"Oh look," Sad Mum said, "coats all over the place. Could you hang them up, please?"

The kitchen door opened and Right Madam appeared, clutching the jackets they had been wearing when they came in. She moved cautiously toward the space under the stairs, holding the coats ready to throw on their hooks.

Skerridge grinned to himself. He let out a soft, slow

hiss. Right Madam stopped. Her eyes got very wide and she took a deep breath.

Skerridge let his own eyes glow a little brighter. She wouldn't see them, but she would feel him watching.

Right Madam stayed still, her gaze searching the shadows, her breath coming in short huffs. Any minute now, thought Skerridge, she's gonna cry.

Then, in one jerky movement, she stepped forward and plonked the jackets right over him. Skerridge blinked in the sudden darkness. He hissed again—this time not for Right Madam's benefit. Usually Skerridge liked to terrorize a kid for at least a month before snatching them, but this one wasn't being half as much fun as usual.

"Pah!" he muttered to the lining of the jacket. "Playin' games, are we? We'll see about that!"

Perhaps it was time to move things along.

When the house was dark, Skerridge got to work. Because he had a lot to do he moved at superspeed whenever he could—so fast that he was just a blur.

First he took out a thin, sharp spindle. Skerridge had made it himself from a stray bone he had found in the House. It was etched with tiny shapes and swirls and had taken him ages to do.

Using the spindle skillfully, he began to draw all memory of Right Madam out of her mother's head. When he had done that, spinning the threads into a tight ball, he went on to her grandmother, her grandfather and her best friend.

The nature of the universe was such that once he had removed all trace of the girl from the minds of those who loved her most, anyone else who simply liked her, knew her or happened to bump into her from time to time forgot about her too.

This was the part of his job that Skerridge enjoyed most. It took skill not to break the thread and to catch every last strand of it. He loved the way it spun into a bright, shining ball like a pearl full of strange colors. Once it was done he tucked the ball carefully into the small bag made of spider silk that he carried in a secret pocket hidden in his vest, and moved on to the next task.

After all, there was no point erasing the girl from memory if he left bits of her lying around all over the place. There were her clothes to get rid of, not to mention her books, toiletries and other personal items. Photographs too, and postcards, school projects, all manner of things scattered about the house, the town and even the country.

This time he used the spindle in a different way, turning it counterclockwise instead of clockwise. As he did so, all the physical things that Right Madam had left around became less and less THERE, until they quietly and completely evaporated from existence. The only personal things left would be the ones she was wearing or holding. All Skerridge would have to do was a little tidying up afterward to make sure the gaps didn't show. Like filling empty wardrobes with somebody else's old jackets, that kind of thing.

Of course, even magic wasn't perfect and sometimes, very, very rarely, an item would get missed. It never mattered, because even if some much worn sweater or grinning photo image did slip through, one thing alone was never enough to unlock a memory pearl. People just thought, "I wonder where that came from?" and threw it in the bin.

At last, when night was creeping into the early hours of Wednesday morning, it was time for the girl herself.

To his surprise, Skerridge was feeling nervous about this one.

She was asleep, judging by the bump in the bed. Skerridge dug out his sack and drew a deep breath. He was going to wake her with a scream. Simple but effective. It would have her instantly confused and terrified, and easy to pop into the waiting sack before she had time to realize what was going on.

A second before he let rip, Skerridge noticed that the bump in the bed wasn't breathing.

Shock slammed into him like an Intercity train at full speed. He, of all creatures, could not possibly be caught by the old pillow under the covers trick!

A sound behind him made him spin around. Armed with a hairbrush, Right Madam stepped out from her hiding place between the chest of drawers and the wardrobe. She glared at him.

Skerridge hissed.

Right Madam pointed a wobbly finger.

"You," she hissed back, "you stole my brother!"

"You," hissed Nin at the Thing on her bedroom rug, "you stole my brother!"

It bared a set of crazily jagged teeth at her and flicked the sack it was holding so that it fell open. Then it tensed.

Nin looked around wildly. To get out of the room she would have to get past the Thing and that didn't look like an easy job. Not to mention the fact that she was nearly paralyzed with fright. Her legs felt like rubber, and if she tried to run for it she would probably end up on her face.

The Thing looked like it was going to pounce on her. Now seemed like a good time to use the hairbrush she was holding, in case she needed to hit anything, so she threw it. The hairbrush caught the Thing right in the middle of its forehead. Bristles-side out.

The Thing yelped and looked surprised.

Nin took her chance and ran.

The Thing leapt.

Nin screamed as the sack scraped her head, the rough cloth nearly covering her. She twisted sharply, slithering forward. The Thing gave a snarling hiss, the sack slipped off her and she was free.

She wasn't sure how she got to the stairs. Once there she half ran, half fell down them. It might have been more sensible to go the other way, toward her mother's room, but instinct told her to head for the front door.

Glancing back, Nin gave a shocked gasp. The Thing wasn't bothering with the stairs. It was scurrying down the wall and along the lower hall ceiling on all fours, looking like some huge, awkward spider. She screamed again.

A door sprang open and Lena Redstone appeared in the upstairs hall. She flicked on the light.

The Thing on the ceiling froze, then dropped on to the floor just in front of Nin. It glared up at the woman in her pajamas, her hair in a tousled mess.

Nin felt a wave of relief as her mother hurried down the stairs. It was all over now. Mum would fix it.

Lena came to a stop right next to the Thing, which crouched back against the wall. She was even standing on a corner of the sack, but she was looking only at Nin. For her, the Thing wasn't there at all.

Open-mouthed, Nin looked at it. It smirked at her.

And then something even more horrible happened.

Lena Redstone stared at her daughter, her face stern.

"Who are you," she said, "and what are you doing in my house?"

Nin didn't stop to argue. She'd seen what had happened with Toby, how completely he had been removed from her mother's mind. There was no point hanging around trying to make her remember.

She ran for the front door and her hand found the latch just as the Thing tried to go after her. It jolted to a halt with a bump and a squawk. It was still hanging on to the sack, which was anchored to the floor by her mother's foot.

The door flew open onto night air and the empty road. Nin fell through it.

"You're lucky I haven't called the police!" yelled her mother after her and then the door was shut and Nin was running up the path, out onto the street and down the hill.

She hadn't gone far when she bumped into somebody.

"Not so fast!"

She shrieked and tried to pull back, but whoever it was had her firmly by the arms. She lowered her head to bite, but then he said something that got her attention.

"It'll come after you, y'know."

Nin stopped struggling and looked up. It was the boy she had seen around town a few times. The rough one in the black coat and the red scarf. He was tall and looked like he hadn't eaten properly for a long time. His eyes were gray and not unkind, and his greasy hair might have been blond if it had been washed. He smiled.

"Time for introductions later," he said. "Follow me, right?"

He led her quickly down the hill. Nin followed in a daze.

"Number 27," said the boy over his shoulder. "It was burned to a shell about four years ago, remember?"

Nin nodded. Number 27 was mostly hidden behind a high wall and all anyone walking past it could see were the boarded-up top-floor windows and the broken roof.

"Y'know what everyone says about it?"

"Um . . . yeah," she croaked, hurrying to keep up with him. "People died in the fire and at night, like, you can hear them dragging themselves about."

Down by the side of number 27 was a path that went nowhere except to a locked side gate. Fired by nerves, Nin's imagination must have been running riot, because as they hurried down it she was sure she heard something dragging itself about inside the ruined house, scratching at the walls like it wanted to get at her. The boy kept going and Nin went after him, thinking she must be mad. Still, since her life had shot down a side alley from normality anyway, she figured she might as well. Right now she didn't have a better plan.

So she followed him down the path that went nowhere and ended up someplace else.

Bad Things Don't Like the Light

Everything went dark. Everything.

"Um . . ."

"It's okay," said the boy, "it often takes people like that. We're in the Drift. Skerridge won't think to look for you here, he'll think you're still in the Widdern."

"The what?"

"My name's Jonas," he said, ignoring her.

Nin thought he must have brilliant night vision because he set off confidently into a darkness that was completely empty of house lights, street lights, or any other lights at all. She shivered. Although she could sense the wall of number 27 as a wedge of solid darkness to her left, to the right there was a feeling of open air. A definite lack of Next Door.

In fact, now she came to think about it the world had gone silent too. No distant murmur of cars, no . . . Well, it was nighttime so there wouldn't be any people anyway, but something was still missing. The underlying hum of a fair-sized town, the sound that went on even while everyone slept, had gone too.

"Wait!" She hurried after Jonas, stumbling on the

uneven ground of a hillside that suddenly had grass instead of pavements.

"You're Nin," Jonas was saying. "I've been keeping an eye out for you. I guessed he'd be after you next, once he'd dropped Toby off."

Nin stopped dead. "Toby?" she demanded. "What about Toby?"

Jonas paused, turning to face her. By now, Nin's eyes were adjusting to the dark and she realized that there was light after all. The stars were brilliant in a sky of inky velvet and a wedge of moon touched the landscape with silver. Her eyes fixed on something that rose against the northern horizon like a distant wall of hazy white.

"Sorry," Jonas said ruefully. "Couldn't help him. Can't take them on, you see, they're too powerful. I was just watching to see if either of you managed to get away. As you did." He looked up at the sky. "We'll shelter in the woods till dawn. The Drift isn't a good place to be out in at night."

Nin started toward him then stopped, unsure of what to do. "My mum will worry."

Jonas watched her for a moment. "No, she won't," he said gently. "She won't even wonder where you are."

For the first time since all this horribleness began Nin felt her eyes fill with tears. Jonas set off again, making his way down the grassy slope of the hill toward the darker shadow of the trees.

Still crying, Nin followed him. There was nothing else she could do.

She got the tears under control on the trip down the hill. Although she stumbled often, she was grateful for the dark. At least he couldn't see her face.

At last, they reached a small copse and groped their way

under the trees. The shape that was Jonas sat down with his back to a broad trunk, so Nin settled next to him. She felt safer in the copse because the gentle rustle of leaves and the twitter of the odd night bird did a lot to cover the unnatural silence that didn't belong to the Dunforth Hill she knew. Fortunately, the leaves also covered up the skyline with its rounded silhouettes of trees instead of the usual hard-edged ones of roofs and chimneys.

"So," she said firmly. "Why have all the lights gone? And what wood is this?"

"This is the Drift," said Jonas patiently. "The lights have gone because it's another world and not many people live here. The wood doesn't have a name, there are too many woods in the Drift to give them all names."

Nin was silent. There were so many questions tumbling around in her head, all trying to get out at once, that they were stuck in a kind of mental traffic jam.

"Anyway," said Jonas conversationally, while she tried to get a grip, "how did you do it? Get away from Skerridge, I mean. No kid has ever managed that before."

"That THING stole my brother," Nin burst out, before she realized she was going to say anything at all. "It stole Toby and everyone forgot about him except me." She paused, remembering the dark shape under the stairs, the silent breathing in the shadows. "Then, I knew it had come back for me, so I stayed up all night and waited for it."

Jonas watched her intently; she could feel his gaze in the darkness, like a cool touch on her face.

"Skerridge must've left your memory behind when he took Toby. That's not like him, I can tell you. It's part of their magic." Jonas sounded sad. "To steal your loved ones' memory, so that everyone else forgets too. If you hadn't been so close to Toby, your memory of him would have faded with the night."

"Like everyone's memory of me will be gone too," said Nin flatly. It wasn't a question and Jonas knew it. "Although"—she looked over at his shadowy shape— "if you were watching me before . . . well, *you* still remember me?"

"I'm already stolen, already on the outside, see. The memory spell wouldn't find me because in a way I don't exist."

"And that's why you don't have a home, because you got stolen too?"

"Yep. Mind you, it was Polpp who snatched me, not Skerridge."

"Why did you look out for me?"

His gaze slipped away from her face then, she felt it go.

"Like I said, I knew there was a BM around so I kept watch. You never know if a kid's going to get away."

"BM?"

"Bogeyman. Anyway, your brother went and you seemed like a possible too, so I waited to see if the BM came back. Got nothing better to do. Course, I didn't realize then it was Skerridge or I might not have bothered."

"I'm glad you did." Shivering in the darkness, Nin sneaked out a hand. Jonas must have known because he took it and gave her fingers a friendly squeeze. She inched close enough to feel his shoulder, solid against hers. She was cold, although it was a mild night, and she ached with the hugeness of it all. The next question struggling out of the maelstrom in her head was, "What exactly is this place anyway?" but something bigger got there first.

"How many kids go missing like this?" She gasped. "I mean, how many have disappeared that nobody even knows about?"

"These days, there are only a couple of dozen BMs left and mostly they like to hang around scaring a kid for weeks before they do the snatch. So, I dunno . . . say . . . up to a hundred kids every year? Of course, that's peanuts in a population the size of Britain, but . . ."

"That's *awful,*" gasped Nin. "Can't somebody do something about it?"

Jonas burst out laughing. "Like who? The police? Round up the BMs and bung them in prison, I s'pose? If they could see them to round them up, of course. Not to mention they'd be toast in a second."

"Toast?"

"Bogeymen have Firebreath. I mean, *real* Firebreath, not just post-onion firebreath."

Nin blinked at him. It was getting lighter. On the horizon, at least the bit of it she could see from under the hanging branches, the sky was tinged with soft gold.

"Anyway," he went on, "BMs don't just go for any kid, they like a particular sort. The shy or nervous or thoughtful ones. You know, the sort who see faces in the pattern on the curtains, or make sure the closet doors are closed at night so nothing can come out. And if they find a kid with brothers and sisters who are the same, they, or one of the others, tend to go back."

"Like me and Toby?"

"Uh-huh. So although most families get away with nothing, others can lose every single kid. Now that is truly awful!"

"What happens to the ones that don't escape? Like Toby?" cried Nin, suddenly afraid. "What happened to him?"

"Kids that don't escape, which is most of the ones that get stolen in the first place, get dropped off at the Terrible House," said Jonas, watching her carefully. "After that"—he shrugged—"nobody ever sees 'em again."

"The Terrible House?"

"Uh-huh. They get handed over to Strood . . ."

"Strood?"

"And that's it. Gone."

Nin opened her mouth and then shut it again. She had been about to say "gone?" but she was starting to feel like some kind of echo so she bit it back.

Her confusion must have shown on her face because Jonas grinned at her in the half-light.

"Look," he said, "I'll tell you what I know, but not just now. By the feel of things, the sun is about to come up and I don't think you'll be paying any attention to me for a little while."

Nin raised an eyebrow and turned to look toward the horizon. It was deep gold by now and along the edge of the world, where the land curved away against the sky, burned a rim so bright she could barely look at it. She got up and took a few steps forward, coming out from under the trees to stand in the open where she could see better. She had a weird feeling inside, like caged electricity, as if something huge was about to happen.

The dawn ignited.

Even in the face of everything that had happened to her, it took Nin's breath away. It honestly looked like the sky was on fire.

"It's all right," said Jonas, "the sky is on fire, it'll calm down when the sun's up properly."

Nin shifted her gaze to him. But only for a second. Overhead the flames burned on, lapping up the night in dragon tongues of smoldering amber and fierce yellow. Around them the hillside was bathed in molten light.

"A lot of things here are what people make of them," said Jonas. "Take number 27 for starters." He nodded his head back up the hill the way they had come, so she turned to see.

Looking somehow closer to them than it should, number 27 towered against the flaming sky, huge and grim, its eyeless windows watchful. Nin could see shadows coming off it like steam.

"On the Widdern side there's nothing in there." Jonas laughed. "Just a lot of empty, burnt-out rooms. This side, it's a place you don't want to go!"

The flames grew dim and went out, leaving a pale blue sky full of gentle sunlight. At last, Nin got her first real view of the Drift.

All the houses were gone. The hill swept before her, its coat of grass strangely vivid and speckled with buttercups that shone like gold. Away in the distance, she could see the lazy curve of the river, but it was not the one she knew. Its banks were no longer edged with parks or neatly kept houses. Instead it had a fringe of dark and ragged woodland that turned to open meadow further upstream. Here and there, white trees stood out among the green like the bone-dead casualties of some weird attack by lightning. And beyond the wood, rising above the shadowed trees, was that bank of cloud, sitting on the horizon like a white cliff against the sky.

"The Raw," said Jonas before she could ask. "It's like

a kind of fog. You get patches of it all over the Drift, but it doesn't go away."

"Fog always goes away," said Nin, puzzled.

"I only said it was *like* fog." There was an edge to his voice, as if the mist made him nervous. "Sometimes the patches kind of . . . explode outward. Or sometimes a whole new patch just appears somewhere else. But wherever it is, once it's there it never goes away again."

Nin was only half listening. She had just spotted a concrete hump that looked seriously out of place.

"That kind of looks like the underpass to the park."

"That's because it *is* the underpass to the park," said Jonas. "It's a partial gateway. You can get to the Widdern through it from the Drift, but not back again. From the Widdern, it only goes where it's supposed to go, under the road."

"Huh," Nin snorted. "I don't s'pose it's any friendlier in the Drift than it is in the Widdern."

Out of the corner of her eye she saw Jonas smother a grin. She turned to look at him, but he just stretched and shook himself.

"It's morning," he said cheerfully. "Bad things don't like the light. They give up when the sun rises."

"And that'll include Skerridge, will it?" said Nin fiercely.

"Probably." Jonas grinned. "Bet he's right ticked off about you!"

Skerridge was steaming. It was coming out of his ears and nose in thin streams, and every time he opened his mouth to curse he let out a cloud of scalding vapor. He stamped back up the hill, dragging the sack behind him and peering at the dawn light growing on the horizon. Somehow Right Madam had given him the slip. He couldn't believe it had happened. He, Skerridge, Chief Bogeyman and Champion Kid-Catcher, given the slip by some nasty girl-brat. He stopped to scream with rage, sending billows of hot mist spurting into the early-morning air. Then he threw the sack on the ground and pounced on it, shredding it with his bone-yellow claws. When it was a rag he chucked it aside and stared again at the horizon.

Dawn. BMs hated the dawn. They loathed the sun. Despised its nasty, sizzling glare that gave them no place to lurk.

Skerridge bellowed again. The steam hissed above him in a cloud, faintly golden in the growing light.

Thing was, he had a reputation to keep up. Other BMs might lose kids, but not Skerridge. Never Skerridge. Even the half-eaten one didn't count as a loss. Exactly. His mind made up, Skerridge stood his ground.

The rising sun crept above the lip of the world, flowing over empty streets and sleeping houses and one creature of yellowed bones wearing torn trousers and a fancy vest, its red eyes blinking warily in the light.

When it was fully day, Skerridge got moving.

5

Dandy Boneman

By now the sun was up and a cool breeze blew white clouds across the blue expanse of sky like ships fleeing before a gale. Nin squinted up at them.

"They've got sails. A bit ragged, like, but still sails. And portholes!"

They settled on the outskirts of the copse, where Jonas arranged some stones in a ring and began building a fire in the center. He lit it with the help of a box, dug out from his bulging pockets, then crouched next to the flames, feeding them with twigs and chunks of branch. Nin watched him, glad he was there. She didn't like to think how she would be feeling if she was all alone right now, homeless, with no one to help. Soon she would have to decide what to do next, but for now, sticking with Jonas seemed like a good idea.

"Right, I want you to sit here and warm up. I'll fetch some water from the stream and see about making you a hot drink . . ."

"What of?"

"Water and honey. 'Cept the honey and my brewing can are in my pack, which is down by the stream where

I left it when I went to watch for you. Get used to it,"
he added, seeing the look on her face. "No cups of tea
or bottles of fizzy pop here. Drift honey is probably
more nourishing than your average dinner, though. It'll
warm you up."

Nin was about to tell him that she wasn't cold, then
realized she was shivering. Must be shock, she thought,
it's not every day you get your life stolen. She giggled,
feeling light-headed.

"I need the bathroom."

Jonas pointed to a bush. "I'll be back in ten minutes."

In fact, he was back in five. Nin was huddled over
the fire, trying block out the memory of her mother's
voice demanding to know who she was. She stared up
at Jonas miserably.

"It'll get better," he said, "believe me. You might not
want it to, you might want to hang on to feeling bad
because it ties you to what you've lost, but it will get
better anyway. You won't be able to help it. And one
day it'll slip so far into the past . . ."

"NO!"

"Okay." Jonas gave her a warm smile and set about
putting a large can of water on to the fire to heat up.
"I've only got one mug, we'll have to share."

Nin gazed over the landscape. It was beautiful, no
doubt about that. The colors were vivid, without being
harsh, and the air was so clear it filled her head with
light. Without the ever-present trace of car fumes, she
could smell grass, cool water and the smoke from the
fire which had an odd scent, like roast apples. Soon the
musky-sweet smell of honey drifted into the air too.

"Would you like some cakes to go with that?" asked
a voice behind her. "I'll do you a deal."

Jonas, who had been paying attention to the fire,

sprang to his feet. Nin looked around, startled.

A man was standing a little way up from them, on the slope of the hill. He had been walking in the shadow of the trees and now he stepped into the light. He was short and wiry with a pointed, foxy face and ginger hair twisted into tangled ringlets. He wore a long coat of green silk over a yellow top and leather trousers with knee-high, brown boots. All this Nin saw in a flash, but what really got her attention was the thing in his hand.

It was taller than a man and the top end was fashioned into a snarling dragon's head engraved with complicated symbols. The whole thing gave off a silver haze that evaporated in the sunlight. It looked like it was made of bone and she wondered briefly what kind of animal had bones that big. Out of the corner of her eye she saw Jonas give the thing the sort of look you might give to a Samurai sword in the hands of a lunatic. Then she caught sight of the objects lined up behind the stranger and forgot all about the bone.

Jonas stepped forward, putting himself in front of Nin. She peered around him, still staring at the what-evers.

"Dandy Boneman," the stranger said. "No need to worry. Just traveling, like you." He smiled, showing teeth that were broken and black on one side.

"Sure," said Jonas, his voice guarded. "We were just having breakfast." He didn't offer their names.

"I saw." Boneman turned, beckoning to one of the objects at his heels. "I have some cakes, but no honey. You appear to have honey, but no cakes. How about we combine resources?"

Nin gaped. Trotting forward with a huge pack balanced on its head was . . . well, she wasn't sure what it was exactly. It stood about thigh high, was roughly man-shaped, but gray in color and crumbly in texture, and had two glowing red eyes.

"Mudman," said Jonas shortly. "Sort of like the Quick legend of golems, only not."

The mudman came to a halt in front of Boneman and stood there while its owner rummaged in the pack, finally pulling out a package of greasy paper wrapped around a handful of small cakes. He held them out. His hands were slim and very white and Nin noticed an ancient-looking ring on his middle finger. It had a large red stone and a lot of symbols that made her skin prickle to look at them.

"A half-dozen, plenty to go around."

"Thanks!" said Nin brightly. She hadn't realized it before, but she was hungry. It didn't seem right to want food when your life had just been turned upside down, but the small, golden cakes looked good and the stranger was smiling at her, his blue eyes bright and innocent of harm. She thought she heard Jonas sigh.

Boneman walked around to the other side of the fire and Nin got another look at his mudmen servants. There were five of them, all burdened with pots, pans, blankets and packs. Boneman sat down with the mudmen ranged in a row at his back. Jonas stirred more honey into the boiling water.

"Um . . . don't they want to put those things down?"

"They don't get tired," laughed Boneman. "They are just lumps of earth, you know." He gave her a look that she didn't understand. Like he was working something out in his head. Calculating.

Nin looked at the creatures, which stood there, unmoving. Their red eyes had dimmed a little, but that was all. One of them was crumbling on the left side, a chunk of its mud had fallen away leaving a hollow.

There was no expression, no self-awareness, not even in the ember eyes. She shuddered.

"Are you newly stolen?" asked Boneman. "You'll get used to it. What do you think of my staff?" He nodded at the bone rod, which was now lying close to his side, then began to divide the cakes.

"Is it, like, magic?"

"Sure. It's a sorcerer's staff." He gave her two cakes, then turned around and pulled a tin mug from the jumble piled on mudman number three, handing it to Jonas.

"Are you a sorcerer, then?"

Boneman laughed gently. "I wield a sorcerer's power."

"All the sorcerers are gone," explained Jonas, handing back mugs full of steaming liquid. "Except possibly one and that's only a story. A staff like that has the last of its maker's power stored up in it, like a battery, see." He pointed to a symbol like a fancy T running along the back of the staff's carved head. "That's the mark of the sorcerer who made it. All sorcerers had their symbols, their trademark, that would be branded, carved, or burnished onto anything they made."

"But an ordinary person can still use it?"

"Sort of. The sorcerer who owned this could have cast fantastic spells with it, but all a Quick can do is force the remaining energy outward in a blast of power. And that's hard enough. Eventually the stored-up magic will run out and then the staff will return to what it was before the sorcerer shaped it, just an old bone."

Nin, halfway through a sip of her honey tea, glanced up and saw the look Boneman sent Jonas as he talked. She coughed. When she looked again the expression, like he could have willingly put a knife through Jonas's heart on the spot, had been replaced by an affable smile and a nod of agreement. She thought she must have been mistaken, but her nerves were still jangling with shock.

"It makes a fair weapon, for those Quick who can master it." Boneman's voice was calm, unconcerned. "I found it abandoned in one of the old northern castles." He put down his mug while he ate.

"And what about the . . . mud . . . things?"

"Oh those! Anyone can do that." Boneman waved a hand dismissively. "The magic is in the Land, all you need to do is use it right. Mud to make, fire to bake, words to wake. Simple. Once you've baked them hard, just tap them on the head, give them a name and tell them what you want them to do. You don't need sorcerer power for *that*."

Nin nodded through a mouthful of cake, th the crumbs from her fingers and returned to which was turning out to be pleasantly war glanced up, feeling Boneman's eyes on her. The very bright, almost turquoise. He smiled.

"So, girl, do you know where you are?"

"It's called the Drift," she said flatly. "But that's it."

Boneman laughed, gulping down the last of his honey tea. "Here goes, then. But I don't want any of that, 'I don't believe in faeries' stuff. You obviously do or you wouldn't be here."

Indignantly, Nin put on her grown-up face, though she suspected it just looked like she had swallowed a wasp. So she gave up. She was too interested to pretend.

"What you have to understand," Boneman began, "is that everything you see around you is not made of atoms as you understand them. It is fashioned from raw magic. The clouds, the trees, the rivers,"—he swept an arm over the landscape—"even the animals that run in the woods and the birds that fly in the air."

Nin was quiet, watching Boneman intently. He was on his feet now and his hands wove pictures in the air as he spoke, using the staff like a prop, to point or gesture. In the background, the lumpy shapes of the mudmen stood still in the sun, casting odd, misshapen shadows on the grass.

"The Long Land, to give it its rightful name, is the way things are in people's hearts. The essence of dread and desire made real. Take the gateways, for example. The Quickmares, as we call them, that link the two worlds always open up in places where dread or desire is strong." Boneman laughed. "Which is the reason that they are always moving from one site to another as people's hearts change. But not their deepest hearts, of course. The fears and longings in their deepest, most unspoken hearts are always constant."

"So what lives here? Magical people?"

"The Fabulous. Faeries and worse. Giants, dragons, elves, the lot."

"Sorcerers?"

"Of course. Sorcerers were the most powerful of all, the rulers of the Fabulous. No witches, mind. They are just ordinary Quick who use the Long Land's magic for themselves."

"Like you and that staff," put in Jonas.

Nin glanced at Boneman, looking for some sign of the malevolence that had shown on his face earlier. There was nothing. She must have imagined it.

He ignored Jonas and went on. "Like the Land and everything in it, the Fabulous are made from raw magic, but they are much more potent than the birds and animals because they have intelligence and power, terrible power. Although you might think you know what a giant, a goblin or a faerie is, you don't. The Fabulous are creatures born from dread and desire, not just foolish Quick legends, so they might not be quite as you expect." He smiled, his blue eyes vivid. His voice dropped to a husky whisper. "You should see the tombfolk, girl. Fear and desire all rolled into one awesome package."

"And death," snapped Jonas.

"That too," laughed Boneman.

"What are they? Like . . . vampires or something?"

"And much more! They are so beautiful you would consider it an honor to feed them." As much as the words, Boneman's soft voice gave Nin a chill up her spine.

"Get on with it!" Jonas scowled.

Boneman took up the story again, speaking more normally.

"Back in the great days, the mighty days when magic ruled the hearts of Quick and the Fabulous *were* magic, the Long Land was a glorious place. The Fabulous called it Celidon and it was full of wonders. And terrors, of course. Never forget the terrors."

"But it changed?"

"Of course. All things change."

Boneman sighed, his face becoming solemn. Nin could have sworn that the turquoise of his eyes faded as his expression altered.

"There was a plague. It came from nowhere and nobody knows how it began or why. But a terrible darkness swept through the land of Celidon, cutting down the Fabulous like a scythe cuts wheat. The faeries and the elves were first, along with the dragons. Then the giants and the wood and water spirits and so on. At last it reached the most magnificent of all the Fabulous—the sorcerers. They lived here, in the east and the south of Celidon, and when they realized that the plague had begun to take them as well, they took shelter in the beautiful city of Beorht Eardgeard. They barricaded themselves in, refused to let any travelers stop there and killed any Quick stupid enough to turn up at the gates. It did no good."

"It still got in?"

"Believe me, this plague could get through any wall. And when it did, it destroyed them so fast that in the end the dead lay piled in the streets!"

Nin shuddered.

"Oh, they fought hard to stay alive, but it was no use."

"They all died?"

"They all died or ceased to be sorcerers, which is more or less the same thing." A shadow crossed Boneman's face and he turned away, but Nin caught a glimpse of something in his eyes like an old, bitter rage. When he looked back it was gone. He smiled wryly. "And when the sorcerers met their end, Celidon ceased to exist."

"You mean like, it went back to being the Long Land?"

"Oh it's always been the Long Land. Celidon was what the Fabulous called it. Like the Quick call it the Drift."

"The plague can't have killed all the Fabulous? What about the . . . the bogeymen?"

"Some Fabulous survived, but not many. And although the worst is over, it's still out there, slowly destroying the few that are left. Even the bogeymen are a dying breed."

"Doesn't stop them being horrible!" grumbled Nin. "What happened next? Is there more?"

"Sure there's more. There's the tale of the Seven Sorcerers, for a start. About how they tried to cheat

Death. But that's not really the story of the Long Land. The story of the Land is still going on, because after the plague had taken out the sorcerers, something worse happened. Something far, far worse." Boneman paused and leaned toward her, his eyes turquoise again, bright in his brown face. "The plague began to kill the Land."

"The Land!" breathed Nin. "How?"

Quickmare

Boneman smiled slowly. He straightened up, taking a firmer grip on his staff. "It's mid-morning, we should be getting on."

"What!"

"Best tradition of storytelling, girl," he said evenly. "Get them hooked and leave them on a cliff. Right?"

Jonas was shaking his head. Nin burst out laughing. "Okay! But I want the rest, you can't just leave it. I HATE not knowing the end of a story!"

"I'll tell you on the road. Thought we might travel together a while." Boneman smiled, then turned to the mudmen.

"Nemus, Enid, Senta, Crow, Dark, get moving."

Underneath their burdens, the mudmen creaked into life, the reddish glow of their eyes brightening again. They shuffled forward and stood ready.

Jonas sighed. "Look, no offense, but . . ."

Boneman laughed and this time the chill was right there in his eyes. "Are you going to tell me that you prefer to travel alone? Well, I have other plans. You could be useful. She could be useful." He nodded toward Nin. "A girl child lost in a strange land. Believe me, it will open doors. You'd be surprised how much more people trust you when you have a kid in tow. They think it shows a caring nature." He laughed and Nin felt her skin prickle with fear.

"No," said Jonas in a voice like steel. He flicked a look at the ring on Boneman's finger, then at the staff, then fastened his gaze on Boneman's face.

"Don't anger me, boy." Boneman's eyes turned the color of dark water, his hand curled more tightly round the staff. He seemed taller suddenly, taller and colder. "Mind your manners and I might let you live. For now at any rate. I could do with a Quick servant. The mudcreatures have their limits."

Jonas was slowly backing away, his eyes still fixed on Boneman, one hand stretched out toward Nin. She reached for it. Jonas pulled her toward and behind him.

Boneman whirled the staff, aiming the dragon's head in their direction. Jagged, blue fire danced across Nin's vision. She heard it crackle and a smell like scalding water filled the air. The lightning bolt hit the ground just in front of Jonas and he leapt backward, forcing Nin to scurry out of the way. Jonas landed awkwardly, slipping to one knee and staggering up again. The grass at his feet was a mess of ashes. Nin gazed in horror at Boneman, now gripping the staff with both hands. He smiled. It was a playful smile. Dandy Boneman was having fun.

The staff twitched to the left, pointing at Nin and tilting slightly down.

"Her leg first, I think. I can do plenty of damage without killing her. Then we'll see how you feel, boy, when she's screaming."

Nin didn't waste breath on a cry. She slithered backward, turned and ran, hoping Jonas would follow.

Blue light sent an eerie glow over the landscape, but Nin was gone. She hurtled down the hillside toward the concrete mound of the underpass, remembering what Jonas had said about it being a one-way gate. She didn't care how unfriendly the thing was, it would get her home and away from this dream that was really a nightmare.

Its mouth loomed ahead, for once almost welcoming. She just had time to hear Jonas scream, "NIN—NO!" before she was over the threshold and into the underpass.

As the sound of feet on concrete died away, a slender figure wearing a long coat and ringlets came to a halt a few feet away from the tunnel mouth. The mudmen, still carrying their burdens, clattered to a stop at his heels. The one that was crumbling had lost part of its leg by now and was lagging badly behind.

Dandy Boneman stared thoughtfully into the darkness. After a moment, he shrugged and switched his attention to the mudmen. He frowned. Then he took the bundle of clothes and the large saucepan away from the damaged one and divided it between the others, heaping their burdens even higher.

And then he turned and walked away.

The four laden mudmen trotted after him. The fifth stayed where it was as the light faded from its eyes and it began, quickly, to crumble back into the earth.

Nin kept going. Ahead she could see the blank wall where the tunnel turned sharply to the right. In a heartbeat she was there and around the corner.

Where she stopped dead.

The bull turned its head and looked at her.

It was huge. It filled the tunnel. Its black hide was

glossed with sweat and its hot breath steamed on the air. The smell was like the zoo only hotter, richer.

"Don't move," said Jonas softly from over her shoulder.

Nin had no intention of moving and didn't think she'd have been able to anyway, so she nodded.

The bull pawed the ground with one coarse hoof. It snorted, blowing jets of steam though its flared nostrils. Its head swung slowly from side to side as if trying to get her properly in its sights.

"Back off slowly. We've got until it lowers its horns. When it does that it's going to charge."

Around the bull, splintered bones lay scattered and a skull watched with empty eyes, half crushed at the back. Something old and dark stained the tips of the bull's yellowed horns. Bizarrely, in the background the steps still ran up to the High Street and Nin could hear the murmur of traffic. It sounded a universe away.

"Then we run," went on Jonas.

"I can't move," said Nin, her voice faint, hanging at the point of dread.

She felt Jonas put a hand on her shoulder and squeeze. "Yes, you can." He pulled her gently backward. Her feet resisted for a moment then fumbled into life. One step. Another.

"When I say go, run. Okay? And keep running. Don't stop or look back until you're out. It won't cross the threshold. Once you're out of the tunnel you're safe."

The bull snorted again. The slow swing of its head stopped. Red eyes fixed on her.

"And, Nin . . ."

"Uh?"

"If I should fall or anything, don't stop."

"Don't you dare!" she hissed.

She couldn't see him, but she knew from his voice

that he was smiling. "I'll stop for you, but don't you stop for me. That's an order, kid. I can move faster than you. You can't afford to waste time, got it?"

The bull lowered its head.

"GO!"

Nin turned and ran. She got around the corner and nearly stopped from the shock of what she was seeing. But Jonas was yelling at her so her feet just kept going, taking her with them. The underpass had changed.

Around the corner, what should have been a few yards back to the entrance had become a long, dark tunnel, stretching on and on to a dot of light far in the distance. The bull reached the corner. Nin heard the thud of its heavy body as it turned its bulk too late. It bellowed and the sound was huge. Nin would have screamed, but she didn't have any breath to spare.

Then it was around the corner and on the move again, its hooves filling the tunnel with thunder.

If it hadn't been for Jonas behind her she would have given up. She would have collapsed in a sobbing heap and let her bones join the ones crumbling under her feet. But Jonas was there so she kept running. Sweat misted her eyes and her chest hurt with the effort. She couldn't feel her legs.

Behind her the thunder drew closer as the head start they had on the bull was eaten away. It seemed like the distant point of light would never get any nearer, but just as she thought her lungs would burst they plunged out of the darkness and into the light.

Nin dropped like a stone.

She lay on the grass, red mist clouding her vision, blood pounding in her ears, her lungs full of hot coals. Jonas stood over her, gasping.

After a minute she heard him say, "Get up, Nin."

She raised her head, remembering Dandy Boneman and his fire-spitting staff. There was nobody there. Silence stretched out as Jonas scanned the scene.

"He's gone. Probably thought we were as good as dead."

"Charming," muttered Nin to the grass.

"We better get out of sight, come on."

She pulled herself up, hanging on to Jonas, her chest still heaving. Together they stumbled down the slope, turning away from the tunnel, until they reached more woodland.

"What was that?" gasped Nin. "I mean, in there. I know it was a bull, but it was . . . so . . ."

"Ectofright. It's part of the Quickmare, it couldn't exist outside." Jonas was scanning the hillside carefully, looking for any sign of life. Then he pointed to a gap between some bushes on the edge of the wood. "Stay there."

"But . . ."

"My pack. I need it. I won't be long."

Nin waited, in knots of fear, for him to come back. She didn't like to think what might happen if he ran into Boneman again. Both to him and to her. Without him she would be lost in this strange world with its unnatural ways. She shuddered, remembering the blank, mindless mud things. Of course, she could always go back to the Widdern, but without home and family, would that be any better? And what about Toby?

The bushes rustled and she barely managed to stifle a scream. It was Jonas, his battered leather pack with its tarnished buckles slung loosely over one shoulder. He was also clutching Monkey.

"Yours, I think? Didn't I see it tucked into your waistband?"

"Do you mind!" she said indignantly, snatching the toy. "It was Toby's." She stuffed it back into the waistband of her pajamas and smiled at him. "I kind of kept it with me, just in case I ended up forgetting like everyone else."

"You're stolen now, remember. Outside that particular magic. It would only work if the rest of your life went on as normal and kind of filled in the hole left by Toby."

"I'm a pretty long way from normal right now," said Nin mournfully. She shuffled out of her hiding place after him.

"And getting further every minute," said Jonas cheerfully. "Right, we should move on. *If* Boneman thinks we're dead already, I'm hoping he won't try coming after us. But, just in case, I'd feel happier living somewhere else for a while. There's a town, Hilfian. I know someone there who will give us shelter."

He was already settling the backpack properly into place. Nin watched anxiously.

"I'm sorry," she said, "I mean, for getting us into trouble. And for running away like that. I was so scared I didn't know what else to do."

"Don't worry about it. Running away is a great survival technique, so get used to it. We'll probably do a lot of running away." Jonas started walking purposefully. Nin scurried after him.

"Not that you asked," she mumbled, getting in his way, "but I didn't say I was coming with you. I—I have to go and look for Toby." Fear uncurled inside her at the thought of heading off on her own.

Jonas stopped and turned to face her, his gray eyes looking seriously into her blue ones.

"Nin, you have to understand, once a kid is taken to the House of Strood they're gone. Really gone. As in never heard of again. Believe me, if I thought there was a chance I'd tell you. Anyway, you wouldn't last five minutes alone in the Drift. You've got a lot to learn about surviving here. Like not to trust every cake-offering stranger you run into. Got that?"

"Okay, okay!"

"I mean it. Especially when the balance of power is not in your favor, right?"

"You're talking about the staff?"

"Uh-huh. Anyway, my point is, you'd do best to stick with me, okay?"

Nin looked up into his steady gray eyes. Right now, he was the only person in the whole world, both the worlds, who knew her name and she just wasn't brave enough to leave him.

"Just so's I know," she asked cautiously, "if I *was* going to look for Toby, which direction . . ."

"North," said Jonas cheerfully. "And yes, I'm going north too, so you can go with me and still be looking for your brother, for a while at least." He looked her up and down, then sighed. "You're a real sight, you are. Not to mention that you can't run around in a torn T-shirt, pajama bottoms and fluffy socks."

Blinking back tears of relief, Nin looked down at herself. Her T-shirt was a wreck with a big tear right across it and a sleeve dangling loose. Her once pink socks were caked with earth and her pajama bottoms were filthy.

"I liked those socks," she said mournfully, curling her toes.

"We need to get you sorted out before we go anywhere." He started walking again. She noticed that he was heading back up the hill, toward number 27. "So first off, we'll go back to the Widdern and see if we can find you some things."

"What? Do you mean steal stuff!"

"Look, if your mum knew about all this she'd want to help you, wouldn't she? You know she'd give you anything you needed."

Nin opened her mouth then shut it again. She thought about it. "I tell you what, Mum puts all the things for charity in a bag in the garage. I bet there's clothes there we could use."

"There you go," said Jonas. "That's where we'll start then."

The Last Breath of Celidon

I t still looked like home. Nin felt dangerously close to tears. She was nervous too, and running about in her nightwear wasn't helping.

"It didn't seem so bad in the Drift," she said anxiously, crunching up her toes in their grubby socks. "Like, when you're being kidnapped by hideous monsters or blown to bits by staff-waving maniacs, hanging about in your pajama bottoms just isn't an issue."

"You're fine," said Jonas. "You're a dropout, no one will even look at you. In fact they'll do their best not to, you'll see."

He pushed open the gate of the Redstone house. Nin edged past him, peering up at the blank windows. Her mother would be at work, her grandmother out shopping, and Grandad? Well, hopefully he'd be upstairs in the flat with his usual newspaper and a cup of tea strong enough to stand the teaspoon up in.

"Thing is, it'll be locked," she said, "but there's a window around the side and the catch is broken." Nin hurried to the small window hidden in the shadow of the trees.

"Nice and sheltered, perfect for a spot of breaking

and entering," she whispered more cheerfully than she felt. Even if she knew that her mother would gladly hand over anything to help her daughter—if she could only remember who Nin was—it still felt wrong.

She watched Jonas make short work of opening the window. She had a nasty feeling he might be used to this kind of thing.

"You'll have to go in," he said, "it's too narrow for me. You can hand the stuff out."

With a lift up from Jonas, squeezing through the gap feet first wasn't hard and fortunately she didn't land on anything painful. In the corner of the garage she found two bin bags, one of clothes and one of books and DVDs.

She pulled the clothes bag open and tipped out the contents. All of the things that tumbled on to the floor were her mother's or grandparents', her own belongings had disappeared along with the world's memory of Ninevah Redstone. She sighed. They'd have to do, though how she would manage with just her socks to walk in she didn't know. She picked out a pair of jeans, two T-shirts, a sweater and a jacket.

"Hurry," called Jonas softly.

Nin pushed the clothes through the window to Jonas and began to shove the rest back into the bin bag. Except that there was one last thing wrapped up in a carrier bag. It was a pair of her old boots. Scuffed and worn, but still boots and still hers.

"That is sooo brill!" she said, scrambling back through the window with a leg-up from an old paint can. "My boots! How did they get missed!" She pulled them on. They still fit.

"It's a million-to-one chance," said Jonas cheerfully,

wrapping the clothes into a bundle to stuff into his pack. "Maybe you're just lucky."

Nin scooped up the jacket to hand to him when she heard a sound. Jonas melted into the trees. Nin was about to follow him when she dropped the jacket. Stooping to grab it, she straightened up and found herself face to face with Grandad.

He was gripping a trowel and his gardening gloves. He watched her through ragged eyebrows, his face stern.

"Um," said Nin, "I needed some clothes."

Grandad looked her over carefully. He took in the torn T-shirt, the muddy pj's and the battered boots, then moved on to her tangled hair and smudged face.

"I can see that," he said gruffly. "Are those leggings? Looks like someone's old pajamas to me."

"It's the pattern," said Nin.

"What's your name then?"

"Nin," said Nin hopefully.

"Where d'you live?"

Nin was silent for a moment. "A world away," she said finally. Which was true if you took it that she kind of belonged in the Drift now.

"Been hitching rides, have you? Didn't anyone ever tell you that's dangerous?" Grandad looked her over again. "You don't look beaten up or ill-treated and you don't look like you've been on the streets for long either. Why did you run away? Had a row with your mum?"

"Sort of."

"D'you know she didn't mean it? Cos I'm telling you she didn't."

Nin felt her eyes fill with tears. She didn't want them, they just happened.

Grandad looked at the tears thoughtfully. "Going back then?"

Nin nodded again.

"I should take you to the police. They'll see you home."

"No! I'll go on my own," said Nin stubbornly.

Grandad looked at her for a long time, then heaved a sigh. He put down the trowel and threw the gloves after it, then rummaged in his pocket.

"If I went to ring the police you'd be gone by the time I got back," he said. He pulled out a battered wallet. "So I'm making a choice here. You can keep the jacket, it's only for jumble anyway. This"—he handed her some notes—"is for a ticket home."

Nin gaped at him. She took the notes stiffly.

"You know what'll happen to you if you don't go home?" Grandad looked stern.

Nin had never really noticed before how piercing his eyes were. She managed a smile and returned his gaze. "The bogeyman'll get me."

Grandad gave her another long look and then his face crinkled into a grin. "That'll do," he said.

Then he picked up the gloves and trowel and ambled off into the garden.

Jonas slid out of the greenery, grabbed her arm and dragged her toward the gate, hustling her out on to the street and down the hill.

"Get moving! Whatever he said, he might be calling the cops now. What did he give you?"

Nin held out the money.

"Not bad!" He started off down the road, walking fast.

She scurried after him, pulling on the jacket as they went.

* * *

Irritably, Skerridge watched them go. His morning had been horrible. He hadn't had time for breakfast, the sun made his head ache and his eyes smart, and the Quick had kept getting in his way as he ran around the town looking for Right Madam. He had reduced several children to hysterics (much to the distress of their parents), had eaten a small dog for barking at him and had set fire to the fire station for . . . well . . . for just being there really. He had searched everywhere but he had not found so much as a sniff of Right Madam.

So, after a lot of thought, he had finally worked out that she would go home. Even if her mother threw her out again, she would still try. With nowhere else to go and nobody to help her, there was nothing else she could do. Skerridge simply had to hide under a nice shady tree in the garden and wait for her to come to him.

Unfortunately, the Bogeyman Code was firm on the point that kids had to be alone when snatched—at least "Never In Front Of Witnesses" seemed pretty clear to Skerridge, whichever way he looked at it—and he hadn't bargained for her turning up with a boy in tow.

Skerridge hadn't automatically known the boy's name, which meant that he had to be one of the Stolen. Beyond that Skerridge knew nothing and cared less. The kid was just an obstacle. A bright one, judging by the way he had slipped silently into the trees (only a few feet away from Skerridge) the instant Old Bloke turned up, but still an obstacle. On the plus side, at least Skerridge now knew where Right Madam was.

He waited a few minutes to let them get a head start, absentmindedly snapping up a small bird that had been stupid enough to land next to him. He munched, then frowned in disgust and spat out the feathers. Birds. Yuck.

* * *

"You know," Nin said as they headed back toward Number 27 and the Drift, "I just worked it out! What Boneman said! Like, if enough people are afraid of something, really afraid in their hearts, then it kind of takes shape."

"Uh-huh?"

"I thought it was just me who was scared of the underpass, but when . . . when Dad died it was in the papers. Only the local ones, but enough people must've read about it. Enough people must go around the corner of the underpass and think about . . . about how he died and be frightened. P'raps avoid using it altogether. So that's why it's here and that's why there's a bull. Right?"

"Sure is," said Jonas calmly. "But sooner or later, people will forget and then the gate'll vanish."

Just as Jonas was about to dive off down the path beside number 27, a chunk-shaped boy with squashed-down hair hurried past them on his way home to lunch.

Nin stopped walking. Then started again. The boy hadn't given her a second glance and a week ago she wouldn't have cared a jot. She sighed. There was so much she could have done and hadn't. Like taking the time to talk to Grandad back when he knew who she was. Like being nicer to Dunk the Chunk instead of snubbing him every time he spoke to her.

She glanced over her shoulder. To her surprise, he was glancing over his. Their eyes met for a single moment and she smiled at him. Dunk went vividly red and nearly fell over his feet. He turned his head away and hurried on.

"What's up?"

"Nothing. Just . . . nothing. I remembered I never

said thanks for listening." She shook her head. "Too late now. Hold on! Now we're off the main road, give me those jeans."

Jonas handed them over silently. They were loose on her and Nin had to roll them up, but they did just fine. The jacket—with the sleeves turned up—covered her torn T-shirt nicely. At any rate, it would have to do, it wasn't like she had much choice.

When they had left the dark hump of the underpass behind, Nin looked back. The hill-that-should-be-Dunforth-but-wasn't rose in a sweep of green up to the clear sky. A soft breeze bore the scent of growing things and fresh water. There was nothing visible to suggest that murder had nearly been done here. Fortunately, there was no sign of Dandy Boneman either. Nin shivered at the memory.

As they traveled, she began to see that the rise and dip of the strange landscape before her matched the one she knew in the Widdern, like the distorted echo of a shape. The same but almost unrecognizably different. It came to her that if the gateways were links from one world to the next, then the two must lie together, the Long Land somehow overlaying the Widdern like a gauzy topcoat. Unseen, but just a step away.

Which meant that by now, they would be wandering across the high street. Buses would be hurtling along right where they were walking. And now they'd be sauntering through the brick walls of the supermarket. She grinned.

"Shame you can't create your own gateways wherever you want. You could be a super-thief. Locked doors, walls, alarms—no problem. Crown Jewels, here we come!"

Jonas laughed. "The security footage would make them sit up!"

A rustle in the bushes to their left caught Nin's attention and she turned to see a fox slinking along in the undergrowth.

"There was something odd about that fox," she told Jonas, trying to work out what it was.

"Yep. Tell me, when in the Widdern did you last see a fox that red and with a brush brushier than an old bootlace? Look, the Long Land is not Alice's Wonderland. You aren't going to wake up and find it was all a dream, it's as real as we are. Real enough to kill. But the things in it, well, they *are* kind of dream-like because they are the idea of things rather than the thing itself. So, the foxes are russet red, with thick bushy tails and sharp minds. Really sharp minds."

Nin glanced back. The fox was watching them, its tongue lolling out and its head cocked on one side. It looked curious. When it caught Nin's eye it flicked its ears nonchalantly and switched its gaze elsewhere.

"They don't . . . talk or anything?"

Jonas gave her a look. "Use that fluff that passes for a brain, please! This is not about stories come to life, right?"

"Okay," said Nin, humbly.

As they walked, Nin watched the woods. She saw tall trees and twisted ones, tiny flowers that glowed like stars in the shadows, and pools of water hung with mist, but no animals or birds at all. She got the feeling that the wildlife knew she was looking for it and was keeping out of sight. She heard birdsong, as clear and sweet as a flute, but couldn't spot the singer. The bushes often rustled behind them, but never in front, and once something thin and dark sprang out of the brambles and back in again before she could get a proper look.

The Long Land knows I'm here, she thought, and the idea was so freaky that she stopped trying to see anything other than the way ahead and stuck close to Jonas.

After the wood came open fields that stretched to the horizon. Far to the left hung the white curtain of Raw, closer now, but still too distant to worry her.

"So, what Fabulous are left then, after the plague and that?"

"BMs, obviously, the tombfolk and the odd werewolf or goblin. Oh, there are a few Fabulous Beasts around too, but all the things you don't want to meet. All the bad things. And the remains of six of the Seven Sorcerers, of course. The things they have become."

"How do you mean?"

Jonas shrugged. "I only know some of it. Basically, the Seven knew that if they stayed as sorcerers the plague would kill them. So they . . . changed. Became something else so that they wouldn't die."

"You mean like, a—a monster, or a great bear, or a wonderful jewel . . ."

Jonas laughed. "Sort of like that, only more complicated. You've already met one, I think. I might be wrong, but there was something about Dandy Boneman that stank of old magic. That ring for a start, the one with the ruby. I think it used to belong to Ava Vispilio."

"And he was one of the Seven Sorcerers?"

"Uh-huh. And if Boneman is wearing Vispilio's ring, it means that Boneman is . . . Well, let's just say that although the body is a man called Dandy Boneman, the thing inside him is what's left of Ava Vispilio. And take those mudmen servants: he'd named them after the other six—Nemus Sturdy, Enid Lockheart, Senta Melana,

Morgan Crow, and Simeon Dark. Just the sort of thing Vispilio would do, like an insult to them, see? He was said to be a nasty piece of work."

"But he's not a sorcerer anymore, just a human using a sorcerer's staff. He can't do sorcerer spells or anything." It wasn't a question. Nin was sure that if Boneman had been able to do real magic they wouldn't be walking around still free.

"You know," she went on, "I bet you're right. I bet it *was* him. He looked daggers at you when you said all that about the staff."

"Honestly, Ninevah Redstone," said Jonas cheerfully, "five minutes in the Drift and you bump into an evil sorcerer!"

Nin shrugged. "It's Wednesday."

They walked in silence for a little way, then Jonas spoke again.

"What Boneman said about Celidon being dead was not exactly true, you know. I think that even though they are no longer sorcerers and can never be sorcerers again, the remains of the Seven are the last breath of Celidon."

Nin looked at the fields of grass, rippling in the scented breeze and splashed with mop-headed dandelions as fierce and bright as tiny suns. Now the sky had clouds scudding across it like vast-winged creatures, their shapes changing as they flew, from pirate ship to coiling dragon to flying horse. The wind was growing stronger and it whipped the summit of the distant Raw into snakes of white vapor that reached hungrily into the air.

"The last breath of Celidon," she said softly. She remembered what Boneman had said about the plague moving onto the Land. The hairs on her skin prickled and she hunched her shoulders, feeling as if the knowledge of something dark was just out of her reach.

After the whole being blasted with magic and chased into the underpass thing, she had been left feeling as if she hated the Drift. Now, having walked a little in its green hills and wild woods, her heart was changing and the tales Boneman had told about the Long Land began to stir her imagination. It was terrifying to know that such a place, filled with such things, could exist, but it was also exciting. To know that all the beauty and the terror were dying and that she would never see it as it once was gave her an ache inside.

Jonas was drawing ahead, so she ran after him as he carved a path through the long grass. It occurred to her that if part of surviving in the Drift was to be careful who you trusted, then she was putting her faith in Jonas far too easily. He turned to grin at her as she tumbled up behind him, panting.

"Come on, kid, there's no time for wool gathering, you know."

For a moment he sounded just like Grandad. It's all right, thought Nin, and whatever he says, I've got to trust someone.

Words to Wake

When Nin's feet were too sore for her to go much further, they settled at the top of a low hill to rest, not far from a small stream. To her dismay Jonas had stopped on the way to pick up some rabbits caught in a snare, and had been walking the last few miles with their cleaned and gutted corpses dangling in a bundle from his pack. They would be passing beyond the boundary of his hunting territory soon, so this would be the last free food ready and waiting. Past this point, Jonas told her, was an afternoon's walk to the Drift town of Hilfian where his friend lived. Then came the long journey to the Savage Forest and the Heart of Celidon before she could even think about making it to the Terrible House of Strood.

Turning it all over in her head, Nin watched as Jonas built a fire and began cooking the rabbit. She didn't fancy the Savage Forest at all, though the Heart of Celidon didn't sound too bad. She went cold inside when she thought about the bit where they reached Hilfian and she went on without him.

But she didn't have to leave Jonas yet, so she tried to put it out of her mind and set about making a mudman according to Dandy Boneman's recipe. She wanted to see the Land work its magic, but also she wanted to learn, to understand it better. She was going to need that knowledge.

Digging up a pile of earth with her bare hands, she raked through it to turn out some of the larger stones. The soil wasn't sticky enough so she scooped up mug after mug of icy water from the stream that seemed to whisper in her ear as she leaned over it.

"Streams, rivers, they all do that," Jonas told her. "People call it the Voice of the Land. It always says the same thing, too—Doom and Death. Death Without End. Sometimes, rivers sing at night—you should hear it then!"

"No thanks!" said Nin with a shiver.

She mixed the water with the earth, adding a little at a time to make sure it didn't get too runny. It reminded her so much of cooking classes at school that she got a fit of the giggles. Once she had it just right she began to push it into shape. The mud felt cool and soft under her fingers, but making it do what she wanted was difficult. Jonas watched her with an amused look, but didn't interfere.

When she had finished she dug her finger into its round head to make eyes and used a twig to scratch a mouth, then stepped back to take a look. Her mudman was lumpier than Dandy's had been. It was lopsided and its arms were too long.

Next came the baking part. She realized that if she tried to pick the mudman up and move it to the fire it would fall apart, so instead she took the fire to the mudman. She gathered some branches and twigs and made a kind of pyre over it, which she lit using one of the twigs as a taper.

By now, the rabbit was coming on nicely and the

smell made Nin's mouth water as she settled down to watch her mudman cook. She wondered what she would live on once she had left Jonas. Berries and things would have to do. She made a mental note to talk to Jonas about berries. And things.

Nin shivered as a surge of longing for her mother rushed through her. Suddenly she felt very alone and lost in this beautiful and deadly land. Even though she knew that Toby might be out there, as lost as she was and in need of her help, Jonas was the only wall between her and a world full of danger and leaving him to go on alone would be unbearably hard. Just thinking about it gave her butterflies in her stomach the size of vultures and about as friendly. But however impossible finding Toby seemed, Nin knew that she couldn't give up. Not if she was going to live with herself ever again. There was being afraid and there was being a coward and they were different.

She swallowed hard, fixing her eyes on the glowing shape of her mudman, deep in the flames.

"So, like, when we get to Hilfian and I leave you, will you do me a map or something about how to get to the House?"

Jonas looked up from stabbing a portion of rabbit with his knife to see if it was done. He grinned. "Still thinking about that then, are you?"

"You said that kids who get taken there are never heard of again, but that's not the same as being dead, is it?"

"It might be. The Terrible House isn't a picnic, you know. It's vast and rambling and full of bad things, the sort of place you get into and then never get out of again."

Nin frowned. "And when I've found Toby and

rescued him, then I need to find Skerridge so's I can make him give me our lives back. And you said Skerridge would be at the House too, right?"

"He'll be in and out. But we are talking bogeymen here. Remember them? Scary Fabulous with red eyes and teeth, not to mention the firebreath. Oh and superspeed, don't forget that. And then there's Dandy Boneman, or should we call him Ava Vispilio. He's out there somewhere, remember, and according to stories, Vispilio never lets an insult go unavenged . . ."

"Okay, I get it!" Nin shrugged her shoulders. "I'm still going."

"I know you have to try," he said. "And for the record, just to take that scared rabbit look off your face, I was always going to take you there. I just wanted to know that you were really set on it, see. Because one thing you're going to need is determination."

Nin stared, then beamed as his words sank in. "You'll come to the House with me?"

"Think I'd let a kid your size run around the Drift on her own! Besides, nerve like that has got to have a reward."

Nin leaned over and gave him a clumsy hug, then settled back again. He took no notice apart from a shake of the head and a grin as he prodded the near-done rabbit. She found herself wondering about his past life, about who he had been once, before he was just Jonas.

"Did you go looking for your life back?"

"Nope. I just got on with living in the Drift, but then I'm a different person and I didn't have anyone to look for, like you've got Toby. I think your mudman's cooked!"

Nin looked back at her fire. The flames were dying and the embers were beginning to fall apart, revealing

the mudman in their fiery heart. Stirred by the thought
of making magic, she jumped up and hurried over,
kicking the ashes aside.

"Now what? Words to Wake, right? Tap it on the
head and name it . . ."

"Wait, Nin!"

She was already leaning over, tapping it in the middle
of its lumpy head with one finger. The mud was not
as hot as it might have been, as if all the fire had gone
inside.

"Jack," she said, using her father's name. She was so
keyed up with hope and relief and fear that her voice
came out as a squeak.

"You've got to give it a task!" said Jonas sharply. He
dropped the plate he was holding and got hurriedly to
his feet.

"Um—I dunno—just—um—be alive."

There was a moment of silence and then a deep,
distant rumble. For a second Nin could have sworn that
the Land trembled.

"You said what!" Jonas shook his head. "You're
supposed to give them a proper task to do! Not just . . .
that! Galig knows what you've made now!"

Nin stared at her mudman. It was still lying on the
ground.

"Then again, maybe it didn't work," went on Jonas
cheerfully.

The mudman sat up. It looked at Nin with its red-
flame eyes.

Jonas sighed. "Look, you give them a clearly defined
job, see. When the job is over, or you tell them to
stop, they are fulfilled and go back to the earth. So
how's that one going to end?" He glared at it. "Well, I

suppose, if it's a problem we can just throw a bucket of water over it."

The mudman turned its glowing eyes on him. Jonas looked uncomfortable.

"He's okay," said Nin, hoping she was right. "He's not going to hurt anyone. Are you?" She looked sternly at the mudman.

It opened its mouth and said, "Jik?"

Jonas sighed and shook his head. "Let's hope it just goes back to earth once it realizes you haven't done it right. And whatever you do DON'T go messing with Land Magic again, okay? Not till you know what you're doing."

"All right! You made your point."

The mudman was on its feet by now. It stood where it was and studied the view. Then it turned, this time staring down the hill. "Jik?"

"It thinks that's its name." Jonas began to serve up the roast rabbit. "Eat, Nin. It's the last food you'll get until tomorrow morning. I've got a couple of hunks of bread I've been saving too."

Nin sat, accepting the bread. It was stale, but did very well as a base for the meat, which Jonas cut into chunks with his knife. The mudman watched them patiently while they ate.

"Jik?"

"Um—hello—" she said through a mouthful of rabbit. She studied the mudman thoughtfully. Jik sat— or rather, fell on to his behind—next to her.

"Jik? Jik!"

"You're gonna have to learn a few more words if you want a conversation," she told him. "Try my name, that's easy. Nin." She pointed to herself with a greasy finger, feeling like she was in some corny Tarzan movie. "Me Nin."

"Jik?"

"Nin. N—I—N."

"Jik?

"I think you're on a loser there." Jonas laughed.

He was already on his feet, stamping out the fires. Nin hurried down the last of her food.

"Right. The worst part of the journey will be the Savage Forest. It's pretty deadly if you don't play it right. And Quick can't survive the Heart either, so normally we'd have to walk all the way round it. Only I know this Quickmare just before you reach the Heart; it's pretty nasty, but it brings you out into the Widdern south of London. With the money your Grandad so kindly gave you, we could get a train from London to Bury St. Edmunds. Then, when we get to Bury, we find another gateway back into the Drift, see? Cut out the walk around the Heart, the longest part of the journey, straight away."

"Good old Grandad, I must remember to thank him when I get back." Nin rolled her pajama bottoms up in her top along with Monkey, tying the arms in a knot to make a bundle. She felt like Dick Whittington only without the stick. Jik trailed along at her heels, like Whittington's cat.

"If! Just because I'm taking you there doesn't mean I think you'll succeed. Is that thing following you?" Jonas grinned. "Well, he might come in handy, I s'pose."

"Jik?"

"Yeah, I'm talking about you."

"Yik!"

"So," she asked as they headed across open heath toward a cluster of trees in the middle of a field of daisies. "What can you tell me about the Terrible House of Strood. Like, why's it called that?"

"Because it's terrible. Oh yeah, and it belongs to Mr. Strood."

"All right, Mr. Smarty Pants. I want detail."

Jonas sighed. "Look, Nin, the thing about the House is that people who go in there don't tend to come back out again, so that kind of puts a damper on the exchange of information. See what I mean? Apart from the BMs, of course. They come and go, but then they don't spend a lot of time gossiping to the Quick."

"What about Mr. Strood? Don't you know anything about him either?"

"Nope." Jonas shrugged. "There are tales about him, but a lot of them are made up. Some people say he's a kind of demon. Others that he's a bewitched monster who eats souls."

Nin turned the stories over in her head. She guessed she would find out the truth eventually, if they ever reached the House. Right now, with the sun on her shoulders, Jik at her heels and Jonas leading the way, she was almost sure they would succeed. Almost.

She had been lucky so far, she knew that. She had Jonas, her boots and Grandad's money to prove it. Perhaps her luck would hold. After all, she had already survived more danger in two days than she had faced in her whole life until now.

"I'll just have to trust to luck," she said cheerfully, "because that's all I have."

Their path took them through a cluster of twisted trees standing in a ring like a circle of dancers turned to wood as they swayed and bent. Shadow dappled them and the air was suddenly cool on their faces and hands.

"Luck!" said Jonas. "You need to come up with

something a bit more concrete than luck if you want to survive the Terrible House of Strood, find Toby *and* get your life back."

"I've got a plan," said Nin, as the path took them out again into the sun and alongside the whispering river. "I just don't know what it is yet."

Underneath a nearby shrub a sinister patch of shadow with blood-red eyes couldn't believe its ears.

Skerridge watched patiently as Right Madam and Obstacle, followed by the mud creature, wandered past him at the painfully slow pace anything that wasn't a BM always used. He didn't move until he thought they were far enough down the path that if they glanced back the trees would be just a shaggy blot on the horizon. Then he exploded.

He rolled out of the shrub and back into his own shape, shaking with laughter. He lay on the ground and roared, accidentally setting fire to a patch of feathery bracken. Scalding tears of mirth steamed on his cheeks.

Skerridge had never heard such a good joke in his life. When he had laughed himself into acid hiccups he calmed down and thought about it.

Skerridge had been worrying about how to get Right Madam to the House, but there was no need to worry anymore because she was WALKING TO THE HOUSE OF HER OWN ACCORD!

And if that wasn't mad enough, the kid even thought she was going to get out again. Alive. Some chance! Not if Mr. Strood had anything to do with it. Right Madam was destined for the same terrifying end as all the other kids over all the many years. Or then again, she might just end up as one of Strood's horrible experiments.

Skerridge sniggered. Main point was, the Quick

would cross the Drift on their own. No need for Skerridge to do a thing. But it was a long haul and a dangerous one and at some point they would run into trouble, get separated or simply leave one another alone for a moment. Then he could snatch Right Madam and run, leaving Obstacle to whatever horrible fate awaited him. After all, there were so many horrible fates in the Drift that sooner or later one of them was bound to get him.

Skerridge grinned. He grinned so fiercely that a rabbit shivering under a bush nearby had a heart attack and dropped dead of fright on the spot. Skerridge's sharp ears picked up the soft sound of its crumpling body. Licking his lips, he grabbed a twig, speared the tiny body through and picked it up. Then he gave it a light roasting with his firebreath and popped it in whole.

When he was finished he yawned, scratched himself, straightened his vest, and disappeared.

A Drop of Rain Won't Hurt You

S o when do we get to the Savage Forest?" asked Nin.
It was late in the afternoon. They had left the
river behind and were crossing a stretch of open
meadow. The wall of Raw was still visible behind them,
looking smaller now and less threatening, like a beached
cloud on the horizon. A red-painted barn dominated the
field to their left, its doors slightly open onto darkness.
From the waves of energy that came off it, Nin knew it
had to be a gateway. Beyond the fields to their right lay
a swathe of woodland, covering a range of low hills like
green fur.

"Tomorrow. Tonight, we need to get to Hilfian by
sunset because we don't want to risk the tombfolk.
Indoors they can't smell you. Out in the open your scent
will travel on the air."

"There isn't exactly the chance of a wash out here,"
grumbled Nin.

"Not that scent, idiot! Life has its own aroma. A
Quick wouldn't smell it. A tombfolk will pick it up from
miles away."

Nin glanced over her shoulder to where Jik was trotting along at her heels. Her eye caught something on the

horizon, a band of purple clouds that boiled against the sky, traveling swiftly toward them.

She sighed. "Look at those clouds! We're gonna get soaked."

"A drop of rain won't hurt you," said Jonas briskly, barely glancing at the sky.

"Yeah, but what about Jik? I mean, won't he kind of melt? Get washed away like a mud pie?"

"Of course. That'd be one problem solved, anyway."

"He's not a problem," said Nin indignantly.

Jonas sighed and came to a halt. "Strapped to the bottom of my pack," he said, "there's a roll of waxed cloth. It's waterproof."

He stood patiently while Nin fiddled with the straps. The cloth wasn't big, barely enough for Jonas to lie on, but it would do. Feeling goosebumps run along her arm as the temperature plunged, she draped it around Jik like a stiff shawl so that only his glowing eyes peered out. He looked puzzled. Already it was growing dark.

"It'll keep you dry when it rains. The clouds are coming up awfully fast."

"What?" Jonas turned his head to look. He went pale. "Nin! Don't argue, just run. Toward the wood."

She opened her mouth to ask why, but a glance at Jonas's face made her shut it again and start to jog across the field. The trees were a strip of darker green ahead and suddenly it seemed like they were miles away. Thunder rumbled at their backs, shaking the air and sending a cold wind to lift Nin's hair and chill her blood. If clouds can be pirate ships, she thought, what is it that runs in the storm?

Jonas was doing a steady trot rather than going full tilt, so as not to wear them out. Even so Nin soon found herself gasping for breath. She glanced up. The sky was more than dark, it was a mass of seething purple that swallowed the light in bounds. She struggled along behind Jonas, her hair flopping in her eyes and blood pounding in her ears. They were gaining on the trees, but the clouds were faster.

Lightning slashed the sky with brilliance and the thunder that followed was loud enough to make Nin scream. She was stumbling now, hanging on to Jonas for support. A brown object, knee-high and crackling as it ran, overtook her. It glanced back and she saw Jik's eyes glow from under the waxed hood as the first drops of rain hit and ran across its slippery surface.

The trees were dead ahead, lit by another slash of white light. Just a little further, she thought, and tripped.

Her scream as she fell was lost in breaking thunder that shook the ground. Jonas was at her back in an instant, shielding her with his body and hauling her to her feet. Around them the air was filled with the clamor of baying hounds and suddenly she knew what it was in the storm. Rain came now in a wall of ice that beat her head and drowned her eyes. And then Jonas lifted her in his arms and fell past the first trees into shelter.

They lay in the gloom, listening to the Hounds rage over their heads, unable to come to ground without tearing themselves into slivers of dank air on the branches. Nin was gulping quietly, trying to hold the tears back. Jonas stared up through the canopy of leaves, his eyes bright with fear. Keeping under the waxed cloth, Jik watched anxiously, nothing visible save for the reddish glow of his eyes.

"I'm sorry," said Nin as soon as she could speak.

"It wasn't your fault, kid. They move fast, the Gabriel Hounds."

"W-what are they exactly?"

"The Gabriel Hounds *are* the Storm. They're not physical, more like shapes made of cloud and energy. They hunt the Quick. If they come close enough to touch you, then they think you are theirs and never let up until they get you. And when they do, you get swallowed up and made like them. You never escape. You forget everything and hunt with them. Give it a while and you become one yourself."

Nin was silent, tears near to the surface again. "I felt their breath, was that close enough?"

Jonas turned a pale face to smile at her. "No, kid. Not quite enough. They didn't touch you."

"You then!" She began to feel panicky. "They'll come back for you?"

Jonas sat up. He shrugged. "Better make sure we keep our eyes open and stay out of their way, hadn't we."

"Listen," whispered Nin, staring up.

The Hounds were rising higher into the sky and as they left the Land behind, the heavy rain slowed quickly to a halt. Even so, drops still pattered down from the trees and Jik stayed huddled nervously under his make-shift umbrella, his flame eyes glowing in the half-light. Nin shivered, listening to the low rumbles of thunder from the Hounds as they circled high overhead, waiting for their prey to come out.

"I'm crazy, aren't I?" she asked. "I mean, to think that a four-year-old kid could still be alive in a world where even the storms can swallow you whole."

"Changing your mind about going to find him?"

Nin didn't even have to think about it. She sat up.

"No! I didn't mean that. Even if I think it's mad, I have to try, because he's my brother and I want him back."

She meant it. Thinking about him lost in this dangerous world, perhaps hurt or frightened or lonely, made wanting to find him feel like a huge, painful knot inside her. She shook her head, her ears filled with a high-pitched ringing that brought her out in goosebumps.

"Can you hear that noise?"

"Probably just a rabbit."

Jonas was on his feet, checking his pack. Jik settled his wrap more comfortably over his head and looked in disgust at the wet woodland floor.

"It's not *that* sort of noise," mumbled Nin getting up carefully. She was worried she might have twisted an ankle during their tumble into the wood, but it took her weight all right.

"Okay," said Jonas, "we'll have to stay here until the Hounds move off—and I warn you, they could trap us in here for days. Still, being under cover makes it harder for tombfolk pick up our scent, so that's good. Problem is, if they *do* happen to come close enough to smell us, then the trees won't stop them. Gabriel Hounds are only made of cloud and the branches break them up, but tombfolk are different. When they are in the air, tombfolk are like ghosts and can fly through anything in their way. And then there are the bears to worry about, of course."

"Bears? Cool."

"You won't think that when they're gnawing on your leg-bones!" Jonas grinned at her, his face pale in the gloom. "Still, it's a chance we'll have to take." He glanced up through the rain soaked trees to the storm clouds beyond.

Brushing off the wet leaves that clung to her jeans, Nin paused, turning her head to stare into the darkness between the trees. For a moment she thought she heard that eerie ringing again, but there was nothing, only a faint rustle away to their left. Probably just rain trick-ling through the greenery. Or a rabbit. She shivered. The wet woods had an earthy, graveyard smell.

"I just thought," she said nervously. "Tombfolk. I mean, I know it's still day and all that, so they won't be out hunting, but what if they *live* in here?"

"No, too much light. Anyway, they like to live around tombs. The clue is in the name, you see."

Nin thumped him gently on the arm. Something beyond him caught her attention.

"Anyway, what's *that*!" She pointed.

Rising through the dark shadows of the woodland was a pale column, gleaming wetly in the storm light.

"I thought it was a dead tree, but it's not."

Jonas studied it, then moved closer, picking his way carefully through the undergrowth. Nin and Jik followed in his tracks. A few paces from the base of the column, they stopped to stare. It was twice as broad as Nin and shaped more like a flattened oval than a round pillar. The whole thing was curved too, not rising straight from the ground like Nin had expected, but round like the outer rim of a vast wheel. Three pairs of eyes followed the line of it as it swept up, its top almost reaching the canopy of leaves overhead, and then down again the other side.

"It's like an arch, only the wrong shape, too round," muttered Jonas, frowning as he tried to work out what it was.

"Jik!"

The mudman pointed deeper into the woods. There were more of them. A few feet away, looped in ivy and hemmed with thick moss, was another strange arch-like shape. And beyond that, almost hidden in the green shadows, shone the pale gleam of a third.

Although discolored and scarred by weather and time, their creamy color showed through, glowing against the dark trees. Nin looked behind her.

"It's like a row of weird arches and we're in the middle."

"I wonder how many there are? I can see three in front of us and two behind, but there are probably more hidden by the trees. They're pretty old too; this wood must have grown up around them. Look, that one's broken."

Jonas pointed to one of the row that had splintered into a jagged point halfway down, revealing a honeycomb of porous rock inside.

Nin craned her head back, picking out the line of the arches just below the thick spread of leaves that formed the roof of the woodland.

"They join up at the top, look, there's something running along from this arch to the next one. Like a kind of bridge, only it's not that. It reminds me of something, but I can't think what."

Jonas was frowning. "You're right the shape does seem familiar . . ."

There was a sudden crack of thunder from the storm clouds above. Nin gasped as something small and inky swirled around them, followed by a cluster of others, then hurtled upward. An eerie screeching filled the air.

"Bats," said Jonas. "Thunder disturbed them, I guess. You're not afraid of bats, are you?"

"Nope. No worries." Nin sent him a worried look. "So long as they're not the blood-sucking sort?"

"Don't get vampire bats in the Drift as far as I know. Just vampires." He looked up at the swirling cloud as it disappeared into the space beneath the arches. "Must be a nice place for them to sleep."

"I s'pose," said Nin doubtfully. "I'd just like to know what it is. I mean, I'd think it was ruins, but it doesn't look right for a building at all."

Jonas's gray eyes went wide with astonishment. "I've got it!" A smile crossed his face as, for a moment, he forgot about the Hounds. "You're right, it's not a building. It's too *natural*. This wasn't made. This GREW, like you and me."

Nin looked bewildered.

"It's a giant. Or the remains of one. Look, Nin."

He dragged her closer to the arch, near enough to touch the rough surface of the stone. Only it wasn't stone. It was bone.

"A skeleton! The ribcage, see. The skeleton is lying on its back and these curved columns are ribs. They rise to join at the breastbone, which is that bridging bit at the top. I bet if we dug underneath we'd find the backbone. Buried under decades of leaf mold and tons of bat dung. The rest of him is probably buried in the wood or crumbled away. Wonder what happened to the skull!"

Nin was silent, staring. Trying to imagine a person so huge that their chest would be as big as a castle hall. A glimmer of lightning made the white bone flick into sharp relief against the dark trees. High above, the storm rumbled again.

"Think of that," she breathed, "lying there dead with whole trees pushing up through your ribcage where your lungs used to be, and hundreds of bats fluttering in your heart space." She smiled. It was grisly, but it was pretty fantastic too. "A real giant!"

"Giants didn't normally live this far south, but people say that when they were all dying, the oldest and strongest of them all, the last of his kind, got lonely and left the Giant Ridge to come and live down here where there were other Fabulous still alive."

Edging closer, level with the columns of bone, Nin could see the inside of the giant's ribcage, festooned with bats hanging from the joining ridge and the upper sides like some kind of weird lining. Below, the ground was thick with their droppings and she wrinkled her nose at the squelching underfoot. Peering at the bats, she thought something glinted, shining out at her once from the depths of the shifting, rustling, leathery mass far above her head, then disappeared. There was something silver up there, caught just where the rib dipped to join the breastbone. She wondered how it had got there, carried by the bats perhaps?

"What's that?" She cocked her head, listening. It was that ringing again, cutting through the sound of distant thunder. It reminded her of the noise a tuning fork makes, a high, silver humming, calling her. From up above, deep in the sea of bat wings, came a glint of light that pierced her eyes and was gone.

"I dunno," said Jonas, but he wasn't hearing the same thing as Nin. Eyes suddenly sharp and every muscle tense, he was staring into the trees where something rustled stealthily.

"Nin, be careful. I think someone else might be hiding in here with us."

Ignoring him, Nin stepped forward into the dead giant's chest space, regardless of the bat droppings. All she could hear was that silver ringing. Her skin tingled as the sound ran through her like electricity. There was only one thought in her head. She wanted the shining thing and she wanted it NOW.

"I'm coming," she murmured, her eyes searching the darkness overhead for that bright gleam.

Jonas glanced after her, startled.

"Nin? Where are you going?" His expression turned to one of fear as he saw her put one foot on the slope of the rib and begin to climb. "WHAT THE HELL ARE YOU DOING!"

And in that moment, as Jonas stared the other way, Dandy Boneman stepped out of the shadows.

10

Giant's Rib

Boneman was alone this time. Unlike Jik, his mudmen hadn't made it through the storm. He didn't say a word, he just took aim at Jonas and fired.

Jik sprang, leaving his waxy overcoat behind as he flew through the air. Before Jonas worked out what was happening, Jik got him in the midriff and the two of them crashed to the ground and rolled just as the blast struck, right where he had been standing.

I've killed us, Jonas thought, as he lay face down in the damp earth, I should have guessed Boneman would be heading for the town. The storm must have driven him in here too.

He pushed himself up, leaping back on to his feet. Jik was already standing.

Boneman snarled, his eyes glittering in the half-light. His coat was so drenched it looked nearly black and his hair hung in dripping rat-tails. In the gloom the staff shone, radiance coming off it like steam. One hasty glance at Boneman's face was enough to tell Jonas that he was right. The body might be that of a mere Quick, but inside was the once-sorcerer, Ava Vispilio.

The only shield to hand was the great column of the giant's rib, so Jonas edged sideways fast, keeping an eye on the staff as he went. Boneman tracked him, steadying his aim, but Jik bunched his fists and jumped into the line of fire, eyes glowing. The staff wavered as Boneman took a surprised step back.

Jonas stopped and grinned savagely. "Give up now," he said. "I've got a mudman and he's aimed at your heart. The staff won't stop him because he was born in fire and believe me, he's ready to take you out."

"Nice try," sneered Boneman. "But Land Magic isn't that strong, boy. The thing is only a lump of earth. One blast and it will shatter into pieces."

Jik leaped aside and the staff followed, blue fire arching from its dragon-tip as it spun, ripping through anything that stood in its path.

Inside the skeleton, Nin was halfway up the giant's rib. Its inner surface had a coat of rough scaling that left gaps and edges where she could wedge her fingertips and the toe end of her boots. She scrambled on, higher and higher, the bats shuffling out of her way with a leathery rustling. All she could hear was the ringing sound, like a bell calling her. All she could see was a dazzle, star-like above her, hanging from the top of the ribcage.

Blue-white and vivid in the giant's shadowy insides, the blast cut the air close enough for Nin to feel its heat through the soles of her boots. It carved a dark furrow in the moss and the bone beneath and a stink of burning filled the air, along with the sound of splitting bone.

Nin screamed as she felt the rib lurch sideways, then jerk to a stop. Her grip went and she hung loose, her left arm flailing wildly as she clung on by her toes and the fingers of one hand. Bats took off in a swirling blur, pattering against her face and body like dark rain and blocking her vision, their high-pitched screech surrounding her. She reached out desperately, feeling their wings under her hand as they curved and dipped, spinning around her in a whirlwind of leathery wings. Then her fingers found bone and she scrabbled for a hold, ripping her nails and grazing her hand, until she was safe again, cheek pressed against the rough surface, heart thudding in her chest.

Far below, Jonas had thrown himself to the ground, just in time to feel the staff's fire graze his back. He rolled, pressing his singed coat into the wet leaves, then looked for Jik.

The mudman was pinned against a tree, held up by the blast. It had shattered his hands and feet but he was still mostly whole. As the stream of fire ended, he slipped to the ground, glowing red-hot.

Boneman howled and fired again. Snakes of flame twisted through the air, ripping the mantle of leaves overhead to shreds. As if in reply, forked lightning split the sky and a tree burst into yellow flames as the Hounds dipped lower. Scraps of burning branch fell everywhere, forcing Jonas to scramble under the outward curve of the giant's rib. Thunder broke loud enough to shake the woodland.

Scattered drops of rain hissed into steam on Jik's baking surface as the mudman sprang to his broken feet and launched himself at Boneman, red-hot arms outspread. Screaming with rage, Boneman fired again and again, the blasts keeping Jik at bay, but making him even hotter.

In the shadows, illuminated by blinding flashes of staff fire and lightning and with burning wood still raining down around him, Jonas scrabbled desperately through the leaves and broken branches, searching for his pack. He had put it down while they stopped to look at the skeleton. Now, there was something inside that he needed.

"Hang on, Nin," he muttered as his hands found the sodden bag hidden in a clump of half-burned ferns.

High above the fight, her breath coming in short gasps and her hands sticky with sweat, Nin struggled on up the giant's rib, feeling her way from one tiny edge to the next. Thunder broke right over her head, a tidal wave of sound that tore at her, as if determined to shake her loose. Fire arched around her and she didn't know if it came from above or below. A spear of light struck the already damaged rib in the center of its curve. She heard a wrenching, grinding sound and felt the bone twist sideways, falling.

But right ahead, right THERE was the shining thing. Nin stretched out one arm to its limit, grazing the thing with the tips of her fingers. It swung a little, sending arrows of light spinning amid the whirl of dark wings, its silver call cutting through the clamor to pierce Nin's head. She reached just a little further, hanging on with her fingernails and with all her weight balanced on one toe wedged in a gap narrower than a pencil. As the rib began to tear itself free of the breastbone that was now only feet away, she felt her foot slide and her grip come loose. For a moment she hung in the air, still desperately reaching for the shining thing. She felt its cool touch on her fingers. And then she fell.

At the sound of her scream, Jonas looked up to see Nin plunging through the air in a whirlwind of bats and lightning. He ran, taking with him the rope he had just dug from his pack. Knocked flying into a pile of wet leaves by a hit from the staff, Jik staggered again

to his broken feet and tottered toward the bone arches.
Boneman's head swiveled, his turquoise eyes vivid in
his white face.

Hurtling down through a whirling sea of leathery
bodies, their dark mass split by flashes of brilliance, Nin
felt as though the fall went on forever, like she would be
plunging toward death for eternity.

And then, suddenly, it was over and she was lying on
the ground, face down in a load of bat droppings with
half her fingernails ripped out and some bruises she
wouldn't forget in a hurry, but still alive. She turned her
head. In front of her, twined around her fingers, there
it was. A thin rope of leather knotted through a silver
wedge traced with a star design that seemed to burn in
the air just above the metal. Beyond her hand, she could
see the white wall of the collapsed rib where it had
crashed to the ground only yards away. She tightened
her grip on the amulet.

"I'm okay," she murmured, hardly believing it,
"though I'm not too happy about the bat dung."

Right next to her, Jonas groaned. He had broken her
fall, so she reckoned his bruises were going to be at least
as good as hers. She didn't have time to get used to still
being alive, before fire blazed over her head, striking
the ground beyond them. They were an easy target, but
Boneman couldn't kill Jonas without hurting Nin and
he wanted her whole. Mostly whole anyway.

"Move away," said Boneman, his eyes like chips of
blue ice. "Move away, girl, because I want to kill him."

Nin hung on to Jonas, both of them struggling up to
stand facing Dandy Boneman. Jonas had a bleeding cut
on his forehead, burns on his hands and was covered in
dung. Nin didn't look much better. She also noticed that
Jonas was clutching an odd-looking rope woven of green

stems bound tightly together, as if each thread had grown into the others.

There was a cracking sound of trampled twigs and Jik hurtled into view behind Boneman. He was stuck all over with leaves and lopsided, but his red eyes were glowing.

"Oh for Galig's sake," hissed Boneman, "is that mud rat still going!"

Swinging the staff by its lower end he whacked at the mudman, felling him to the ground and smashing his legs. Jik glared at him and began to struggle up.

Nin felt Jonas push past her. In the time it took Boneman to turn back to them Jonas had walked forward, swinging the rope of stalks like a lasso. His eyes were fixed on Boneman and blazing with something that made Nin shiver. She could have sworn that as the rope swung, the green stems began to writhe and twist as if they were alive.

Boneman paled. He knew what Jonas held in his hand. He also knew that it would take him two seconds to reposition the staff and fire.

It took Jonas one second to throw the rope.

Nin couldn't believe what she was seeing.

The rope coiled around Boneman, binding him from head to foot, forcing him to drop the staff. Where it touched it sent out shoots that burrowed into him, pushing through clothing and skin. Boneman screamed. The shoots burst through the other side and went on growing. Wiry stalks twined around him and leaves unfolded from his ears, nose and eyes. Buds appeared at his fingertips, splitting the skin and sending the ring flying into the air where it arched in a flash of gold, hitting the ground and rolling into the shadows. He opened his mouth to scream again, but only green fronds came out. Staggering, he fell to the ground. The shoots went on bursting out of his chest and limbs, unfurling into fierce purple blooms, their petals touched with scarlet. Dandy Boneman thrashed briefly and then was still.

Jonas watched until there was nothing left but a man-sized patch of purple flowers and a lot of leaves. Above them, the dark sky boiled and the rain began falling in earnest. The flaming trees hissed and smoked. Nin looked up.

A funnel of clouds dark as night was pouring toward the gap in the woodland canopy. In front of them, with the trees reduced to jagged, smoldering trunks, the wood was open to the sky. Nin could see the cloudy shapes of jaws and hound-heads as the Storm dived towards them.

"Run!" she screamed.

Jik was already lurching along on his half legs, heading as fast as he could to shelter. As the baying of the Hounds grew louder and the cold rain slashed through the air like knives, Nin grabbed Jonas and pulled him toward the deeper woods. He shook her off and stepped forward.

"Jonas!"

The Hounds were almost on him as he leaned down and picked up Dandy's staff. He stood again, looking up into the open jaws and lightning eyes just a heartbeat away from his own. Then, as the first Hound lunged toward him, he turned the staff and hurled it down-ward, ramming it head first into the Land so that it stuck there, quivering like an ivory sapling in the gale.

The ground shuddered as the staff earthed itself, pouring all of its stored magic into the Land and drenching the wood with power. Blue light irradiated everything. A scorching wind burned outward, smashing through the Hounds and scattering them, forcing them to turn and race back toward the horizon. Nin screamed and ducked as the magical force seethed about her, whipping her hair and stinging her face like a desert wind. Still clutched in her hand, the amulet burned and hissed against her skin.

And then the light winked out, leaving behind it a big animal bone stuck upside down in the ground. The staff was dead, drained of its magic, its eerie glow gone as if it had never been.

When Nin straightened up the first thing she saw was Jonas, staring up at a clear sky filled only with twilight and a gentle evening breeze.

Stars lit the nighttime forest, shining through the wreckage of the leafy roof. From underneath a bush, Skerridge watched the two Quick as they patched up the mudcreature with new feet and hands made from dark woodland mud and put him by the fire to bake. Then they settled down for the night in the mortal remains of the last giant, Scardoom Thunderfoot. It didn't seem terribly polite, but dead was dead and Scardoom wasn't in a position to complain.

Skerridge had been following the whole affair with interest and was shocked to find that he almost wanted to join in. He had crushed the urge at once. It didn't do to get involved with the Quick.

He chuckled. This whole chasing his target across the Drift thing was turning out to be quite an entertainment!

Watching Right Madam bewitched into risking her neck for the amulet had given him some nervous moments, though. After all, she'd be no use to Mr.

Strood in pieces. But sorcerer magic liked to belong to the kind of person who wanted something badly and Right Madam had got the amulet's attention all right! As it was, the kid probably thought *she* had found *it* instead of the other way around. The Quick just didn't appreciate the nature of spells.

Skerridge yawned, stretched and settled down again, but sleep was a long time in coming and he lay awake for hours, watching the stars grow brighter and a half-moon rise slowly in the sky.

Pictures paraded through his head, old Thunderfoot in his last days as the plague devoured him, his eyes haunted by the knowledge that he would soon die and, with him, his entire species. The city of Beorht Eardgeard just before it fell to the Raw, its streets layered with dead and the great Hall of Galig towering against a sky the color of old iron, the lights in its spires finally extinguished.

And even when he finally dropped off, Skerridge only dozed fitfully, his dreams laced with images of the Final Gathering, when the Seven Sorcerers had come together to weave a spell big enough to cheat death. Skerridge had been there, had seen it all and it was an event that was bound to live on in the nightmares of every witness. An event that had marked the last chapter in the story of Celidon and the first beginnings of the Drift.

Because soon after the Final Gathering, the Sorcerers had gone forever, Mr. Strood had taken over and, for the BMs at least, everything changed.

11

Grimm

Skerridge snuffled irritably. It was early morning and the mudman was standing, propped up against old Scardoom's rib, staring at him.

Skerridge stared back.

Fabulous couldn't make mudmen, it took a spark of Quick life to do that, but Skerridge knew all about them. And what he knew was that they were not insolent things that stared back at you. He didn't know what Right Madam had done to it, but the thing was getting on his nerves. It was an unknown quantity and it made him feel uncertain. Skerridge didn't like uncertain.

Through the gaping hole left in the woodland, a tinge of gold was burning a line across the horizon, and the air buzzed with the electric feel of raw magic. The tinge grew to a flicker as flames licked the rim of the Drift. Then the sky ignited.

Skerridge turned his gaze to watch. As much as he hated the sun he had to admit (grudgingly) that its rise over the Drift was dramatic. Raging across the heavens from the east horizon to the west, the boiling flames lit Scardoom's broken ribs to pillars of gold.

Unknown Quantity tilted its head back, now staring

at the sky instead of Skerridge. It was an improvement.

Curled up among the giant's remains, Obstacle and Right Madam stirred, awakened by the dawn. Right Madam had slept badly, Skerridge knew, her night filled with dreams of pursuit by something that never gave up, never grew tired and never forgot. But then, if any Quick was stupid enough to go messing with the Gabriel Hounds, let alone Ava Vispilio, they weren't going to get any sympathy from Skerridge.

When the sun was finally up, Obstacle got to his feet and stretched.

"Come on, Ninevah Redstone," he said, and another day began.

Jonas, helped by Jik and Nin, spent ages raking over the forest floor looking for Vispilio's ring, but in the end he had to give up. It was lost somewhere amid the chaos of leaves, ferns and shrubs. Hopefully it would stay that way. But he did find Boneman's pack hidden behind a clump of trees, and while they ate their breakfast of cold roast rabbit he went through it looking for anything useful. His best find was a net, woven from the same stalks as the rope that had killed Dandy Boneman.

"Fantastic! A crowsmorte web. That's the flower, see," he added, nodding at the purple patch of ex-Dandy. "Crowsmorte. Named after the sorcerer who made it, Morgan Crow. The web will hide us from the Hounds."

Jik ikked doubtfully and Nin raised an eyebrow.

"Just so long as it won't turn us into flower beds!"

There was something for Nin too. A small backpack. Pink. With a fairy embroidered on the side. She stared gloomily at the fairy. Once she wouldn't have been caught dead with it, but she needed something to carry stuff in and the world of choosing what to own had long gone. The pack had probably belonged to the last kid Boneman used to gain the trust of innocent people and Nin just hoped that whoever she was her fate hadn't been too nasty.

Peering suspiciously inside she found a pink hair-band, a small bottle of clear liquid and a yellowish candle with flecks of purple in it. According to Jonas, the liquid was bee venom, a good painkiller, and the candle was mixed with crowsmorte to bring peace of mind. She added Monkey and her pj's to the contents and they were ready to go.

They left the ruins of the giant's rib behind and were quickly out of the wood and into the hills and open fields beyond. The morning sun was warm and the air fresh, blowing from a sky of clouds like skeletal horses with manes and tails that flew behind them in threads of twisted white. And on the skyline ahead was a familiar cloudy wall.

"I thought we'd left that behind?"

"We did, this is more. There are patches of Raw everywhere, remember. And if you think that's big just wait till you see the Heart!"

At around midday, they saw the only other person, apart from Dandy Boneman, that they had met on their journey so far. He came striding toward them, clutching a sack that hung over one shoulder.

"Just keep walking," said Jonas in a low voice. "No reason to suppose he's gonna be trouble."

As the man went by, he nodded at them in a friendly way, so Nin risked a quick glance up. Her first impression was of a brown man with a heavily lined face. Then, with a flip-flop of her stomach, she saw that his eyes were red and that the hands clutching the sack were oddly hairy, with thick fingers and sharp claw-like nails. He caught her glance and grinned, showing the pointed teeth of a wild animal. She whipped her head around, eyes dead ahead, and bunched up against Jonas. Jik scuttled closer, bumping into the back of her legs.

"Grimm," said Jonas, when the man was a reasonable distance behind them.

"Yeah, it was a bit unnerving."

Jonas laughed. "No, I mean he was one of the Grimm. Half Fabulous, half Quick. It happens, but only with those Fabulous that are born the same way as Quick. You'll always know them by their eyes, even the ones that look quite human otherwise."

In the afternoon they found the river again, though it was too far away for them to hear it whispering. Now, their path ran along higher ground and the water stayed in view below them for the rest of the day. There was no sign of the storm, and Nin began to hope that maybe the Hounds had forgotten about Jonas after all.

Although they stopped for a break once or twice, it was never for long and as the day began to fade they reached the next stage of their journey.

12

Twilight

So, that's the Savage Forest, is it?" asked Nin nervously. They were standing on the crest of the hill, looking down at a swathe of woodland that cut across the landscape. To the left, it ended in the banks of the river they had been following all afternoon, here grown larger and more rapid. To the right, dark trees marched onto the horizon. Nin shivered, as if she could feel its shadow closing about her already.

"It's huge! I mean, even if we're just going across it the thin way, it's still huge."

"For tonight, we'll camp at the bottom of the hill. Tomorrow, we'll have an easy morning hanging about here, plus I'll catch a rabbit or two. Then we'll head into the Forest after lunch in nice time to get to the oak for night fall."

"So it's too late to start now?"

"Far too late. It's nearly sunset and Sturdy's Oak is at least three hours' walk into the wood. You can't cross the Savage Forest comfortably in one day. It's best to do it in two parts, spending the night at the Oak."

"And we'll be safe there will we?"

"Uh-huh. The Oak is a protected place. It's magic,"

he added, seeing the question on her face, "you'll find out when we get there. Next morning, we start off early and it's about four or five hours' walk out of the Forest. We'll keep going until we reach the Quickmare into the Widdern, then we catch a train, and then back to the Drift on the other side of the Heart. After that, we're on the last stretch to the House. Got that?"

"Yep."

"Got a plan yet?"

"Same one I always had. Trust to luck."

Jonas laughed and glanced at the sky where the sun was beginning to sink in earnest, its molten light dusting the shadowy woods with gold. They stood, taking a moment to watch. Sunset in the Drift wasn't the inferno of sunrise, but it had a strange, liquid beauty. Jik shuffled at Nin's side and she glanced down at him. The glow in the sky made the fiery points of his eyes look brighter.

"Nice, isn't it? Like . . ." She smiled. "Like the sun is drowning in its own light. Anyway, I won't be sorry to wait until tomorrow, I'm pretty tired as it is. Are you okay, Jik? What are you staring at?"

The mudman had turned around and was looking back the way they had come, away from the setting sun and towards the darker horizon. Nin followed his gaze. There was something odd about the skyline. It was wavering in the way that air wavers in the heat. Ripples ran through the deep turquoise, like a fine veil floating on the edge of twilight. As she watched, the ripple effect changed direction and began flowing towards them.

"Hey, Jonas," she said, "there's a funny kind of see-through cloud thing."

Jonas went white. "It can't be! It's too early, they come out as the sun starts to go down, so they can't have had time to find us yet!" He stared at the sky for a moment and groaned. "It is. Oh hell, we must be close to a nest."

Nin could see the thoughts flicking through his head, reflecting like shadows in his gray eyes. He came to a decision.

"Too late for the crowsmorte net, they're headed this way, they've probably got our scent already. So, no choice. Nighttime or not, we'll head into the Forest and hope for the best. Maybe we'll lose them in there."

"It's not the Hounds . . ." Nin looked bewildered

"Tombfolk," said Jonas grimly.

Nin threw a glance at the horizon. The tombfolk were moving fast, drawing a soft veil over the sky as they flew through the dusk, the evening light shining through their bodies. They looked so beautiful that she almost wanted to stay and watch.

Instead, she followed Jonas, rattling down the hill, her pack bouncing on her back and her hair flapping about her eyes as she leapt over tussocks and prayed that neither of them fell. And then they were at the foot of the hill and the Savage Forest lay before them, a great wedge of darkness with a pale ribbon of track leading into the shadows. They hurtled down it, plunging into the wood, the tall trees closing around them.

Skerridge had been taking it easy under a bush, watching Right Madam and Obstacle as they trundled slowly toward him. When they finally got around to overtaking, he would superspeed on to the next hiding place, somewhere just outside the forest, and wait all over again.

He wondered how it was that Quick could bear to live at the speed they did and was just chuckling to himself about how, from a BM's point of view, the Quick were anything but, when things went horribly wrong.

He was puzzling over why they had suddenly speeded up (as far as a Quick can) when something went "IK!" in his ear.

Skerridge nearly jumped out of his skin.

"Oy! Where'd ya pop up from then? Ya was over there a minute ago!"

"Jik gik kik," said Unknown Quantity irritably, "Ik!" He pointed to the horizon.

Skerridge's heart sank. Tombfolk. Headed this way.

"Blast," he muttered. "Blimmin' ik all right! Wha' d'ya 'spect me t' do?"

Unknown Quantity looked at him.

Skerridge sighed. He had a choice. Run for it, or try to delay them long enough to give the Quick a chance to reach the Forest. Of course, no normal forest would provide shelter from the tombfolk, but the Savage Forest was different. The Savage Forest was anything *but* normal.

He chose. As soon as the Quick had thundered past, Unknown Quantity hid under a bush out of sight, leaving Skerridge to come out of hiding and get into position. To feed, the tombfolk needed to be on the Land. This meant that as soon as they drew close to their prey, they would sweep low in the air and skim along just feet above the earth until the victim was surrounded. At which point most Quick gave up and collapsed with terror, allowing the tombfolk to land and have a nice dinner.

Skerridge stood in the middle of the path into the forest, watching as the airy forms swooped down from the sky, gliding toward the Land and the fleeing Quick. As soon as they were close enough, he tipped back his head and sent a blast of firebreath into the air. It got their attention at once. They stopped, hovering just a little higher than his head.

"And what do *you* want, bogeyman?" said one.

It was a female. In wraith form she was almost part of the twilight sky. Her hair made waves of misty silver in the dusk and there were stars in her empty eyes. She was so lovely it made Skerridge want to weep for the Celidon that was gone, even the deadly parts.

She wasn't the leader though. Their king watched Skerridge with eyes like silver whirlpools, a whole galaxy of stars.

Skerridge swallowed nervously. It would have to be the king's hive, wouldn't it. The Daemon of the Night. Not that this was his real name of course, the king had left that behind long ago. Skerridge summoned up all his nerve and grinned.

"Jus' a minute of yore time, tha's all."

The tombfolk swirled, some of them fanning out, ready to sweep past him as soon as their king gave the word. But the Daemon of the Night stayed where he was, gazing at Skerridge with interest.

"We are thirsty, bogeyman," said the female, "and what we want a drink of is behind you. Why should we waste time on you?"

Skerridge swallowed hard. The tombfolk lived on the life force generated by a Quick soul, but they weren't above snacking on magical energy if it was around. To a tombfolk, magical energy was like wine—they couldn't live on it, but it had a nice flavor. So even if they really wanted the Quick, it didn't mean they wouldn't attack Skerridge too.

"Ya see, problem is, Right Madam 'as a place booked in me sack. So if yer eats 'er, it's gonna make fings tricky fer me."

"And how do you plan to stop us, bogeyman?" She sounded amused.

Skerridge scratched his head. As soon as the tombfolk set foot on the ground they would become as solid as he was. And then he'd be done for. Fully formed, the tombfolk were indestructible. But right now . . .

"S'like this see. Right now yer made of vapor. An' yer know what 'appens to a cloud o' vapor when it meets a ragin' inferno!"

He drew in a deep breath and held it, ready. He didn't know if he could manage all of them, not spread out as they were, but he would get the king and his lady head on.

There was a pause. The tombfolk looked at their leader. He floated in front of Skerridge like a purple stain across the deepening blue of the evening sky. His silver eyes glowed.

"Skerridge, isn't it?" Daemon spoke in a voice as soft as a night breeze. "Mr. Strood's Champion, with an unblemished record." He smiled a smile that chilled even Skerridge to the bone. "But not for much longer."

Skerridge hung on to his breath. He wondered how far the Quick had got, because pretty soon this little game would be over.

"Because we WILL have them," went on Daemon. "Your firebreath can only reach so far, and we have the whole sky to fly in."

Already the hive was moving, those closest spiralling up far higher than Skerridge could blow flames. Those further away just drifted around him, floating through the trees like ghosts. Soon, only Daemon was left, watching the bogeyman with a smile that was part sneer.

"I can still see them, bogeyman. Your precious Quick move slowly, even when they run."

A thin sound rose into the air. It was like a scream only colder, sharper, cutting the air like a knife. It wasn't the Quick and it wasn't the tombfolk. It came from the heart of the Savage Forest.

Skerridge let out his breath in a hot sigh. "But ya know what THAT was, don' ya? An' if I carn' stop ya, THAT will."

For a moment, Daemon looked unsure. It didn't suit his face. He sent Skerridge a look full of icy fury.

"Then we'll get them before it knows we're here," he hissed.

And he was gone, leaving Skerridge in an exhausted heap on the ground.

Something screamed, a high, chilling sound that rose from the heart of the forest, but Nin was too focused on running to pay attention. Her breath rasped in her throat and her blood pounded through her body, making a sound in her ears like thunder.

Suddenly, the air rippled behind her, sending chills across her skin. Without thinking, she glanced back. The tombfolk were there, gauzy shadows swooping low in the air. One was flying ahead of the others, eager to reach them. For a moment his silver whirlpool eyes met Nin's. They looked . . . starving.

Jonas grabbed her hand and they fled on down the white path, its chalky earth crunching beneath their feet. The gauzy shapes drew steadily closer, catching them up, surrounding them. Nin thought she heard laughter and felt something like cool silk drifting over her, THROUGH her.

Dragging her along with him, Jonas ran faster. But in her heart Nin knew that it was hopeless. Any moment now she would collapse with terror, the tombfolk would land and she and Jonas would be dead.

And then, just as the last edge of sun slipped below the horizon and Nin's legs finally gave way, the scream came again, slicing through the still air and turning her blood to iced water. It was louder than before, closer. Much closer. As she cried out and fell toward Jonas, she saw his white face staring up, full of astonishment.

Because the tombfolk were leaving, sweeping up through the trees and fading fast into a sky that was just tipping from twilight into night.

Nin hung on to Jonas, staring after them.

"Don't tell me," she gasped through burning lungs, "there's something in this wood that even the tombfolk are afraid of."

Jonas gave her a strained smile. "I'm sorry, Nin, we've got to keep running."

Skerridge sighed. "Better get in there after 'em, I s'pose." He studied the Savage Forest, lying like a sea of darkness at the foot of the hill. The tombfolk had gone, spiralling up out of the trees into the deep bowl of the sky where the last dregs of daylight barely reached.

"Yik. Wik ik?"

"Yer 'eard the screamin', right? That screamin' what turned all yer blood inter iced water? Well, not exac'ly blood in yore case, but ya gets the point."

"Yik. Ik."

"We'll tha's it. Tha's what the tombfolk are afraid of. The Dark Fing What Lives in the Wood." Skerridge paused to gaze at the last stain of light fading swiftly from the horizon.

"Sleeps in the 'eart of the forest all day, then comes out to 'unt at night, ya know," he went on conversationally. "So oo's goin' first? Yew or me?"

Silence fell.

So did the night.

13

Savage Forest

As the last trace of day vanished, so did the path. Nin lurched to a halt, staring around wildly. Her legs were shaking and her heart thundered in her chest.

"What happened!"

"Forest used to be faerie territory," gasped Jonas, "and they loved to play tricks on the Quick. Like, lure them in with a path then make it vanish just when they need it most."

"How do we get to the oak now?"

Jonas didn't answer. For a moment the forest was silent save for their ragged breathing. Nin shivered, smelling bracken and earth and dead leaves, all mixed with the night air that cooled her burning lungs. Her legs steadied a little.

"Keep going in a straight line and we'll make it," he said at last. "This way."

Although he spoke firmly, Nin saw the look on his face and her blood froze. It's a faerie wood, she thought, as she followed him into the maze of trees, and I'm betting that even two steps into a faerie wood is enough to get a Quick lost. But she said nothing. There was no point. Either they made it to the Oak or they died.

As they ran, a hunched bird shape appeared, keeping pace by gliding from branch to branch, its monstrous hooked beak and hungry stare looming out of the shadows every time it flew past. A thin gray shape snaked out of the darkness to their left, then another. And another. Eyes shone like pale discs. Something snarled. Two somethings, one on either side. Wolves.

A thunderous crashing from deeper in the forest made Nin yelp. Whatever made that noise was far bigger than a wolf. The thought of BEAR came into her head. A dark-furred one with horrible eyes like coals and huge yellowed claws. Probably hungry and drooling.

And then the scream that had terrified the tombfolk came again. Nin's cry of terror was lost in the sound that echoed through the forest, making the air quiver. They ran. Diving through columns of tall trees, leaping over dead branches and down mossy hollows and dips. The scream came after them, always at their backs, always close. The wolves and the bears were forgotten.

Nin thought her heart would burst with the effort, but she focused on the dark shape of Jonas and kept going. They plunged on through the night forest, and Nin knew that they were hopelessly lost, they would never find Sturdy's Oak. The screaming thing would get them and they would die here in the Savage Forest.

Something came hurtling through the undergrowth behind them, catching up fast. Horribly fast. Red eyes burned in the darkness, and then . . .

"Jik!" gasped Jonas.

The mudman burst out of the trees and kept going, overtaking them and plunging off to their left.

"Jik tik yik!"

Jonas changed tack, hard on the heels of the mudman.

"Follow," he gasped. "I think he knows the way."

They ran on, chasing the twin beams of Jik's eyes that lit up the way ahead with a reddish glow. The deeper in they went, the more the forest changed. The trees, which had been straight and heavy with leaves, became gaunt, their ghostly shapes twisted and thick with ivy.

The screaming thing screamed again and the air grew colder, the last scrap of moonlight vanishing, leaving only the red glow of Jik's eyes.

"It's near," she wailed. "Whatever it is, IT'S NEAR!"

"Keep going!" cried Jonas, and Nin heard something in his voice that made her look further ahead.

There the dark was not so dark. A faint hope uncurled in her heart and Nin forced herself to keep running, each breath like a hot knife in her lungs, blood pounding through her head so hard that flashes of light pricked her eyes. But now, right in front of them, the dark was giving way to a soft golden glow that grew as they hurtled towards it. She knew it wasn't possible to run any faster, but somehow she did.

And then the golden glow was all around them and the horrible screaming stopped.

"It's okay," gasped Jonas, "we've made it!"

Breathless and exhausted, they sank to their knees in an open space of soft, green grass scattered with daisies, their petals curled in sleep. In the center, its branches spreading out over the whole clearing, was a vast oak. The moonlight filtering through its leaves was strangely golden. It was wonderful and Nin knew that they were safe. She could have cried with relief. More than anything, the silence was beautiful. Wherever the screaming thing was, it wasn't here.

"Look at it," Jonas said staring up through the green

roof of leaves, "I've never seen branches that . . . complicated. Or a trunk so . . . knobbly."

"This moss down here round the bottom, it's really springy." Nin crawled over to it, dumping her rucksack next to her. "Smells nice."

"Here," called Jonas, pointing.

In the middle of the trunk, etched into it in a way that appeared to have happened naturally rather than been done with a knife, were the words:

NEMUS STURDY

"We'll be all right now, thanks to Jik." Jonas dropped his pack next to hers and settled on to the soft moss.

"Yeah! Thanks, Jik. Aren't you coming in?"

The mudman stood on the edge where the dark forest turned into moonlit grass, just outside the reach of the branches.

Jik sighed. "Jik, nik."

"I don't think he's allowed," said Jonas quietly. "I think this place is just for Quick."

Jik drooped. Nin got up and went over to him. She bent down to pick him up. The mudman hopped back sharply just as Jonas said "NO" very firmly.

"Don't try bringing him in! You don't know what will happen. You might find *yourself* barred and if that happens you could be in real trouble!"

"Yik."

"You'll be all right out here, will you? Are you sure?"

Jik stared at her vacantly.

"And don't pretend you don't understand."

"Nin," said Jonas gently. "There isn't any choice. He's not allowed in."

Nin looked around. "Well, I guess nothing will want

to eat you," she said at last, "cos you're not meat. But if
that screaming thing comes, bury yourself just in case."
She pointed to an earthy patch next to him. "I'll dig it
up for you. It'll be the perfect hiding place."

Jik watched her as she knelt on the edge of the
protected place and leaned to break up the earth with a
dead branch, turning it over so that it was loose. Then
she went back to where Jonas had stretched out on the
moss and sank down next to him. In seconds they were
both asleep.

14

The Dark Thing That Lives in the Wood

I t was pitch black. The moon might have been shining outside the forest, but it didn't get a look-in here.
Skerridge sighed.

Unknown Quantity heard him and turned to look.

"S'all right fer Quicks," muttered Skerridge. "They're safe enough. Don' need t' worry about them."

"Yik."

"Good fing ya knows yer way about," added Skerridge admiringly. "Still I reckon yer made of earf, so yer oughta know the lie of the Land all right. It was fun doin' Wild Bear, too. S'a while since I've done Wild Bear. Not much opportunity fer it these days, what wiv the spread of urbanization in the Widdern."

Jik sent him a stern look.

"Don' complain! I kep' the wolves off 'em didn' I? An' them bird fings what like to eat eyes!"

Skerridge sighed and looked up anxiously. Jik followed his gaze.

"Dik fik wik lik ik tik wik?"

"Yep, it's out there somewhere. An' we Fabulous ain't got any protection in the Savage Forest. Not that a bitta Land magic like yew qualifies as Fabulous." He squinted at the mudman. "Though it's up fer discussion, I'll grant ya. I mean, yer ain't exactly an av'rage mindless Land Magic neiver. Land Magic's ain't s'posed t' be *alive*, an' tha's what Right Madam made ya, eh?"

"Yik!"

Skerridge chuckled. "Not fer much longer, mind, if the Dark Fing gets a whiff o' ya! Don' kid yerself it eats Quick, neiver, cos it don'. It only plays wiv the Quick, what it likes ter eat is Fabulous. So stay quiet an' keep still an' 'ope it won' find us. Not that it's much of an 'ope. An' if ya feel like makin' a fuss jus' remember that I can stomp on yer as easy as that!"

"Yik yik."

"Right. We've got an understandin' then."

There was a faint scuffle from Unknown Quantity. Skerridge guessed the mudman was hiding himself in the earth.

"S'all right fer some," he muttered.

Normally BMs liked darkness, but Skerridge knew what this darkness hid and so he wished he could light a fire to make the darkness not so dark. It would be a stupid thing to do, though, so he didn't. His last, best hope was to stay utterly quiet.

Unknown Quantity was doing a good job of being a lump of earth. You wouldn't know it was there. Even the glow of its eyes had gone, buried in the covering soil. Of course, it had an advantage over Skerridge in that it didn't have to breathe. Skerridge tried to join in by slipping into Dark Shadow in the Forest shape (With Eyes), but changed back again straight away. The darkness all around was so very dark he was afraid he might lose himself in it and never get out.

The night stretched ahead of him. Long, long hours until dawn.

Something freakish stirred deep in Skerridge's insides. He had a nasty feeling that it might be fear. It wasn't very comfortable and he wished it would stop.

Nin was dreaming about Toby. The dream started that Wednesday morning when her brother disappeared and went on through everything that had happened to her since. Sometimes she was living it all again, and sometimes she was telling it all to somebody, like a story. At the end of the story she woke up. Sort of.

She was lying on the moss under the oak tree, but Jonas was nowhere to be seen. In his place was an old man with a long white beard and long hair, all tangled with oak leaves. His face was the same wrinkled brown as the bark of the tree and his eyes were moss green, the color of the robe he was wearing. He smiled. Nin returned it nervously. There was something about him both wonderful and terrifying.

"Where's Jonas?"

"Ahh. Your companion is asleep, as are you." The old man's voice was deep and earthy. It made Nin's skin prickle. "Thank you for telling me your story."

"Is it you, protecting us in here?"

"It is. But there's a price," the old man leaned close. "All you have to do is remember me."

"Shouldn't be too hard. Who are you exactly?"

"You know."

She frowned, then her brow cleared. "Nemus Sturdy," she said firmly.

The old man chuckled. "Tell, me, do you know the story of the Seven Sorcerers?"

Nin shook her head. "I know they were the last Fabulous sorcerers ever to live and that they tried to cheat the plague by becoming something else, but Jonas never got time to tell me the rest."

Nemus Sturdy smiled. "Then, since you've given me your story, I'll give you ours," he said.

Above Skerridge the darkness swirled. It was something the bogeyman felt rather than saw. And then it was there. "So, what might you be?" said a voice like black velvet.

Skerridge swallowed hard. "Erm . . . I'm jus' an ordinary ole bogeyman."

The Dark Thing settled around him.

"Are you Fabulous? You don't look very Fabulous."

Skerridge cleared his throat. "Ahem. Erm . . . yeah, kind of Fabulous."

"You're sure about that? I sometimes eat Fabulous, you know." The Dark Thing moved closer. It wasn't something Skerridge could see, but it felt awful.

Skerridge came over all clammy. He took a deep breath. He could lie about it, but then again . . .

"Um . . . yeah, I'm Fabulous," he said gloomily.

"Good. Because I only *sometimes* eat Fabulous. I *always* eat liars."

A trickle of sweat ran down Skerridge's back. He cleared his throat again. "Um . . . might I arsk 'ow ya decide which Fabulous to eat?"

"Oh, I don't decide. It's up to you."

Skerridge sighed. He had a nasty feeling he knew what was coming next. He had to ask anyway, the Dark Thing obviously expected him to.

"Um . . . 'ow does that work then?"

The Dark Thing laughed. "I get hungry when I'm bored," it said softly. "Keep me amused until morning and you might live."

Skerridge sighed again. Dawn. Must be, what, three,

four hours away? He could feel the Dark Thing watching him. Not that it had any eyes. Eyes he could deal with, but this kind of seeing without seeing business freaked him out.

"Jus' so's I know, like," he asked humbly, "'ow d'ya eat wivout 'avin' any mouf?"

The Dark Thing chuckled. Or it might have been more of a snigger.

"I can be anywhere, even inside you. And, because you are Fabulous, inside *you* is magic. Magic feeds me. So I will slip inside your heart and suck up every last ounce of magic. And it won't help if you run away because I will be with you. And when I've done there will be nothing left but a husk. What remains of you might just make it to the edge of the wood before you go to the Raw. Possibly."

Skerridge gave a small whimper. "An' I'll be gone forever?"

"Forever. Like all Fabulous when they are unmade. So you had better be very amusing, hadn't you?"

Skerridge gulped. "Um . . . jus' so's I know, like. 'Ow many Fabulous 'ave ever kept yer interested long enough t' live?"

It sniggered again. "One," it said. "Just one."

"Crumbs! 'E must've been somefin'."

"Of course. He beat me, didn't he?"

"What was 'e then? Elf? Them elves are good at talkin'."

"Oh, I've eaten plenty of elves," sneered the Dark Thing. "They can talk, but it's all poetry and singing. Noble words might work on the Quick, but not me."

"A faerie, p'raps?"

"Vain creatures," it said sniffily. "Beautiful, but so self-interested it's unreal. Taste good though."

"Uh-huh. What about King Galig? 'E was brilliant! Warrior an' wizard all in one. Gotta be."

"Nope."

"Hmm. Some great sorcerer then, I 'spect?"

"One of the greatest," said the Dark Thing grandly.

"Well, 'e'd 'ave t' be."

"Quite."

"So 'oo was 'e? No, no. 'Ang on, lemme guess." Skerridge thought hard for a moment. Then he grinned. "Was it 'im? Was it Merlin 'imself? The greatest of 'em all."

The Dark Thing sniggered. "Nope. Not him."

"So, not Merlin, but anovver powerful . . . Ooo, was it one of the Seven Sorcerers?"

"One of the last great seven who tried to cheat the plague? Yes, it was one of them."

"Crumbs!"

"I'll give you two guesses."

Skerridge thought fast. It was all very well wasting time, but it wouldn't do him any good if the Dark Thing rumbled him and got annoyed. And after all, the answer was obvious.

"I don't fink I'm gonna need two," he said proudly. "There's only one of 'em what really did it. I mean, the ovvers might've 'ad some success wiv the endurin' fing, but it wasn't what yer'd call livin' now, was it?" He chuckled. "I'm gonna guess Simeon Dark!"

There was a long silence. At least it was probably only a second or so, but it seemed like ages to Skerridge. He began to think he might have annoyed the Dark Thing anyway.

"Right," it said lazily.

"Tha's nice. Do I get a reward? Like, to go?"

It laughed. "It's not that easy, Bogeyman."

Skerridge gave a heavy sigh. "Fort not. Wodja wan' me t' do then? I can sing?" He broke into a verse of "She Was Only The Alchemist's Daughter."

"Please! I have sensitive hearing, you know."

"Dance?" He capered across the clearing and fell over.

The Dark Thing laughed.

"It's too dark in 'ere even fer me. I carn' 'ardly see where I'm goin'," grumbled Skerridge.

"Don't worry. I've no interest in watching a bundle of bones like you prance about like a jack-in-the-box."

"Fanks," muttered Skerridge. "I'll 'ave ya know I'm very ryvmic."

The Dark Thing snorted. Which can't have been easy without a nose.

"Tricks?" Skerridge crisped a nearby bush, which fell instantly into ash. Then he spat out short bursts of fire, lighting flame-candles on all the branches of a small tree.

"Hmmm, pretty, but limited."

"Change shape?" Skerridge did Manic Clown, Hunched-backed One-eyed Monster and Hairy Thing With Big Teeth, one after the other.

"Interesting, but, again, limited."

"Or I can move as fast as lightning," he said craftily.

"Don't even think about it," said the Dark Thing smoothly. "No matter how fast you move, I'll be there before you."

"Okay, okay, just a thought."

"Well, don't think."

"Nope, no worries."

"I'm getting bored."

"Wait! Stories! What about a nice story. We bogeymen get around y'know. We know all sortsa stuff."

"Mmmhmm?"

"Like, oh, oh, um . . ."

"There's one you could tell me," it said. "Last chance, Bogeyman. Tell me this one story and who knows, I might let you go."

Skerridge gulped. "Um . . . right . . ." He said nervously. "An' what story would that be?"

"You said that there was only one of the Seven Sorcerers that really beat the plague. You said that although the others survived in one form or another, there was only one of them who actually STAYED A SORCERER."

"Ahh. Simeon Dark."

"That's what you said, Bogeyman. So tell me the story of Simeon Dark and you might survive. Might. If you tell it well and if I believe you. Make it up and you're gone. Got that?"

Skerridge let out a long, slow breath. "It's tricky," he said.

"But you do KNOW it? You do KNOW how the Seventh Sorcerer managed to go on being a sorcerer when the plague sent all the others to the Raw?"

Skerridge scratched his head. "It's a long story. Y'see to appreciate it properly ya gotta know about the other six. Do ya know about the other six?"

"Some," said the Dark Thing.

"I 'ave t' start at the beginnin' then."

It sighed. "Get on with it! Or I'll eat you where you sit."

"But then yer'll never know," said Skerridge quietly. "Will ya?"

15

Seven Sorcerers

L ike ev'ryone knows," Skerridge began in his storytelling voice, "Celidon was doin' jus' fine until the plague came along an' wiped out all the Fabulous, 'ceptin' for some o' the Dread ones. There was remains ev'rywhere and the sun rose in flames the color of old blood."

"I know," said the Dark Thing gravely. "Terrible times."

"They were indeed," sighed Skerridge. "Anyway, the seven greatest sorcerers still livin', which didn' include Merlin who'd already gone t' the Raw on account of 'im bein' incredibly old, were determined not to let it get 'em. First of all they worked on a spell to put off deff. Ya know about that I 'spect? About 'ow it worked, but was so terrible that they didn' wanna use it?"

"Uh-huh. The Deathweave. I know all that."

"Right, I won' go frew it again then. So, they 'ad to give up on that and fink of somefin' else. Each one of 'em came up wiv their own solution."

"But none of them came up with a solution that meant they could actually stay being a sorcerer . . ."

". . . 'cept Simeon Dark."

"He really was amazing," said the Dark Thing thoughtfully.

"Remember what 'e looked like, do ya?"

"Tall. Silver eyes, like many of his kind, but strangely flecked with gold. Thin. Fair hair."

"Crumbs! Still I s'pose ya would remember the only one 'oo ever got past ya."

"Get on with the story."

"Okay, okay! Anyway, where was I? Oh yeah. So, the first sorcerer, the most powerful, was Nemus Sturdy."

"Do you know the real difference between you and a Fabulous? Apart from just the magical one."

Nin shook her head.

"In each Quick is a soul, the essence of their being, and when that Quick dies their soul goes on. When a Fabulous dies, the magic they were made of becomes one with the Raw again. In turn, that raw magic will be used to make something else. A rock, maybe. Or a bird or an animal. But their essence, *all they were*, is gone. In one sense you could say they never die, like a drop of rain does not die when it falls into the ocean. But that drop of rain will never come again, its singleness, its individuality, is . . . nothing."

Nin shivered. "And the Seven Sorcerers just didn't want to end?"

"That's right. But the only way we could go on living was to stop being what we were and become something else."

Nin stared at him. She took in the green eyes, the oak leaves twined in his beard and hair and the lined skin. "You *are* the oak tree, right?"

"I am. What you see before you is just a dream image. Now all I am is the oak tree."

* * *

"So the first Sorcerer is just a tree," said Skerridge. "That tree."

"The one that protects the Quick?"

"Uh-huh. The key is that every Quick what comes this way 'opes in their deepest 'eart that the stories they've 'eard about 'im really are true, cos ovverwise they face a nasty deff in the forest. An' even if they've met 'im before an' know 'e exists, they're petrified in case 'e won' be there *this* time."

"Ahh. Dread and Desire," mused the Dark Thing thoughtfully. "Clever, but a bit tame, don't you think?"

Skerridge shrugged. "Point is, so long as the Quick remember 'im, which they're gonna do, the essence of Nemus Sturdy lives on, see? Anyway, after Sturdy comes Enid Lockheart, the only one of the Seven 'oo had any time for the Quick. Rumor 'ad it she actually liked 'em."

"Ahh, so she must be the healer?"

"Tha's it. Could mend almost anyfin', could Enid Lockheart. So she took a leaf outa Sturdy's book . . ." he sniggered.

"What?" snapped the Dark Thing.

"Leaf . . . geddit? Him bein' an oak . . . Oh, never mind. Anyway, she set up an 'ospital for sick an' dying Quick an' poured all of 'er magic into the walls. What was left of 'er physically went to the Raw, but 'er essence is still there, livin' in the 'earts and minds of the patients."

"So, sick and dying Quick hear a whisper about this place that makes it all right again and they want so badly for it to be true, even though most of them will never find it, that it's enough to keep her essence alive? Hmm. Rather cutesy if you want my opinion."

"Dunno about that, but she 'ad the nerve to put it right

under Mr. Strood's nose!" Skerridge sniggered again.

"Really? You would have thought he'd notice."

"Well, 'e 'as blocked up all the winders so 'e carn' see out."

"Doesn't he ever leave the House?"

"Why would 'e wanna do that? 'E's got servants to run around after 'im, guards to guard 'im. Doesn' need t' go out. Everyfin' 'e wants is brought right to 'is door."

"Hmmm. What about . . . FUN. Doesn't he like fun?"

Skerridge sent a look into the darkness. "The life or deff of every livin'—or dyin'—fing in the 'Ouse belongs to 'im to play wiv. That's fun enuff fer anyone, take it from me. They don' call it the Terrible 'Ouse fer nuffin'."

"I wouldn't disagree."

"If ya like I'll tell ya about some of 'is experiments wiv livin' bein's?"

The Dark Thing thought about it for a moment. "Maybe later . . . What about the third Sorcerer?"

"Morgan Crow. The only one of the seven 'oo didn' succeed. He 'ad this darft idea, see, about growin' anovver of 'im and transferrin' 'is bein' into it. But then jus' cos 'e was powerful doesn' make 'im bright."

The Dark Thing cleared its non-existent throat. Skerridge suspected that the Dark Thing, like Crow, thought it sounded like a neat plan and didn't want to let on in case it meant that it was as daft as Crow. While the Dark Thing was feeling mildly embarrassed about things, Skerridge rambled off on a long story about Morgan Crow and a fortune-telling potion that proved exactly how dim the Sorcerer was. By the time the Dark Thing realized that he was rambling, it was already curious.

"He said that! To a fortune teller?"

"Yep."

"And then drank the potion?"

"Yep. Well, you can imagine the nightmares. 'E was never the same again. Got into 'is blood, it did. 'E was so embarrassed about it 'e never told anybody ever. Not that yer can keep a secret from a bogeyman, o' course. Yer'd be surprised at the stuff we BMs know."

"Really . . . ? Like what?"

"Like . . . like . . ." Skerridge remembered the mudman, buried somewhere nearby, ". . . the girl what *made a Fabulous.*"

"Ridiculous! No single Quick can make a Fabulous." The Dark Thing wobbled for a moment, torn. "NO! Get on with Morgan Crow."

"Ahem. The reason it was a darft idea, as ya prob'ly worked out, is that 'e weren't lockin' 'imself into anyfin' that was likely t' survive. I mean, where's the Dread or Desire in that!"

"Ahh, yes of c—exactly what I thought," said the Dark Thing swiftly.

"The idiot planted a simple poppy, fed it on 'is own blood an' said growin' spells over it. Its petals went darker an' darker till they were purple 'an' its stalk an' leaves got thicker an' more twisted ev'ry day, and ev'ry day there were more an' more of 'em. Then 'e lay down in the middle o' the patch an' said the spell that was meant to pour the last of 'is magic into the flowers an' make 'em grow a strong, new body around 'im." Skerridge paused dramatically.

"Go on! And?"

"They ate 'im."

"Ate him!" The Dark Thing sounded horrified.

"Tore 'im apart and ate 'im. 'E'd given it a taste for blood, see?"

"Crumbs," said the Dark Thing.

Skerridge grinned inside. "An' that's how we got crowsmorte."

"I never knew that."

"See. We bogeymen know stuff. Tha's why it 'eals as well as kills, because it was designed to grow a body. I bet ya can guess why makin' it into a potion an' drinkin' it gives ya weird dreams that might or might not be the future?"

"Because of the fortune-teller thing," said the Dark Thing excitedly. "Getting into his blood and all that! Crumbs."

"Right! Well, number four was Azork. Vain and selfish, even by Sorcerer standards. Anyway, 'e quickly figured out that the simplest way to go on existin' was to become a Dread Fabulous, cos dread is so much stronger than desire. Fear bypasses years o' Quick evolution and takes 'em right back to their oldest ancestors. It's like, primeval."

"It didn't save the faeries, they were a Dread species."

"Well, yeah, but they was jus' too fancy. Us wha's left, we've got the real edge on fear wiv a capital eff. Show me a kid what doesn' dread the bogeyman an' I'll eat me vest. An' as to the tombfolk, when it's dark and an' they're alone ya won't find a Quick livin' what doesn't wonder if there ain't somefin' nasty in the night wiv 'em."

"So, what? Azork became a tombfolk?"

"Tha's it. As yer know, sorcerers carn' lose contact wiv the Land. If a sorcerer is stoopid enough to try flyin' then 'e becomes a spirit of the air an' fades away. No turnin' back eiver. Sever that connection jus' once and it's gone. Doomed to a slow deff. Unless . . ."

"Unless he chooses to prolong his existence by feeding off the Quick?"

"Uh-huh. "'Course, sorcerers tended to look down

on the tombfolk as being kinda dumb to give up all that sorcerer power just so's they can float about a bit. So Azork likes to call 'imself a Daemon of the Night, but what it boils down to is tombfolk. I know, I met 'im jus' the ovver night!

"Quite," said the Dark Thing loftily. It was silent for a moment, thinking about it. "Still, must be more interesting than being a tree or a bunch of bricks. Not a bad solution. Next?"

"'Ang on a mo. S'firsty work, all this talkin'. Got a drop o' honeymead?"

The Dark Thing gave him a look. Or at least as near as it could come to one, what with the no eyes problem.

"Okay, okay. I'll settle for a splash o' water. Parched I am."

"Dig under that stone, the flat one over there. Be quick about it."

Skerridge nipped over to the stone and heaved it up. He dug, quickly enough not to be seen to be dawdling, but not nearly as quickly as he could have. After a while, water began to fill the hole.

"Are you done yet?" snapped the Dark Thing.

"Found it. Coupla moufuls, tha's all." He drank deeply. "Ahh tha's better." He took another slurp, making it last as many seconds as he could. Skerridge was counting.

"Okay, fink I can go on now."

"Too right!"

"Don' be like that. I may be Fabulous, but I'm still physical. Bet ya don' 'ave to worry about fings like that, eh? Mus' be 'andy."

"It is very useful in many ways, but . . . GET ON WITH IT!"

"Am doin'! Was jus' int'rested is all! Right, where was I?"

"The fifth Sorcerer."

"Fifth was anovver sorceress. Senta Melana, the beautiful one. She chose to earf 'erself. Cut off 'er 'and to make an exit point an' poured all of the magic inside 'er into the Land. Must've taken some doin', spoilin' 'er own perfection like that. Anyway, she went to live in the Widdern as a n'ordinary mortal. Wivout a soul o' course, cos ya can't jus' get 'old o' one o' them."

"Wouldn't that kill her?"

"Not straight away. She'd've 'ad a few years left until 'er body crumbled."

"Then she's dead?"

"She realized that Quick live on in their children."

"How so?"

"Don' ask me, I'm jus' a pore ole bogeyman! Anyway, she married a Quick and 'ad kids, an' then they went on to 'ave ovver kids an' so on. Out there in the Widdern there's probably some of 'er line still livin' on."

"Seems a bit unsatisfactory to me. Next?"

"Ava Vispilio," said Skerridge in a dark voice. "Vispilio's idea was like Morgan Crow's, but far deadlier and more efficient. Crow planned to transfer 'imself into anovver body grown in 'is image. Ava Vispilio planned to transfer 'imself into anovver body too. But he wasn' gonna make one, he was gonna steal somebody else's!"

The Dark Thing gasped.

"Mean eh? He wasn' daft. Vispilio knew 'e'd need a body wiv its own source o' life. 'E also knew that he wouldn' be able to take 'is magic wiv 'im. Although 'e would still be sorta livin', it would really be just some ovver pore git wiv Vispilio in charge!"

"What happened to the . . . you know . . ."

"The pore Quick what got taken over? Dunno. But

I reckon that they wouldn' die, they'd jus' 'ang around in there wiv 'im. Powerless to stop 'im doin' anyfin 'e wanted wiv their body. Nasty eh?"

"Dreadful," said the Dark Thing with admiration.

"It was a powerful magic. He got a ring an' cast spells to tie 'is bein' into it and make anyone what's wearin' it belong to 'im. When the body e's in gets old or sick all 'e 'as to do is give the ring to someone else. They put it on and there you go! Vispilio's got anovver body."

"What if they didn't put it on?"

"Why wouldn' they? Only need to slip it on for a mo'."

"But if they didn't?"

"Clever ain't ya. Yer've spotted the one weakness."

The Dark Thing preened.

"If, for some reason," went on Skerridge, "nobody would put the ring on, Ava Vispilio would die."

"So," said Nin, "if nobody put the ring on, he'd die?"

"Not straight away. But he would be trapped inside the ring, with no source of energy to sustain him and eventually he would die. So remember, never take a ring from anyone. Here in the Drift you don't know what it really is." Nemus Sturdy sighed. "Of course, you met him didn't you? It was Vispilio inside Dandy Boneman. Shame you didn't find the ring. You could have brought it to me. Buried it in my roots. I'd have kept it safe. But now I fear it's still out there, and remember this," he leaned close, his green eyes looking into hers, "you would not know it again for it changes every time, depending on the soul it's captured."

"Don't worry," Nin said firmly, "it's lost in the bracken where no one will find it."

"We can always hope," said Nemus sadly.

"So, tell me about the last one, the seventh Sorcerer."

"Ahh, Simeon Dark." Nemus Sturdy shook his head. "There are a lot of stories I could tell you about Dark, but not what happened to him in the end. He just disappeared, you see. Legend has it that of all the seven he was the only one to find a way to stay alive and *still be a sorcerer*. Unfortunately no one knows if that's true. Now, dawn is only a little way away and you have a long journey ahead, so would you like to sleep without dreams a while?" asked Nemus kindly. "It will clear your head."

Nin smiled at him. "Thank you. And I feel like I know a lot more now."

"If you come back this way we can talk again. There's more I could tell you. About the way things were and about how they became what they are now." Nemus sighed. "My beautiful Celidon, you should have seen it."

"I wish I could," said Nin as she felt herself drifting towards sleep, "thanks again."

"You are welcome," the once-sorcerer smiled, "just remember me."

"And now," said the Dark Thing eagerly. "The seventh Sorcerer. Simeon Dark. Tell me about how Simeon Dark managed to cheat the plague! Because if there is a sorcerer still alive, as you say, then the might of Celidon has not gone altogether. So, bogeyman, tell me where the last sorcerer is now!"

Skerridge blinked at the Dark Thing.

"Come on, bogeyman, I'm waiting! Because if you've been lying to me . . . !"

"Fing is," said Skerridge slowly, peering upward. "Fing is, yer never, ever gonna know. D'ya know why yer never gonna know?"

The Dark Thing snarled.

"The reason yer never gonna know," said Skerridge carefully, "is cos that up there . . ."

The Dark Thing howled.

". . . is daylight."

16

Angel

When Nin woke up the morning sun was shining through the leaves of Sturdy's Oak on to her face. Skirting the edge of the clearing was a chalky strip of path, trying to look as if it had never been anywhere else.

"Good sleep?" asked Jonas. "It's later than I would have liked, so are you ready to go?"

"IK!"

"Jik? I take it you didn't have a good night then?" Nin grinned at him. "I'm glad you're okay, though."

Jonas was already on the path and looking impatient. Nin hurried to grab her pack and catch him up, with Jik falling in at her heels as usual.

The rest of the trip through the forest would have been enjoyable, if they hadn't been too busy worrying about the things that lived in it. Jonas kept glancing over his shoulder and Nin got the feeling that something was following them, keeping pace slightly behind and off the path. Jik didn't seem worried, though, and somehow Nin found that reassuring.

They stopped once to eat some of the rough bread and salted meat found in Dandy Boneman's pack, but that was all. Even so, when they finally tumbled out into a field of poppies that flickered like tongues of scarlet flame, the sun was already past its height.

As they cut a path through the field, the poppies' bright glow winked out under their feet, exploding into the air in a shower of sparks. Looking back, Nin could see the trail they made, dark against the red leading from the forest, which reared against the sky, a wall of trees that looked almost impenetrable. She could hardly believe they had just walked through it. When she looked back again, several fields later, the forest was just a ribbon of shadow on the melting horizon.

Ahead, the sky was filled with a misty haze that turned it the color of amethyst. Jonas told her they were getting near to the Heart and what she could see reaching into the sky was the vast patch of Raw that the Heart had become.

"Why is it called the Heart of Celidon?"

"It was once the great city of Beorht Eardgeard, where the Sorcerers went during the plague. It was also the first part of the Land to become Raw and they say something terrible lives there."

As they drew closer, Nin watched the towering wall of Raw nervously. There was something menacing about the way it looked like fog, but didn't behave like it, staying where it was, dense and unmoving in the still air and the sunshine. On its misty edge, shadows gathered, stirring restlessly. A dead tree reached out with bone-white branches and a nearby stream sobbed quietly. It all felt like leftovers from the end of the world. Which, in a way, it was.

She felt her skin prickle as understanding dawned and she suddenly worked out what it was.

"The Raw! Dandy Boneman said the Land and

everything in it was made of raw magic and that the plague was killing it. And that cloudy stuff is called the Raw. So I'm guessing it's like, bits of the Land that have died of the plague, right? Land that has gone back to the Raw?"

"Spot on, kid." Jonas had unrolled the crowsmorte net and was cutting it into halves with his knife. "It's getting dark and I don't want to risk the tombfolk, I have a nasty feeling they'll be looking out for us. Here."

Nin looked at her half of the net doubtfully, but pulled it around her anyway, like a clumsy shawl. Jonas glanced at her and smiled reassuringly.

"Don't worry about what the killing rope did to Boneman. This is different, it won't hurt you and it smells of Fabulous, so it will cover our Quick scent and hide us from the tombfolk."

"And that's because there's a little of Morgan Crow in it," said Nin, remembering the story.

They got moving, heading across the field longways and keeping the towering Raw to their right. The last light trickled from the sky and the stars came out, brilliant in the dark blue night. The air was cool and silky, and the Raw looked almost luminous in the moonlight. They traveled alongside it for miles, looking for the Quickmare that would take them into the Widdern.

"Ik." Jik had stopped and was staring at a wedge of extra heavy darkness, streaming in from the east to swallow the stars.

"Hounds," said Jonas tersely. "I'd almost forgotten them!"

He stopped to dig out the waxed cloth and give it to Jik, who huddled under it, glowing eyes fixed nervously on the sky.

"They won't smell us under the nets though, will they? If it works for the tombfolk . . ."

"Yep, that's the idea. But the sooner we get to the Quickmare the happier I'll be. Bad news is, we'll have to walk toward the storm."

They traveled on, sticking close together under their nets. Jik rustled along behind them, casting nervous glances at the lowering sky, where the purple clouds were lit with ominous flashes. Already the breeze was up and the temperature falling. The storm was moving toward them as they moved toward it.

Cold drops pattered on Nin's face and lightning glimmered eerily, throwing a swathe of brilliance over the heath then snatching it away. She felt dizzy with tension and the flickering light. On their left the Raw towered into the dark sky, bleak and solid in the lightning. Thunder rumbled, low key, almost felt rather than heard, but the Hounds didn't see the Quick.

Nin gave a startled gasp as the next flash illuminated an angel, its spread wings stark against the backdrop of clouds, its pale face blank. Beyond it hulked a broken tombstone, and then another. They were in a graveyard.

"At last!" said Jonas. "Right, now this Quickmare has a very limited existence. You see those trees over there, the evergreens, well the gateway opens up right behind them. Story goes that there's a grave behind those trees and no matter how many times they fill it in, *it's always open the next day.*"

"Ugh! Like . . . like something GOT OUT!"

"Yep, and it's supposed to happen at midnight. So we wait and watch and the moment . . ."

"But what if the . . . the . . . *IT* is in there?"

Another bolt of lightning slashed through the air.

Nin screamed.

A figure was standing on one of the tombstones, looming over her. In that brief flash his image was seared on to her eyeballs. A figure made of darkness with eyes that shone like burnished silver.

And others. Everywhere. Tombfolk.

"How good of you," said Daemon softly, "to come to us."

"We've been trying to catch you." It was the female who spoke, her hair shining white against the purple sky. "But we couldn't find your scent. So we stopped to rest awhile and . . . here you are." She laughed.

Overhead, the storm began to move away, the clouds thinning and breaking, but Nin didn't notice. She was staring in horror at the tombfolk.

They're on the ground, she thought, they're solid. She felt her blood chill in her veins and she was sure her heart stopped beating for a moment.

Jonas pulled her close, getting a firm grip on her wrist. He was eyeing the evergreens behind the tombfolk and she wondered what he was planning to do.

The boy just doesn't know when to give up, she thought. He shook her slightly, as if he had read her thoughts. Jik nudged her legs, dropping his waxed sheet and pushing round to stand in front.

Daemon leaped to the ground, coming to land an arm's length away from the Quick. The others clustered around them. Except on the left where the angel was in the way.

Nin looked up at the tombfolk King. He was wearing something close-fitting of dark, velvety purple. It was strewn with tiny gems that glinted in the rays of moonlight shining through the clouds and it was only because of the gems that she could tell where the garment ended and his skin began. It was spooky. Like looking at someone made entirely from night. Without their spiral of stars, his eyes would be a lightless black.

Nin shivered and found herself wondering if she was looking at another of the once-sorcerers. Azork.

Daemon raised a hand and brushed a fingertip against Nin's face, high on the cheekbone. It felt like ice-cold knives sinking into her and drawing something out, some kind of inner strength, though it didn't break the skin or shed any blood. Darkness clouded her eye. Nin gasped and clapped a hand to the cold place where his hand had touched.

"You won't die just yet," said Daemon, "it's amazing how much life force a Quick body can hold. It will take us nights to kill you."

"Don't," said Jonas, his voice low, "please don't. Just let us go. Let *her* go." His grip on Nin grew hard enough to hurt.

For answer, Daemon took a step closer. The hive followed, hands outstretched, reaching for any skin they could find. Nin realized that, even after the thing in the Raw, she hadn't known what real fear was until now.

The next bit happened in a blur.

Jik, fists balled in fury, opened his mouth and a sound came out like rocks grinding together. Shocked, the hive drew back a little. At the same time, behind them, the corner overhung with evergreen grew bigger and darker. The Quickmare was opening.

Jonas took off. He leapt over the grave to their left, grazing the stone angel and dragging the startled Nin with him. Daemon howled.

They hurtled over the ground, lichen-spotted tomb-stones springing at them from the dark as they headed for the gateway. The darkness clouding her eye was still there and Nin ran half-blind tripping and stumbling after Jonas, bruising herself on rough stone. A cold wind rose behind them as the tombfolk took to the skies in pursuit, mouths gaping and eyes wild with fury.

As they raced toward the gateway, a black space between overhanging branches that stank of earth and mould, Nin could feel the tombfolk drawing close. A chill breath touched her neck and she heard the eager hissing of their voices.

Darkness opened in front of her. Tumbling into it, Nin lost her grip on Jonas. Her feet sank into loose earth and she fell on to her hands and knees. Before she could rise again, freezing air blew around her and she screamed, knowing that the tombfolk were at her back. Instinct made her turn to face the danger, twisting so that she was on her behind, scrabbling backward on her elbows, staring up into the silver eyes of Daemon as he streamed toward her.

"Move!" yelled Jonas, "if it closes before we're through we'll be trapped . . ."

"They've got me!" she screamed. "Jonas!"

A smile stretched Daemon's face as he curled downward, his feet reaching to touch the Land. He was almost there when two things happened at once.

Something reared out of the darkness, heaving itself from the earth right where Daemon was about to land.

Jonas grabbed Nin by the backpack and began to pull.

Dragged along at a cracking pace, Nin gulped back a scream. She saw a look of disgust cross Daemon's face as the ectofright clambered right through his shadowy form. He recoiled, swirling up into the air. She felt a moment of relief. Now, by the time he landed, Jonas would have dragged her into the Widdern. She prayed he wouldn't follow them there.

For a fleeting moment, Daemon's whirlpool eyes fixed on hers, full of something dark and unfathomable. Then he turned back to the Drift and was gone.

Nin switched her attention to the thing in the grave.

A skull, one eye still in its socket, swiveled to fix on her and the ectofright began to move, crawling fast over the ground toward her, catching her up, its skeletal hands reaching. Bony fingers gripped her ankle.

Nin kicked and fought, but the skeleton hung on, rattling along behind her as she bumped over the ground. Its one full socket glared at her with demented fury and it began hauling itself up her jeans leg, clacking its pointed teeth as it drew closer to her unprotected throat. Screaming like crazy she battered at it with her bare hands, feeling the cold bone against her fists, a few thin strands of hair still clinging to its skull.

When she slithered out of the grave behind Jonas, its bare-bone face was barely an inch from hers. It let go suddenly, unable to travel outside the gateway. A hot gust of wind streamed over her and Nin saw the ectofright flatten itself to the ground, its horrible grimace turning somehow to a look of surprise as its bones bounced apart and scattered. It was almost comical.

And then it was all gone and they were in a perfectly ordinary graveyard with a small church in front of them, outlined against a clear night sky.

As a furious Skerridge hurtled through the gateway at superspeed, the ectofright that had been doing a good job of terrifying the socks off Right Madam tried to get out of his way. Skerridge gave it a whack as he shot past. The look of horrified surprise as it fell apart improved his temper for at least a nanosecond.

He was angry because he had lost track of his target,

which was a dreadful thing to own up to. But he had been tired after a hard night fending off the Dark Thing and so had dropped off under a tree while they dawdled along in their slow Quick way. By the time he had woken up things had got seriously out of hand.

Fortunately, Unknown Quantity had distracted Daemon for just long enough so that Obstacle and Right Madam could make a break for it.

Unfortunately, the blow Daemon had aimed at Unknown Quantity before giving chase to his rapidly escaping dinner had only knocked the mudman several yards through the air into a puddle of mud. Shame. It would have been one less witness to worry about.

The wretched thing had landed near Skerridge, rolling about in the mud as it struggled to its feet looking like a small, mud-made sumo wrestler. So he had crisped it by way of letting it know he was annoyed and had racked up the superspeed, tearing through the tombfolk so fast that even they couldn't see him.

Racing past the Quick, Skerridge whipped around the side of the church, found a handy bush and swapped into Dark Shadow (With Eyes). It had been a close thing. Two seconds later and he would have missed the gateway completely.

"What I don't understand," said Nin, "is why the tomb-folk turned back."

"I think the King was once a sorcerer," explained Jonas as he rolled up his crowsmorte net. Nin had lost hers somewhere in the flight through the graveyard.

"Azork?"

Jonas nodded. "He had an ebony wristlet with a symbol on it like an A made of lightning. That's Azork's mark." He led them over to the church porch and settled down to wait for morning.

"But why does that mean they can't come through?" said Nin, curling up next to him. She was feeling a lot better already. The cold patch on her cheek had gone and the darkness clouding her eye was disappearing fast.

"Sorcerers can't leave the Land, which means they can't enter the Widdern. And although Azork isn't a sorcerer anymore, I'll bet he doesn't fancy the idea of being trapped here for a whole day until the gateway opens again. We were nearly in the Widdern and he'd have had to follow us through, so he turned back."

Nin thought for a moment. "Senta Melana went into the Widdern. But then I guess she wasn't a sorcerer anymore, she'd already earthed all her magic, become mortal."

"It would still have been terrifying for her. But then, according to the story, she was a brave woman, braver than any of the others, I think."

"Talking of brave, I hope Jik's all right on his own."

Jonas was silent for a moment. "Look, Nin, you know it would be dangerous for him to go through the Heart. He's going to have to walk around it . . ."

"But the Heart is HUGE!" wailed Nin. "It's gonna take him forever. I won't see him again and I never got to say goodbye!"

"Look, he doesn't have to stop to sleep or eat like we do, so he can keep on going. He'll be waiting for you when you've found Toby and your memory pearls and managed to escape again." Jonas smiled into the night.

"You don't think I can do it, do you?"

"Ninevah Redstone, if I didn't think you had a chance I wouldn't let you go. You're lucky . . ."

"I know I said that," wailed Nin, "but I'm not so sure now. I mean, look at all the things that have been after us! We spend all our time running away."

"Yeah," said Jonas, "but that's the point. You're still alive to do the running. Take it from me, after all that, most people wouldn't be."

17

Secret Heart

A cold wind made Jik look up to see the tombfolk leaving, their airy bodies rippling into the night sky. He had been keeping as still as mud, hoping that they had forgotten him. Now, at last, he was free to move.

Jik knew that going through the Heart would be horribly dangerous. He also knew that going around the edge would take too long for him to find Nin again before she reached the Terrible House. And although he could follow her inside when he finally got there, he also knew that before she made it that far she would need her friends. He could feel it in his mud. Something bad was going to happen and it wasn't far away.

He tottered into life. The extra layer of mud that covered his body from top to toe made him waddle, but at least it was now rock hard. It was very kind of Skerridge to sort out that little problem, though Jik wouldn't like to bet it had been meant that way. At any rate, the new top coat had given him a better hope of survival.

Because, however deadly it might be, Jik wasn't going around the Heart. Jik was going *through*.

* * *

If the road hadn't been enough proof, the ordinariness of the trees would have told them at once that they were back in the Widdern. The grass was just doing grassy things, shadows stayed properly in the shade and the only thing that the clouds looked like were clouds. Or possibly bits of cotton wool, but that was as far as it went.

"Better tuck that out of sight," said Jonas, nodding at the amulet around Nin's neck.

Here in the Widdern the charm looked out of place, the star shape burning in the air like hot wire. Nin slipped it inside her T-shirt, where it hung, fizzing against her skin.

"I still don't know what it's for," she said.

"You'll find out sooner or later." Jonas shrugged. "Sorcerer magic isn't predictable, you know."

They left the road and followed a track that led through fields and trees, finally opening out into a green valley. On the other side, the track took them up the hill again to a path with a signpost, pointing to Coulsdon Common. Nin glanced back over the valley, wondering how Jik was getting on and wishing that she could have said goodbye. Just in case.

"Right," said Jonas, "civilization, here we come."

"Do you think we'll see him again?"

"Jik? Dunno, but if there's one thing I've learned, it's not to underestimate the mudman."

The path took them to a pub called The Fox, a main road and a bus stop. On the other side of the road were more woods.

"Call this civilization?" said Nin. "One pub and a load more trees."

Two cars whizzed past. Jonas stuck out his thumb.

"No change for the bus," he said. "Anyway we'll need our cash for the train. So, I'm counting on the fact that you are the lucky sort."

Almost at once a small blue car pulled over.

Wincing in the bright Widdern sun, Skerridge stared after the blue car with mounting irritation. It wasn't that he would have any trouble keeping up with it, but dodging all the other vehicles on the road wasn't going to be a picnic.

Everything went well enough until the road the blue car was on joined another, busier road. This busier road was chock-full of cars and buses. Even then it wasn't too bad until Skerridge realized that the blue car he was following was the wrong one.

Then things got really tricky.

Hilary Jones was having a bad morning. It was her second month in a new job and her boss was a stickler for punctuality. Unfortunately for Hilary, good time-keeping was not something she did well and today, she was running horribly late.

She was speeding around the corner toward Old Coulsdon when she saw a boy and a girl standing by the road. The boy had his thumb out. Her brain went into overdrive along the lines of: "I can go past because it's not my problem but if I read in the news that horrible things happened to two kids on this road I'll never forgive myself because I'll always know they would have been safe with me and I'm late anyway."

So, not without a sigh, she pulled over and said, "Get in."

They got in. She had a moment of ice-cold fear when she got a proper look at the boy. He had long, unwashed hair tied back with string, a worn black coat over his worn clothes and the whole package didn't look too clean either. But then she saw the girl and relaxed a little.

"Where are you heading?" she asked as she pulled away.

The girl was staring at her openly. It didn't bother Hilary because she was used to that sort of thing. The boy nudged the girl hard and she blinked, looking away for all of two seconds. He smiled at Hilary, meeting her eyes in the mirror. Suddenly things seemed a lot better, because even if *he* looked a mess, his eyes looked like eyes you could trust.

She took them all the way to Croydon where she dropped them off within a few minutes' walk of the station. The girl was still staring. The boy managed to say thank you and goodbye with only a slight blush. Hilary was impressed. Normally boys that age went nova and couldn't look her in the eye.

As she tried to pull back into the flow of traffic—not that it was doing a lot of flowing—she realized that something odd was going on behind her. Everything had ground to a halt and a couple of men were out of their cars, shouting. Hilary craned her neck to see. She could just make out a huge dent in the roof of one of the cars. In fact, both of them had a bashed-in look.

Suddenly, horns began to go off all over the place. One car up and to the left a mother with two children was having a problem keeping the kids under control. Hilary couldn't work out if the dented roofs and shouting men were connected to the outbreak of screaming kids. Then, a horrible thing happened.

There was a huge CRUMP overhead. She screamed and ducked instinctively. When she unraveled herself and looked up she saw that the roof of her car was crumpled in like a dented cardboard box. There was a scraping noise and the car shook. Several long scratches appeared out of nowhere on the nicely polished hood. Two things struck her at once.

First, there was absolutely nothing there.

Second, she had a really bad feeling that, although there was nothing there, SOMETHING was staring in at her through the windscreen. Staring right into her eyes.

The car bounced. More scratches appeared in the hood and then all was still. Her heart thumping madly, Hilary threw open the door and scrambled out. Arguments were breaking out all over the place.

"Parts from a passing plane," barked a large man with a purple face. "You hear it all the time on the TV."

"Meteorites," said a boy on a bicycle, staring enthusiastically at the sky. "Falling so fast that even a small one has enough impact to dent sheet metal. Then they just lie there, looking like ordinary stones . . ." He switched his gaze to the ground.

Shivering, Hilary sat down by the road and waited for the mess to sort itself out. The sense that invisible eyes had been watching her still made her skin tingle with fright. She wished very much that her day had begun a little differently, because deep in her heart she knew that she would never feel really safe again.

Skerridge had been nipping between the cars, trying to keep the blue one in sight, but it was a tricky job. As soon as he realized that he had been following the wrong one for the last few miles he decided to go over instead of around.

Jumping, from one roof to the next and occasionally

on to a hood if it was convenient, he went looking for the right blue car. He could feel roofs and hoods buckling underneath him due to the weight of all the magic in his bones, but the yelling Quick didn't cause him any bother so he ignored them and kept going.

A bunch of kids stared out of the windows of a bus. Their names tripped quickly through his head, but since he didn't need to know who they were he ignored that too. He reached the bus and ran up the back of it on to the roof. Inside, the kids hit mass hysteria and the panic-stricken driver screeched to a halt, yelling into his radio for help.

At the front edge of the roof, Skerridge paused. He looked ahead. Away in front was a car of the right shade of blue. Right Madam and Obstacle were just getting out of it.

Swiftly, Skerridge leaped from the roof of the bus he was on to the roof of the one in front and then on to the roof of the blue car. His targets had just disappeared around a corner. Skerridge hopped down onto the hood and was about to hop off it again onto the road when he happened to glance in through the windscreen.

He stared for a long moment, his heartstrings pinging in his chest. He'd know that face anywhere, even diluted by several generations of Quick blood. He smiled right into the eyes that were just the color of rainwashed skies. It was nice to know that Senta Melana's offspring were still around.

Then he leaped on to the road and went to find Right Madam.

"She was, like, so BEAUTIFUL," said Nin for the umpteenth time.

"Yep," agreed Jonas. "And nice with it. Didn't

complain about you staring at her, for a start. Look, this must be the station."

It looked like a sort of glass and plastic ship and was bustling with people. Just outside was a flower seller and just inside was a kiosk selling coffee and dough-nuts. Nin forgot about Hilary Jones and breathed in the aroma. She hadn't had a doughnut in forever. Or coffee come to that.

"No," said Jonas, before she could ask. "We need to get tickets first."

They joined the line. It was a short one and they were at the window in no time.

"Two halves to Bury St. Edmunds, please," said Jonas politely.

The ticket man, whose name badge said he was Rajinder Singh, looked back doubtfully.

Nin shuffled forward. "We're going to see my auntie," she said brightly.

The man glanced at Nin, who looked him in the eyes and beamed. He relaxed slightly.

"Two halves?"

"Yep. I'm fourteen and my sister here is eleven, so that's two halves."

Nin kept smiling so as to distract the ticket man from the fact that Jonas looked at least sixteen.

Mr. Singh sighed. "Got any ID?"

"ID? No, sorry, should I have?"

Mr. Singh considered things. The girl seemed all right, even if her brother was rather . . . well . . . rough looking.

"I'd advise you to get some ID because the next person might not be such a soft touch, right? Sure you want singles, not returns?" Mr. Singh smiled at Nin, then tapped on his ticket machine, which spat out two oblongs of card. Jonas handed over the notes and got some change.

He dragged Nin over to one side and grinned at her. "You're quite handy really, aren't you?"

"Oh thanks," Nin said mockingly. "Nice to know I'm *some* use!"

They hurried down an enclosed ramp onto the platform, and onto a train with Thameslink written on it. As soon as they had found a seat the doors whined shut and they were on their way around the heart of Celidon.

Raw filled the sky in front of Jik, the pallid disc of the sun gleaming like silver through its misty wall. It frightened him, but there was no choice save to go on. This was the quickest way to reach Nin and so he stepped forward into the Heart.

At once, curls of mist rose from his mud as the Raw began to unmake him. Everything in the Land was formed from raw magic, including its Fabulous, and right now, the raw magic that made up Jik was trying to become one with the raw magic swirling all around him, as a single drop becomes one with the ocean.

He couldn't stop the Raw from unmaking him, but if he focused hard on who he was and what he was doing, Jik knew that he could slow the process down and maybe stay whole enough to reach the other side. His new outer layer meant there was more of him to last, but even so, if he made it through, he'd end up worn to a strip. And if he lost his focus for even a second, the Raw would take him apart.

Because this Raw was so old, the rock that was the center of the Land, that lay beneath the grass and the earth like bones lay beneath flesh, had been unmaking itself for longer. Ahead of Jik lay a network of fog-filled chasms where the rocky skeleton had crumbled more quickly into the Raw, leaving behind ridges like raised pathways. Some of the ridges spiraling out from where he stood would lead nowhere, but Jik knew the lay of the Land, even the parts that weren't there any more, and he chose the one ridge that went on and on, joining with others and branching off again, right across the Heart.

He ran on, following the last remaining ridge of Land, until he reached the center of the Heart. There he stopped to stare, trying to make sense of it all.

Although the Raw still coiled its misty tentacles at his back, in front of him it had gone, leaving empty air. Here even the bones of Land had dissolved. Only his one ridge went on, a skeletal finger of rock like a bridge across the dark nothingness. He could sense that the empty space below had no bottom, nor was there any sky overhead. Just darkness everywhere.

And he'd never seen such DARK darkness before. It was not like the dark of night, because night is still full of things and this darkness was empty. Besides, all you needed to do with nighttime was wait for the sun to come back. This dark was dark because everything had been taken away from it, even the possibility of light.

And then Jik's inner fires chilled as he realized that this was the worst thing ever.

The plague had unmade the Fabulous, sending them back to the Raw. Now it was unmaking the Long Land, sending that back to the Raw too. But even when that was all over, the Raw would never again give birth to a new Land or a different kind of Fabulous. Because now the plague was going even further. It was killing the Raw. What Jik could see before him was the death of Magic itself.

In that moment he understood how late he was. Like

turning up for a train just as the station was closing and the ticket office was pulling down the blinds. He was a new Fabulous, but he would never know what he could become. Long before he had time to find out, the Land would die and so would Magic and so would he. He would be dead forever before he had really lived.

The loss of all his possibilities hurt so much it nearly undid Jik on the spot. But then he remembered Nin and the pain began to recede. Nin was his friend and soon she was going to need him, and when she needed him Jik was determined to be there.

Trembling in every grain of his mud, Jik looked down. It was strange that this one last ridge went on, stretching across the void. He wondered where it led. He would find out soon enough.

If mudmen had been built that way, he would have drawn a quivering breath, or swallowed hard. As it was, the flame in the hollows of his eyes wavered, like a candle in a draft.

Jik bunched up his fists and went on.

18

Nothing Really Bad
Will Ever Happen

Jonas had to dump the remaining crowsmorte net in a trashcan on their way to the main King's Cross station. The stalks had dried up, shriveled into something like straw and begun to fall apart in clumps. It seemed that crowsmorte couldn't survive away from the Land.

They found the train to Peterborough, where they would have to change for Bury St. Edmunds, with ten minutes to spare before it left. Plenty of time to get a takeaway coffee and some doughnuts with the change from Grandad's notes.

"This is like, so Widdern!" Nin said cheerfully. She was feeling oddly delicate, as if she were made of glass. Somehow, being in the Widdern was sharpening the realization of what she had lost. It wasn't that she had forgotten about her mother, but when she was in the Drift, the memory of the Widdern had an unreal quality about it. Now it was the reverse and the Hounds and Dandy Boneman and all the terrible and wonderful things of the Drift were like a dream exposed to sunshine, shrinking beneath the glare of normal things. Things like coffee and doughnuts.

They found a seat near the front of the train and settled down. Nin handed Jonas his doughnut, Jonas passed Nin her coffee. She settled back with a sigh.

"Right," she said, "now I'm looking forward to a nice, peaceful journey!"

Skerridge picked the carriage next door. He settled into the nearest empty seat and gazed around. It was comfortable, even though there were candy wrappers scattered around his feet and a sticky mark where someone had dropped their coffee. The Quick were never the cleanest of folk.

Occasionally Quick would wander up and down searching for a seat. If any of them looked like they were going to try and sit on his, Skerridge hissed faintly and they moved on in a hurried and confused way.

Finally the whistle blew and the train began to move. Skerridge watched the platform flick by and then they were out of the station. He stared blankly at the view for a while, but it was dull so he soon got bored and turned his attention to his neighbor.

Skerridge ignored the kid and watched Knitting's fingers twist the wool into lacy shapes. When she paused for a moment to gaze out of the window, he pulled out one of the needles and gave the wool a tug. Feeling the yarn unravel, she looked down.

"Gaaah!"

Skerridge was surprised an old lady could yell that hard. Knitting looked wildly round the carriage and spotted the boy.

"You! You horrible child. I suppose you think it's funny, ruining an old woman's hard work. . . !"

The boy watched her, frozen with shock. Skerridge

grinned at him and he went as white as a sheet and burst into tears.

"Now hang on a minute!" The boy's mother was on her feet. "My Sammy wouldn't do a thing like that! He's been sitting here quietly all this time. So just you apologize, you old . . ."

"You need to discipline that child . . ." yelled Knitting.

"Don't you hit my boy! I saw you! You were going to smack him, that's assault that is—"

Knitting's knitting went flying across the aisle. The boy ducked and slid under a seat.

Skerridge moved, it was getting dangerous back there. Heads were beginning to turn as the other passengers either watched or joined in.

Four seats up he found a packet of chips, which was nice because he was feeling hungry. When he had finished them he put the empty packet back in their owner's lap. She was too busy reading her book to notice, though how she could ignore the screaming from Boy's Mum and Knitting he had no idea. Bookgirl reached for her chips. Frowning she lowered her book.

"Hey, Sue! You stole my chips! Honestly. Can't you leave anything alone! Just get your own and stop sponging off everyone else!"

"What?" murmured the girl opposite, lowering her own book. "Not me!"

"Well, who was it then?" snarled Bookgirl sarcastically. "Mr. Nobody?"

Skerridge moved on. He had spotted a whole carton of orange juice further down the carriage. Which was nice because the chips had made him thirsty.

"So what now?" asked Nin, following Jonas down onto the platform.

"This is Cambridge, right. We change trains again, but the next one should be the last."

"Wow!" Nin stared into the carriage they were passing, the one up from theirs. "What's going on in there? Looks like a riot. That woman looks like she's really going to hurt someone with that knitting needle. And . . ."

"Come on! We've got to find the right platform."

Nin shrugged and hurried after him.

Behind her a paperback whirled out of the window and hit a station guard.

On the concourse Jonas peered at the departures board and Nin watched three guards and a handful of policemen hurtle toward the train from King's Cross.

Skerridge had a nasty moment when he couldn't figure out which platform they had gone to next. He solved it by doing a superspeed tour of all the trains in the station. Fortunately for the rail company and its passengers he found them on the third one he looked in.

Nin dozed for most of the second trip. When they arrived at Bury St. Edmunds, they had to walk all the way from the station to the center of the town to find the Abbey.

"Problem is," Jonas said, "there's supposed to be a gateway in the gardens of the Abbey, but I've no idea where exactly."

Nin pointed to an extra shadowy place by the bridge where the sunlight didn't quite reach, even though it should have.

"What about that?" she said, nervously.

Jonas studied it for a moment. "Well spotted, kid. Follow me, and stay close."

On the Drift side the bridge looked much older, the wood was rotten, and dangling from one of its beams was a corpse.

Nin looked away quickly, just as its eyes sprang open. She hurried up the bank after Jonas, her feet slipping in the soft earth and covering the sound of something moving squishily behind her. A damp and foul-smelling hand touched her cheek and out of the corner of her eye she saw blackened fingertips and bone. She was so used to it all by now she didn't bother to scream, she just focused on scrambling up the bank and the putrid thing soon slithered away behind her, its hand catching in her hair.

"I wouldn't hang about if I were you," said Jonas, grinning at her. "Things live in Quickmares, y'know."

"Yeah, like I kind of got that!" grumbled Nin glancing over her shoulder. The bridge was eerily quiet. She scurried to keep up with Jonas. "So where next?"

"East. We're heading for the coast. We'll walk the rest of today, then sleep. We should be there by lunchtime tomorrow."

Nin felt a lurch in her middle. "At the House you mean?"

"Uh-huh. Let's just hope your plan works."

"What plan? I have a plan?"

"Something about luck?"

"That's not a plan!"

Jonas grinned. "It's as good a plan as any!"

"What will you do?" she asked nervously. It suddenly hit her that he might be going to leave her at the House and go back. "P'raps we can find your life too," she said hopefully.

Jonas turned to face her. "It's been four years since the BM got me," he said. "Far too long." He smiled.

"Even so, I'm going with you, if that's what you're worried about. Got nothing better to do."

The knot in Nin's middle uncurled. "Thank you," she said meekly.

It was a nice day, by Drift standards. The sky was bright and full of cloudy castles. Ruined castles. Nin was beginning to see how much the Long Land was suffering. Its cry for help was everywhere. She felt sorry for it and wished there was something she could do. Even so, knowing that Jonas wasn't going to leave her, she was beginning to feel very positive about things.

"You know, you're right," she said as they began to climb a low hill toward a ramshackle old hut with its door half off and a crumpled roof. "I mean, look how everything has worked out okay so far. I got away from Skerridge, Grandad gave us the money, bucketloads of bad guys have been after us, but we always escape. So why shouldn't my luck hold, eh?" Nin smiled. "My point is that however frightening things get, nothing really bad will ever happen."

She looked up just as the sun disappeared and the dark clouds raced in with astonishing speed. Lightning cracked and the thunder was so loud and so sudden that she screamed.

"Nin!" Jonas yelled. "RUN! The hut. NOW!"

Rain came down in a sheet of liquid ice, the wind tore at her hair and made her gasp for breath. She ran, her lungs bursting with the effort. Jonas was a dark slash ahead of her and she followed him, unable to see through the rain pouring down her face. They were nearly at the hut, but it was going to be too late because she could hear them coming, baying like wolves only worse. She could feel the cold wind of their breath when Jonas got between her and them. He pushed her toward the broken doorway. She could see empty gloom behind it, but it was shelter.

"Go!" he yelled and she went.

She tumbled in past the hanging door, feeling moss and dead leaves underfoot, then turned to look back. Jonas wasn't at her heels. His pack had fallen and lay trampled in the mud. He stood in the heart of the Storm and the Hounds were all around him, their cloudy shapes and lightning eyes beating him to his knees as she watched. When they howled their breath made frost on the air and when they went they took Jonas with them.

"JONAS!" Nin screamed. She ran back into the open. The rain was still falling, but the thunder was moving away. He didn't come back.

She stared blankly as the clouds above her grew lighter.

Then she started to run.

The rain-wet air sizzled across the fields and Skerridge popped out of superspeed to glare at the sky. He'd only been gone five minutes to track down a bit of breakfast and it was pretty obvious what had happened. The Storm had got them at last . . .

Except there were boot prints in the mud. Small ones. Running. The Hounds had only got one of them and it wasn't Right Madam.

Skerridge brightened up. With Obstacle gone and Unknown Quantity out of the picture for the time being, he'd be able to whip Right Madam into a sack in no time. He studied the boot prints.

"Chasin' thunder eh? Well, she ain't got a Quick's chance in the Heart," he muttered and was gone in a flicker.

19

Chasing Thunder

Silas Penny wondered why he hadn't waited for the rain to stop before setting out toward the nearby town of Rife. The damp wasn't going to help his back any. After he'd twisted it a month ago hauling a sack of dried chestnuts about, he was beginning to give up hope of it ever being right again.

He was peering irritably up at the sky when the girl arrived. Before Silas could do anything about it she had pulled herself up on to the cart next to him.

"Follow that storm!"

To his astonishment, Silas flicked the reins, encouraging the ancient horse to go faster. The cart jolted and bounced along the track and he winced as his back gave a stab of pain.

"My friend's in there!" wailed the girl. She looked muddy and frightened, but something in her eyes showed a grim determination. "He gave himself up so that I could get away."

Silas drew in a sharp breath. "Well, girl, I'll take you as far as I can along this track, but I doubt Ben here will be able to keep up with the Hounds."

He flicked the reins again. The girl obviously had to

have a go or she wouldn't feel right about it. She'd find out quickly enough that trying to catch the Hounds was no use.

Ahead of them the clouds raced full of lightning, drawing steadily away across grassy fields of buttercups and low, purple hills. Thunder rumbled, making Ben whinny with fright.

"Come on, lad," called Silas, although he hardly needed to. The horse was moving faster than he had ever moved before, hurtling over the ground at an astonishing pace, eating up the distance. He was beginning to enjoy it too, with his ears laid back and a gleam in his eyes far younger than his many years.

Silas risked a glance at the kid sitting next to him, eyes fixed on the storm ahead. Now they were gaining on it, though only a little. There had to be magic at work and Silas wondered where it was coming from. He caught a glimpse of twisted leather strands around the girl's neck. Whatever it was that dangled from those strands was glowing, he could see the fiery light reflecting off the bottom of her chin.

"It's going left!"

"Darn," muttered Silas. To his surprise he meant it. "I can't take Ben over the river here. There's a chap makes a living out of ferrying folk across. Down that way."

The girl was already scrambling off the cart as Silas pulled Ben to a halt. He watched her slip and slide down the bank toward the river.

Suddenly there was a rushing sound and something heavy landed behind him. Whatever it was—and it was moving so fast he could barely see it—hurtled across the seat and knocked him off the cart.

Lying spread out and face down, Silas yelled as the thing trampled over him, just missing important areas of his insides by a hair's breadth. There was a frightening crack from his back. He rolled over with a groan and then gingerly clambered to his feet. He straightened up. In fact he straightened up more than he had been able to straighten for weeks.

He stretched carefully, expecting a familiar stab of pain at any moment. It didn't happen. A grin spread over his face.

"Well, darn me," he muttered. Then climbed back on to his cart and drove away.

Hunched in his boat, Stig Lattle watched the Storm retreat. Suddenly a girl appeared, running down the track toward the river. Stig got ready.

She clambered straight into the boat and looked at Stig expectantly. He was about to tell her the price, but changed his mind and pushed off, rowing out toward the middle of the river. Slowly.

Or at least he tried to row slowly, though the boat seemed to have developed a mind of its own. Frowning, he fought against the pull. He had no intention of losing a golden opportunity.

"Please can't you go faster," she wailed. Her eyes were fixed on the storm clouds, watching desperately as they slipped into the distance.

Stig let out a long breath. "It'll cost extra," he said. "More effort, more cash." He increased his backward rowing, forcing the annoyingly self-willed boat to slow almost to a standstill.

The girl gave him an agonized look.

"No money eh? What you got in that pack? That'll do."

"But . . ."

"Along with the bag itself, of course. And—oh, lemme

see—your jacket. And them boots look good and sturdy."

The girl frowned. "Git!" she muttered and jumped over the side.

"Hey!" Stig grabbed at the pack as she went, determined not to let all the booty get away. He caught the strap and pulled hard, nearly yanking her over in the water. She let go and he hauled it into the boat, which had suddenly stopped trying to race to the other side and was now content to bob about on the river like a boat ought to.

He watched her struggle away, the water up to her armpits. She made it to the far side and dragged herself out then half-fell up the bank. By now the storm was well into the distance, just a long bank of purple on the horizon. The sun had come out and overhead the sky was blue.

Stig was about to rummage inside the pack when the air sizzled with hot steam and his boat was suddenly very full of a bundle of angry bones in a fancy vest. Stig screamed.

"Gimme that, goatgob!" The Thing snatched the pack from his hands and shoved Stig hard into the water.

When he finally bobbed to the surface again, the Thing had gone and all he could see was his fiercely burning boat.

Tolley Pinn had been walking all night and was running out of energy. She had stopped in a sheltered dip almost completely hidden by some bushes and what she wanted right now was to cook her lunch. She was gazing miserably at a useless heap of soaked wood, when someone fell on her.

Fortunately, it was a small Quick girl and so didn't land on Tolley too heavily.

"I have to get to the Storm!" wailed the girl, looking wildly around, trying to find a way out of the hollow. Her face showed that she knew it was hopeless. By now the clouds were just a memory on the edge of the sky.

Tolley took in the dripping, filthy clothes and the tearstained face and then spotted the rope of twisted leather dangling around the girl's neck.

"Wait," said Tolley calmly, catching hold of the girl's arm.

The girl looked at her and blinked, startled by Tolley's knotty look and yellow eyes. She probably hadn't met many Grimm. But she stopped trying to run and watched Tolley anxiously.

"Trying to get someone back from the Hounds, right?" Tolley frowned. "Know how impossible it is? Gonna do it anyway?"

"Yes!"

"Then you won't get him out from down here. It's said that the only way is to go in after him and PULL him out with you, got that?"

"Yes!" said the girl eagerly, her blue eyes fixed on Tolley's face.

"When you are in there it will be worse than you can imagine. But never despair, always remember who you are. Look for dry land. It's said there is a moment when you can leave them, just before the rain starts, but you have to be FAST. If you can break away then you will be free of them. They will never take you back. Never, do you understand?"

"Thank you. But it's no use if I can't . . ."

"Get to the Storm? Why chase it when you have that?" She took hold of the leather rope and pulled out the amulet. "It's a wish amulet, only not wishes as in things you want, but things you *need*. See, it's doing what it can, but it's struggling because you've smothered it. So, set it free and let it do its job."

The girl looked at the amulet in surprise, as if she had forgotten it. Now it was uncovered, Tolley could see the symbol on the front, a ragged slash like a zag of lightning. It was already glowing, but as soon as the air touched it, the glow became a blaze.

Far in the distance, the Storm wheeled, changing direction.

The girl gave Tolley a brilliant smile and ran to scramble up the narrow path out of the dip, heading to meet the purple flood spreading rapidly over the sky, tearing in from the north with frightening speed. The sun vanished and a vast cold shadow swallowed the land.

Tolley watched as the clouds boiled overhead and the thunder roared loud enough to shake the ground. Now, lightning glimmered above her and rain fell like knives. Even though the Hounds wouldn't be interested in a half Quick with no soul, Tolley couldn't stop herself cowering. When she looked up again, the Storm had gone and so had the girl.

And then something jumped on her, forcing her to leap nimbly out of the way. She swung around to face it. It was horrible.

She took in the bones barely held together by anything at all, the longer than normal arms and clawed fingers, and the fact that it was clutching a battered-looking pink bag.

"Bogeyman," she said.

"Goin' so fast I missed the blimmin' dip," it snarled, as if it were her fault. "Where's the dumb kid gone now?"

Tolley pointed up.

"WHAT!" it howled, its red eyes blazing at her. It was so angry it was dancing with rage. Fascinated,

Tolley saw coils of smoke escaping from its ears and mouth. The grass under its feet blackened. It let rip.

Tolley dropped to the ground as streams of red-hot flame shot out around and over her. The bogeyman gave one last horrible screech and disappeared, tearing up the bank so fast he caused a minor landslide.

When everything was quiet again, Tolley finally got up the courage to unravel. Around her, a bush, a fallen chunk of tree and her own pile of sticks were flaming merrily.

A smile spread over Tolley's face. Then she set about cooking her lunch.

20

Gabriel Hounds

By the time she got to the top of the hill, Nin was at the end of her energy. She held the amulet up high in one shaking hand and a bolt of lightning cracked from the darkening sky right to its shining tip. The cold wind whipped her hair as she watched the Gabriel Hounds racing toward her, faster now.

And then they were all around her. Their baying filled her ears and she felt herself pulled up, off the ground and away into the Storm.

It was the most wonderful feeling. She was flying, only not flying. She was in the air running on all fours with the clouds at her feet and all around her were the Gabriel Hounds.

For a moment the sky above was clear and blue, but then the clouds rose and wrapped her in their misty gloom and lightning crackled in the air.

Running was easy. She didn't have to worry about getting out of breath because the air filled her lungs and sent the blood pounding round her head without stopping. She knew she would be able to run as far and as fast as she needed to. She would be able to run forever.

Then the dark veil of the clouds fell again and she could see the sky. But this time it was full of stars. It shocked her. Minutes ago it had been daylight. She felt a lurch inside.

"What's my name?" she thought. "I can't remember my name!"

The idea was terrifying, but just as a small part of her brain was telling her that it didn't matter after all because she was one of the Hounds now, an image arrived in her head. A boy wearing a long black coat and lounging against the wall of the underpass, somewhere in the Widdern, way back before she had lost her life.

"Jonas?"

For a moment she thought that Jonas was her name. Then she remembered. She was Nin. Ninevah Redstone. Jonas was the one she had come to find. Relief flooded over her.

She opened her mouth to shout his name, but the wind whipped her voice away. So she began to look for him. And wished she hadn't.

Because when she started to look for Jonas she saw what the Hounds really were.

Skerridge had a problem.

It could be easily solved if he just wrote the girl off as his first loss ever. The only kid he, Skerridge, Chief Bogeyman and Champion Kid-Catcher, had ever failed to deliver to Mr. Strood. EVER.

Skerridge groaned. He couldn't do it. He just couldn't. It was his reputation at stake here. In a way it didn't matter because he would still have the lowest score for non-delivery out of all the bogeymen. Only Pigar was anywhere close and Pigar had managed to lose a whole three kids. But in another way it mattered more than anything.

Simply having the lowest number of losses was nothing like having NO LOSSES AT ALL. Nothing like.

The other bogeymen would snigger at him. The great Champion Kid-Catcher would have finally lost a kid. He would be like them. He would be a bogeyman who could fail.

Skerridge snarled.

Not likely. No way. Never.

So, he was back to the problem. Keeping up with the Storm was easy for a bogeyman, he had been hovering underneath the darned thing for three days. The problem was that the Hounds were not interested in a mere Fabulous. The Hounds wanted souls and only the Quick had those. So even if he could keep up with the Hounds, he couldn't make them pick him up.

Gloomily, Skerridge tried to face the fact that maybe, in spite of all his hard work, he would lose his reputation after all.

The Hounds were everywhere, like a great swarm around her. They were gray and wraithlike with eyes of white fire. Their jaws were huge and heavy and their limbs long. As they loped across the sky they were silent, only a low sighing filled her ears, like something crying far away. Like something lost.

And then it came to Nin that if she hadn't remembered her name she would be lost too. But she *had* remembered and because she knew who she was she could be part of the Hounds and yet still herself. For a while at least.

Her heart turned cold as she began to see in the

Gabriel Hounds traces of the people they used to be. Something about the faces had a human look. Here and there the long cloudy legs ended in grotesque hands instead of paws. In some of them Nin thought she saw ordinary, human eyes behind the white light. She shivered, not daring to glance down at herself in case she looked like that too. She didn't think she could bear it if she did.

With an inner lurch she saw that it was evening, somehow she had missed the day. The clouds thickened and she felt a sickening swoop as they tore down toward the ground, searching for Quick life. Now the Hounds were no longer silent and their chilling howls mixed with the sound of thunder as they clamored after prey. To her horror, Nin found that she was baying too. And worse. Something inside her was angry that if there were any Quick around, they had long since fled for cover.

But for a fraction of a second she saw it. Dry land. Stretched below her, patterned with hills and a herd of horses the color of midnight, racing across the Land on fiery hooves as the Hounds raced across the sky. Then the lightning flashed, the rain began and the dry land was soaked.

And then she knew that she couldn't do it. She couldn't break away in time, before the dry land was gone. She would never be fast enough. It was not possible for a Quick to be that fast. She howled again. And it was a howl like a wolf.

Never despair. That was what the Grimm woman with the golden eyes had said. Remember who you are. Never despair.

The Storm rose, riding high into the sky. Nin pushed the knowledge that it was impossible right to the back of her mind. She had to try anyway, but first of all she had to find Jonas.

She began to scan the Hounds, searching for anything familiar. She was horribly afraid she wouldn't recognize him, but she did. He was further ahead of her in the pack, running on long cloud limbs, his face already changing.

Nin began to move. It was not as hard as she had feared, the Hounds had no real weight and she could push through them in the direction she wanted to go. In no time, or what seemed like no time to her although it was already night again outside the Storm, she was close to Jonas. His eyes were full of lightning and he was baying with the rest of them.

She called his name, but he ignored her. Just once, when she had been calling him for a while, he turned his head in her direction and she thought that he might have recognized her. Then he looked away again.

Nin gave up and tried to think of some other way to do this. If she could just get hold of him then maybe she could pull him with her. If she could spot the right moment, of course, and if she could be quick enough to get out before it was too late.

And all the time the Hounds sped on through the sky in endless pursuit. Nin caught glimpses of the land hurtling past far below, always changing from vivid greens and golds into darker hues as the storm clouds cast their shadow. She wondered if it would always be this like this now, if the only light she ever saw was the gray half-light of the rain-drenched countryside or the brilliance of lightning. Fear made her ache inside. She had to get them both away, but she didn't know how.

She was running shoulder to shoulder with Jonas now. She couldn't hang on to him *and* keep pace so she would have to spot her moment, *then* grab him, *then* get out.

And suddenly, it was dawn.

By the number of days she had glimpsed, at least two dawns must have passed already, but they had happened in those great blanks when time lurched forward. This one happened when she was aware.

First she saw a glimmer of light in the air, drawing a nimbus of gold around her and the Hounds. She could feel the power gathering, an electric quiver spreading through the air. Then the sky exploded. Fire surged through the Storm in a wave of pure energy, turning the clouds to crimson and gold. She felt its hot wind rip through the misty fabric of her body and the force of it filled her with fear and intense happiness all at once. She threw back her head and howled and all the Hounds howled with her.

The clouds boiled in the heat, evaporating around the Hounds and leaving them thinner, ghosts edged in flame and carried on the fierce tide as it burned across the sky. The light was so bright that Nin could see nothing else as they flew at a frightening pace, part of the dawn fire, all sense of time or place lost.

And then it was gone.

It left an emptiness that terrified her. Almost at once the Storm began to thicken again, its dark vapor covering the Hounds like a shroud, giving them back their cloudy forms. Now, they ran in silence, although maybe the sighing was louder. The more Nin listened to it, the more it chilled her. She began to think that if she listened long enough she might hear words, cries for help, not just distant sobbing. But however much that filled her with terror, she also knew in her heart that if she experienced the dawn even once more then she would never want to leave.

If she was ever going to get them out it had to be now.

The clouds were swooping down again, the land rising to meet them at a terrifying speed. Tiny figures dropped everything and fled toward shelter.

Nin could feel Jonas running at her shoulder, and her focus was so clear and sharp that she could see every rock and stone and tiny blade of grass spread out below them. In the middle of it was a small, faraway shape, staring up.

NOW.

She reached for Jonas, catching hold of something that felt halfway between fur and cloth, then turned her face down to the dry land and pulled.

Jonas pulled back. He howled and she saw his head turn toward her. Jaws snapped at her arm. Nin screamed and held on, trying to fight her way down out of the clouds. It was too late.

Lightning cracked over her head and thunder rolled around her. Then the rain began.

She screamed again and thrashed, trying to break free and hold on to Jonas at the same time, but it was no use. The Hounds raised their faces upward again, turning to leave the land behind.

And then something grabbed her arm and pulled so hard it hurt.

Nin scrunched the hand that was holding Jonas as tight as she could. She felt herself plummeting downwards and screamed some more as the ground rushed toward her. Jonas was struggling against her, but she held on so fiercely that he couldn't break free. Then she was out and rolling on the ground, yelping at the stones that bruised her limbs.

Above her the Storm flew out over the sea and was gone.

* * *

Nin bumped to a halt and scrabbled upright. Her shoulder and thigh hurt badly and her left eye was swelling.

Jonas howled. She was about to run toward him when she saw IT. The thing that she had last seen downstairs in the hall, smirking at her as her mother asked her who she was. It hissed steam.

"Wotcha done, dumb kid?" it snarled. "Wotcha wanna bring 'im for? Look at 'im. 'E ain't no use now." The bogeyman stabbed a bony finger at Jonas.

"Skerridge!" cried Nin.

She turned her back on him and ran to Jonas anyway. He was still on the ground and shivering. She put an arm round him, but when he turned to look at her, she pulled back with a cry. His eyes were glowing white.

"See," said Skerridge. "'E's been in there too long."

"Not much longer than me," snapped Nin, "and I'm all right."

"Oh yeah . . ." The bogeyman looked at her thoughtfully. "Now ya come t' mention it, y'do look kinda normal."

Jonas howled again. Nin reached out to touch him, but he sprang to his feet and snarled at her and she drew back in horror. Then he turned away and stood, staring at the sky desperately.

"Wants t' go back, see. Carn be anyfin' ovver than an 'Ound now. Ruined for life, 'e is."

"Will you shut up! If you can't say anything helpful then don't bother!"

She looked around. They were on a broad stretch of rocky ground. Further on, the rock turned sandy. Far out, Nin thought she could see a blue strip on the horizon.

"Is that the sea?"

"Yep."

Jonas howled at the sky. Again and again. The sound

of it tore at her. Nin shut her eyes and bit her lip. She could easily have cried and if Skerridge hadn't been there she probably would have. Instead, she marched over to Jonas and dug in his pocket. He ignored her and went on staring hopelessly after the Hounds. His tinderbox was still there. Nin put it in her own pocket and started looking for something to burn.

Skerridge watched her for a minute. "There's bound t' be driftwood on the beach," he said. "Wan' me t' get ya some?"

Nin struggled for a moment. She would have liked to say no, but Jonas needed help and she wasn't getting anywhere on her own.

"You could," she said.

"Done."

There was a rush of air that made her gasp with surprise. Skerridge was gone. And then he was back, carrying a bundle of wood. Nin gaped at him.

"Bogeymen move fast," he said. "Doncha know nuffin'?"

"I knew that," she grumbled.

Nin picked a spot near the beach and piled the wood up carefully. Then she tried to use the tinderbox. Skerridge watched for a moment then shook his head and sent a quick spurt of flame at the wood. It ignited instantly. Nin glared at him. She couldn't bring herself to say thank you.

Trying to persuade Jonas to sit down was difficult. Watching his face as he howled at the sky made her feel sick. His eyes, when he finally looked at her, made her feel sicker. When he was slumped by the fire, staring moodily into it and ignoring both her and Skerridge, she sat down herself. She had never felt so tired in her life and couldn't think what to do next. She had checked the amulet a dozen times, but each time she looked it was the same. Dead, nothing more than a pretty necklace, the fiery trace gone. There was no help to be had there.

"Callin' the 'Ounds musta taken every last bit o' power," Skerridge pointed out. "Carn' o' been easy."

Nin sighed and tucked it away again. "I'll keep it anyway. It helped me save Jonas. I wish I knew who made it."

"There'll be a—"

"There isn't," she snapped. "I know there's always supposed to be a sorcerer's mark, but there isn't on this. I've looked."

Skerridge puffed out his cheeks. "Well there y'are then. Simeon Dark. 'E always liked to be secretive about fings. 'Is mark was not to 'ave one."

Nin glared at him irritably.

"Wanna rabbit? Makes a nice stew, rabbit. I'll get the rabbit, mebbe a coupla rabbits, an' yew make the stew."

"I've got nothing to cook with," she said coldly.

"I fort you carried the pan while 'e carried everyfin' else?"

"Yes." Nin spoke with exaggerated patience, "But someone stole my . . . Is that my bag?"

Skerridge whipped it off his back and dumped it next to her. "Fort it might come in 'andy."

Nin stared at it suspiciously. "How long have you been following me?"

Skerridge scratched his head. "Oooo, lemme see. Since ya ran out the front door, I reckon."

"So what are you going to do then? Shove me in a sack and . . . You are, aren't you?"

"Sooner or later." Skerridge waved a hand airily. "S'bin quite fun really, what wiv one fing an' anovver. Nearly gave up when ya goes an' gets yerself caught up wiv the 'Ounds, mind! Still, nex' thing I know ya was makin' a break for it. Yer'd never 'ave made it o' course, but ya got pretty close and that meant I got near enough to jump as 'igh as I could an' pull yer out."

"And now?"

"Rabbit stew," said Skerridge and disappeared.

21

The Thief of You

By the time Skerridge had reappeared with two rabbits, some mushrooms and a hunk of bread, Jonas was up and pacing the beach. Nin hovered around him. Every time she tried to touch his arm or speak to him, he snarled at her.

"I can't cook," she wailed. "I've got to look after Jonas."

"Strikes me 'e don' want lookin' after," said Skerridge mildly. "I'd wotchit if I was yew. Looks like 'e might bite."

Nin whirled on him. "Shut up!" she yelled. "Just you shut up!" Her face felt hot and angry and stiff with tears.

"No need t' yell at a pore ole bogeyman like that."

Nin turned her back and gazed after Jonas.

Skerridge scratched his nose. "'Ow about I keep an eye on 'im, while ya get on wiv the stew? They're skinned an' gutted so no nasty work t' do," he went on, waving the rabbits temptingly in her direction.

Part of Nin wanted to go on trying to get through to Jonas, part of her knew it was no good and another part was hurting so much she just wanted to leave it behind for a while.

"I s'pose something to eat might help him?"

"Bound to."

"I'll need water," said Nin reluctantly.

"Over there," said Skerridge. "Nice little stream wanderin' down t' the sea."

Nin set off toward the stream. She was glad to go. She wasn't sure she could have stood much more of it. The worst thing, worse than the lightning eyes and the howling, was the way he didn't want her there. He *knew* she was there all right, he just didn't *care* that she was. Right now, Nin could walk off and leave him and he wouldn't even notice.

She sniffed hard. She had to use her sleeve on her wet eyes and nose because she didn't have a handkerchief.

When she got to the stream she sat down on a rock. The sun, half in and half out of some feathery clouds impersonating a giant eagle with ragged wings, was drying everything and a brisk breeze cooled her face and ruffled her hair. The stream mumbled on about Death and Doom in the usual way.

"You can stop all that stuff," she said to it as she filled the cooking pot. "It will be all right, you'll see. At least I hope it will. I just have to believe it will work out in the end."

She began to see that Skerridge had been clever when he gave her something to do, because she was already beginning to feel better. Like perhaps she could cope after all. Carrying the pan, she set off toward the beach again.

"Hope," whispered the stream to her retreating back. "Believe." But Nin was too far away to hear.

Before she got back someone said . . .

"Jik?"

"You found me!"

The mudman was watching her from a slab of rock. He jumped down and trotted towards her. She had never been so glad to see a friend in her life.

"Are you okay? You look kind of thin. Like you lost a layer or something."

"Yikyik."

"Come on then, better go find Jonas. He's not too good after that Gabriel Hound thing."

"Ik."

"Yeah, it's ik all right," said Nin with feeling.

Jonas was standing on the edge of the sand, staring out to where the sea streaked the horizon with blue. Skerridge was crouched a few yards away, watching him carefully. He looked round when they appeared.

"'Ullo."

"Jik."

Nin glanced at them both. "D'you know each other?"

"O' course. 'E's a Fabulous. Got good senses the Fabulous."

"If you knew he was following, why didn't you say anything?" She gave Jik a stern look.

Jik shrugged. "Tik yik nik."

"How could I possibly know when . . . Oh never mind." Nin shook her head, dumped the pot on to the fire and began to sort out the rabbit and the mushrooms.

"Ooo!" Skerridge fished about in the pocket of his vest. He dug out two twists of paper. "'Ere y'are. Seasonin' fer the stew. Pop in all o' that one and a tiny bit o' that one an' it'll spice fings up jus' great."

"You can cook?"

"Bit out o' practice. Eat on the run mostly, jus' 'ave to grab what I can get. 'M a very busy bogeyman, y'know." He scratched his ear.

Nin couldn't stop herself laughing out loud, although she cut it back quickly. Skerridge looked vaguely pleased.

"Wha's yer name, by the way? Used ter know, but I forgot and I carn call ya Ri—Gotta call ya somefin', ain't I? An' don' look at me like that. I might steal kids, but that don' mean I wanna be on first name terms wiv 'em."

"Ninevah Redstone."

Skerridge screwed up his face. "Bit of a mouful. 'Ow d'ya manage?"

Nin shook her head. "People call me Nin. And he's Jonas."

Skerridge nodded and sighed. "S'a first for me, y'know. Bovverin' to remember a kid's name. But we been frew enough that I reckon we orta be introduced."

Nin frowned to stop herself laughing again. "You really are something else."

"Bogeyman," said Skerridge cheerfully. "Ain't ya gonna get on wiv dinner?"

It took her a while to get the stew going. When it was ready, she steeled herself to go to Jonas. Reaching out, she touched his arm gently.

"Please, Jonas. Come and eat something. Please. It might make you feel better."

"I wouldn' do that 'f I were yew."

Jonas turned on her so fast that she didn't have time to scream. Skerridge moved faster. Jonas had seized Nin's hair to pull her head back, but Skerridge snatched her from the bared teeth just as they grazed her skin.

Dumped in a heap on the rocks with Skerridge holding her still, Nin covered her head and wailed. Her scalp throbbed where a clump of hair had been torn out and the scratches on her neck burned like acid.

"Ain't ya glad ole Skerridge is 'ere?" The bogeyman

grinned, his breath tickling her ear. "'E was goin' fer the jug'lar that time."

Nin fought him off and struggled up. Jonas was still howling.

"He'll get better," she said stubbornly. "And he wouldn't have hurt me really."

"Ik."

"Yeah, see. Even the mudman knows better'n that an' e's only been aroun' five minutes."

"Traitor," snapped Nin.

Jik drooped his head sadly. Nin ignored him and stamped back to the stew. She didn't look at Jonas.

"Let 'im alone fer a while," said Skerridge. "'Ere." He dug a couple of small bowls out his pockets along with a pair of spoons. "Picked 'em up alonga the bunny an' that."

"Do you know where we are?" she asked, trying to block out another howl from Jonas, who was pacing the beach restlessly. Jik had turned to watch him.

"Yer jus' a few miles up the coast from the 'Ouse," said Skerridge as he slobbered down the stew, "and I gotta nidea about 'Ound boy. Ever 'eard of the Lock'eart Sanctuary?"

Nin looked blank for a moment and then she remembered. "Enid Lockheart was one of the Seven Sorcerers! She set up a hospital for Quick. Do you think they can help him?"

"They'll try!" Skerridge grinned craftily. "Know where it is? Right under Mr. Strood's nose."

"Near the House?"

"More than that! It's in the blimmin' grounds, innit! I'll take yer there if yer like."

"Hmm. I guess you've got to get me to the House somehow, right?"

"Never said I was gonna be nice."

Nin smiled half-heartedly. "Shame, I was hoping you might, like, give me my life back? Just for the fun of it?"

Skerridge drew in a breath and shook his head. "Ain't that simple. Even if I didn' 'ave a reputation to keep up. Y'see, all the mem'ries of ya, all the ones I stole, they're wrapped up in a memory pearl. The pearls are all in a secret room in the 'Ouse."

"But you were following me. You wouldn't have had time . . ."

Skerridge shrugged. "Miles are pretty much nuffin' when yer got super-speed. Anyway, point is, yer gotta get 'old o' yer pearl first an' then swaller it."

"Swallow it?" Nin frowned.

"Dunno why I'm tellin' ya this really, cos I'm gonna deliver ya to Strood, make no bones about it! But jus' in case somefin' 'appens an', oh I dunno, ya gets away from Mr. Strood—which is impossible o' course—I fort I'd let ya know what t' do next. But don' go finkin' ya can get away easy. Look at it like this. Plenny o' kids over the years 'ave got away from the BMs, 'cept me o' course. But of all those 'oo didn' get away an' got 'anded over, not one of 'em 'as ever escaped from Mr. Strood. S'impossible."

Nin smiled. "So was getting away from you."

"Yer ain't done it yet, kid," grinned Skerridge. "Yer ain't done it yet!"

By the time they had finished their meal, the day was drowning in its evening light, sinking into clouds like a purple lake. The waves were tipped with foamy horses that gleamed bone white in the dying sun and galloped before the breeze, dragging the sea behind them. It would have been beautiful if Nin had been in the mood to care.

She felt deeply tired. Every bone and muscle ached

with it and she knew they had a long trip ahead. Trouble was, how could she get Jonas calm enough to go with her to the sanctuary?

Jik was rummaging around inside her pack. A moment later he hurried over to Nin and dropped the crowsmorte candle at her feet.

A warm smile stretch across Nin's face. "Perfect! Thank you." She picked up the candle and held it for a moment in silent hope. Then she lit it at the fire and carried it over to Jonas, where he had settled in a sprawled heap on the sand.

Skerridge curled up by the fire and was asleep in a second. Nin followed his example and knew nothing more, not even dreams, until the electric feel of gathering dawn woke her up.

Flames filled the sky with gold and she remembered what it had been like to be up there with the inferno. For a second she was filled with a sense of loss so intense that she wanted more than anything to go back.

That's what it must be like for Jonas, she thought, only all the time. She lay where she was and watched the sky until the sun was up and the flames were just daylight. Then she sat up and looked around. Skerridge was a bundle of cloth and bones in a heap a few feet away. Jik was standing, patiently watching over them. The candle was still burning.

As soon as she moved to get up, Skerridge bounced to his feet.

"Them crowsmorte candles do all they can in one night only, so I'd save the rest. Peace o' mind don' come cheap, y'know."

As she blew out the flame, Jonas opened his eyes. The bad thing was that they were still glowing white. The good thing was that he looked at her and said, "Nin?"

Nin nodded, squeezing her eyes shut against tears of relief. "Um . . . do you . . . like . . . remember anything?"

"Everything." A look of pain crossed his face as he sat up. "You shouldn't have done it."

"I couldn't leave you."

"Why not?" Now something like a snarl had crept into his voice and the white gleam in his eye brightened into light.

"You . . . you would have become one of them."

Now he did snarl. "I am one of them! Stupid brat. They'll never take me back now, will they? You've seen to that. And to think I helped you! Right at the start, I should've left you to be gored by the bull." He turned and strode away.

"No," yelled Nin after him, fighting tears. "You're not one of them! You're not."

Jonas stopped at the edge of the sea and looked longingly up at the sky. "Did you see the dawn? Did you feel it?"

Nin nodded. "But it's not where you belong. You'll see."

At mid-morning they stopped to rest and Skerridge lit a fire, then disappeared off to get breakfast. Nin huddled next to it feeling cold to her heart. Jonas was standing nearby, gazing at the sky again, with Jik keeping guard.

Jonas had said little, but then he hadn't howled or snarled either. He still shook her off whenever she got too close, but at least he did look at her when she spoke to him.

"Jus' bread an' cheese this time," said a voice at her side. "An' I 'ad t' go a few miles fer that!"

Nin eyed him thoughtfully. "How exactly do you pay for it?"

"Pay?" Skerridge looked puzzled. "Oh pay! Y'mean what do they get fer givin' me their bread an' stuff?"

"Yeah."

"Well they don' get anythin' as such."

"So you steal it?"

"Not 'xactly. I makes it up to 'em by not wreakin' 'avoc in their whereabouts. So I s'pose ya could say they gets peace an' quiet. Which is a good bargain if y' arsk me."

Nin shook her head.

"Anyway. Wha's wrong wiv bein' a thief? Tha's what I am. Tha's what I do fer a livin'. I'm the thief of yew."

Nin laughed. "You haven't got me yet, Skerridge," she said cheerfully. "You haven't got me yet!"

The bogeyman paused in the middle of shoving some cheese into a hunk of bread. Then he grinned. Then he laughed.

"Yer quite right." He chuckled. "I 'aven't, 'ave I?"

Nin thought the journey would never end. The sand rolled out forever and she trudged on with her mind empty of everything except keeping Jonas in view.

Skerridge followed Nin, carrying Jik on his shoulders. Beside them the waves rolled in, cold and bleak, the sea stallions frighteningly large as they dashed themselves to foam on the beach. Her legs hurt and her feet were sore, burning lumps. It was early afternoon and they had been walking since dawn.

"We're 'ere," said Skerridge.

The sand had been slowly turning into shingle and now it ended in a cliff that towered against the sky. Sea surged around the rocks at its base, forcing them inland.

"It ain't nat'ral. Made by magic years before the plague, that was. Sorcerers used t' like messin' around wiv the Land. There's a way up furver round."

The way up proved to be a ladder of rock. Nin's heart sank, but she drew a slow breath, wiped her hands on her jeans and took hold of the stone. It was a long, hard climb. Skerridge ran up the wall beside her, offering help that she stubbornly refused. Jik, still perched on the BM's shoulders, hung on grimly, his stubby hands clasped around Skerridge's head.

By the time they reached the top, Nin was worn out. They had come out on a grassy slope edged with tall trees and flowering shrubs. In front of her ran a stretch of lawn, overgrown with wild roses. The remains of a path wound through the shrubbery and up past a white ruined building that looked like a temple. Then up some more.

At the top of the hill was the Terrible House.

It towered against the sky in a jumble of chimney pots and dark stone. Ravens circled the bell tower and the pointed roofs, and all the windows were gone, bricked in and mostly covered with ivy. The House was perched on a corner of cliff and, on the right-hand side, the walls seemed one with the precipice. A wedge of evergreens stood tall and dark against the left. Nin could see no signs of life anywhere. It looked blank and forbidding, a place that kept secrets.

Nin shivered. Her tired legs refused to take her any further and she found herself sitting on the ground with no idea how she got there. She couldn't see Jonas anywhere. Jik had gone after him and Nin could hear the mudman in the distance, calling at the top of his voice.

Skerridge loomed over her, his ugly, tooth-filled face hovering close to hers. His red eyes gleamed in the shadowy light. This is it, she thought, he's going to put me in the sack and I'm too tired to do anything about it.

Then everything went dark.

PART
2

THE
TERRIBLE
HOUSE OF
STROOD

22

Strood

The world turned on its head. Scrunched up in a ball, Nin stuck out a hand and touched rough cloth. She wailed, tears stinging her eyes.

"Yer inna sack, live wiv it," muttered Skerridge. He was already on the move and the bobbing up and down as he hurried toward the Terrible House of Strood made her queasy.

"How could you do this to me after all we've been through!" For some reason Nin felt betrayed, even though Skerridge had warned her. "Do you really NEED to be the champion? I mean . . ."

"Yep."

"Skerridge!"

"Give it up, kid, yer goin' to Mr. Strood an' tha's that."

Nin struggled, her despair turning to anger. "You . . . you . . . !"

"Bogeyman," said Skerridge patiently, "the word yer lookin' for is bogeyman. An' this is what bogeymen do."

She gave up and sniveled quietly. She was too tired to deal with this. It wasn't fair. Her sacking prison shook and jostled.

"We're up at the 'Ouse now. The main part is where Mr. Strood lives alonga the guards. Mostly everyone else lives in the extension. Which is, like, at the back. And down some."

"Down?"

"Yeah. Right down in the cliff, like. Oh, an' out under the beach a bit an' all. The front 'all an' that is traps an' guards, but ya don' need t' know that cos even if ya survived, which ya won't, only a turnip'd try gettin' out that way." Something in his tone made Nin listen carefully.

Skerridge chuckled. "Course, fing is they say there's anovver way out. Seraphine's Secret Way, they call it. No one knows fer sure where it is, not even us bogeymen. Rumor 'as it ya go right down past the storerooms, the livin' quarters an' all that, then frew the graveyard an' there is it."

Suddenly Nin realized what he was doing. "I suppose," she said cautiously, "once you've handed me over you're still champion kid-catcher. If I, like, got away then it would be Strood who lost me, not you."

Skerridge snorted with laughter. "Ain't nobody gets away from Mr. Strood."

Her small, cloth world jerked for a moment. She wriggled, trying to get the right way round. There was a thud, like someone banging on a sturdy door, and then the sound of bolts being drawn. Lots of bolts.

"It's Bogeyman Skerridge," said Skerridge. "Gotta delivery."

"Righty-oh. In yer come then. Mind the traps."

"Ow!" Something knobbly got Nin in the ribs. She tried to kick it.

"Tha's better. They're usually strugglin' more'n that. Mr. Strood likes 'em alive." The guard sniggered. "All in one bit, is she? No bites taken out of 'er like ya did that ovver one? Gone down in 'istory that 'as."

"Pah," snorted Skerridge angrily. "The kid deserved it."

Skerridge hefted the sack on to the other shoulder. Nin yelped. "Mind you, took a lot o' self-control, this one. Caused me a lot o' trouble."

"You did what?" demanded Nin as they hurried down the corridor and up some stairs.

"Quiet," snapped Skerridge. "It were ages ago and only a coupla bites, more or less. Now, lessee. Two steps left, three to the right . . ." There was a loud twang. ". . . an' tha's the poison-tipped arrows gone. Then we got the whirlin', jagged-edged cuttin' fings. Better duck 'ere . . ." (Some nasty swishing sounds.) ". . . quickly follered by the hidden crushin' fings . . ." (Some grinding noises.) ". . . are ya gettin' all this?"

"Best not go this way, is what you're saying."

"Good-oh. Now we got the inner guards, so shut it. 'Ullo, Stanley. Big spear ya got there."

"Nice t' see ya, Skerridge."

"Floyd. Like the knobbly club!"

"Fanks, mate."

"Sconce . . ."

"Okay! Okay!" muttered Nin. "I got the point."

They hurried on. Nin was beginning to feel really sick. There was a pause and some shuffling about of the sack. Skerridge cleared his throat loudly.

"Erm . . . before we go in . . . I was gonna say . . . Well, it's been fun. Following yer across the Drift, not t' mention the Widdern. Gettin' yer outa scrapes.

A bogeyman don' get much variety in 'is workin' day mostly, so I jus' fort I'd let ya know."

"Thanks," said Nin grimly.

"Don' worry. 'E'll pro'bly jus' ask ya some questions and then frow ya to 'is Deff. It'll be quick an' it won't 'urt as long as ya don' try to fight. Got that?"

"He'll what?"

"Frow ya to 'is Deff. Right, 'ere we go then."

Nin didn't have time to be puzzled before she heard him knock on a door and a voice said, "Come in."

There was a shuffling sound and the swish of perfectly oiled hinges as the door swung open and Skerridge edged forward. A moment later, he tipped her out of the sack on to a thickly carpeted floor.

"Ah, Skerridge," said a warm voice somewhere above her. "Got here at last, I see?"

"'Ad a bitta trouble wiv this one, Mr. Strood, sir, but 'ere she is."

"Hmm, still the champion, eh?"

"Yessir!"

Nin scrabbled up from lying on her face with her mouth full of carpet, to sitting propped on her hands. She shook the hair out of her eyes and looked up. She blinked.

"Well, now, what have we here," said the voice in a friendly tone. "What's your name, little girl?"

Nin frowned. She wasn't keen on the little girl part, but she could feel Skerridge's eyes burning into her anxiously.

"Ninevah Redstone," she said, then added "sir" rather pointedly.

"Hmm." Strood wagged a thin finger at her. "Are you the girl who made a Fabulous? Fascinating. You must tell me all about it."

He gave her a twinkling smile. Nin shuffled back

a little way on her behind until she bumped into Skerridge's ankles and had to stop.

Strood chuckled. "Making a Fabulous AND giving my champion kid-catcher such a hard time! Goodness, you'll be trying to get away from me next! That's all for now, Bogeyman Skerridge. Off you go then."

There was a swish and a thump. Nin felt the draft from the door as Skerridge left in a hurry. She was alone with Mr. Strood.

Mr. Strood's sitting room was filled with rich dark hues. Wine-colored silk lined the walls, the carpet was a deep plum and the huge, soft armchair was a purple so dark it was almost black. Even the ceiling had been painted to look like a sunset in shades of rose with only a touch of gold. She could see no windows at all and the light came from many lamps fixed to the walls and perched on the surfaces. Everything was spotless.

Strood dropped gracefully into the big armchair and waved a hand at a smaller one opposite. Nin got to her feet and fell into it. She was staring. She couldn't help it. She had a horrible feeling that her mouth was hanging open.

"I know, I know," Strood sighed wearily. "You can't imagine how someone can have got so many scars and still be alive, right?"

Nin nodded. It was close enough. In fact she hadn't got past the "how can anyone have so many scars?" part.

Strood waved a hand that looked like a road map in hand shape.

"What you have to understand," he said smoothly, "is that we are only talking about one mishap. If you can call being deliberately and cruelly thrown to the wolves a mishap, which I doubt."

There was a timid knock on the door. It swung back on a small woman with glossy dark hair, wearing a brown dress with a white pinafore. She was carrying a tray laden with a plate of cakes and one of pastries, a tea cup and a teapot. Her neat fingers were tipped with pearly nails that were just short of claws. She carried the tray over to the carved oak table at Strood's elbow and set it down, then bobbed a curtsey and dashed out of the door.

Humming to himself, Strood inspected the cakes and poured a cup of black tea from the pot. He sat back and took a sip.

"Excellent! Now, where were we?"

"Wolves," said Nin again.

"Oh that," he shook his head. "No, no. Enough about me, tell me about yourself?"

"So that's it really," finished Nin. "Though I don't understand why just telling him to be alive makes him a Fabulous?" She had made the story of Jik last as long as she could because she didn't have a plan for getting away from Strood, so the longer she could put off being fed to his Death the better. Whatever that meant anyway.

Mr. Strood steepled his fingers and looked thoughtful. "Land Magics—mudmen, sand cats, and so on—are mindless things governed by set rules. With mudmen, when you wake them, you give them the one task that rules them. It gives them purpose, but means that they are just tools with no sense of themselves. They'll last until their task is done and then go back to being earth."

"But I told Jik to be alive, which isn't just a task that you can do, right? So that makes him . . . different."

"And if you have created something from the Land that

will live until it dies, something with free will and a *self*, then you may just have made a Fabulous. See?" Strood chuckled. "Now, tell me about how you got away from my chief bogeyman! That must've been quite a feat!"

He poured himself more tea while she talked. It obviously didn't occur to him to offer Nin any, or to give her a cake from the pile on the tray, which he hadn't bothered with at all. She finished the story with the part where her mother accidentally stood on Skerridge's sack, trying to make it as funny as possible. It seemed to work because Strood laughed, but Nin got the feeling that the friendliness wasn't real. At least not in any normal kind of way. She didn't think it would stop him killing her whenever he felt like it.

"And that's when you ran into that young friend of yours, right? And where is he now?"

Nin opened her mouth, then shut it again. Although she was pretty sure Jonas would be with the Lockheart Sisters by now, Strood didn't know about the sanctuary being in the grounds of the House.

She had an idea. "I don't know." She sighed. "He's not been well since I got him away from the Storm Hounds."

Strood stared at her over the rim of his cup. He raised one eyebrow. The other didn't seem to be moveable

"You got him away from the Storm Hounds," he repeated.

Nin gave a nod and then waited patiently while he looked her over thoughtfully. He smiled. He had a nice set of teeth, considering the rest of him was such a mess.

"All right," he said. "You can tell me that one too."

On his way out Skerridge stopped at the big gazebo at the top of the hill, which had huge clumpy columns and a roof that looked like a wedding cake from a gothic nightmare. He sat on a marble bench inside the pillars, clutching a feebly struggling squirrel that he had grabbed on his way. He was also clutching a sheet of paper that he had nicked from Secretary Scribbins's desk on the way out. Skerridge had done the nicking part at superspeed so all Scribbins had felt was a warm draft that blew his neatly arranged papers around the room.

He put the paper on the bench next to him and smoothed it out. It was singed around the edges because he had been going so fast, but still usable. Skerridge frowned at it. He hadn't done much writing in a while. Bogeymen had no need for it in the normal way of things. Around him the day crept on toward evening, bringing out the shadows that had been lingering under the tall evergreens. The harsh cries of the peacocks echoed over the garden and high above white doves flew in bright splashes across the sky.

Skerridge munched the squirrel absentmindedly as he thought about what to say. Then he reached for the pen and scowled. He had forgotten to nick a pen. Skerridge looked at the remains of the squirrel. There was just about enough over.

When he had done writing the note, he stuck it on to the sanctuary door with splinters of squirrel bone and went to find another kid.

Nin was running out of things to say. She smiled brightly and moistened her dry lips with her tongue.

"You must have interesting stories to tell?" she asked, hoping to stave off the inevitable.

"Oh plenty," said Strood warmly. "I love stories. In fact," he leaned toward her confidingly, "I write poems, you know. Not the flowery sort with lots of unnecessary words, of course. I write ballads that tell a story."

"Aren't they a sort of song?"

"No! No! Well, sometimes. I did try having them put to music once. Ran out of musicians. They could never get the harmony quite right. Screamed very tunefully though."

"Um. Could I hear one?" It might be worth it, if they were good and long.

Strood waved a hand. "Oh I don't read them out loud! But you should try the *Ballad of the Last*, that's a good one." He chuckled. "Except, of course, that you won't get time before you die. Shame. I think you'd like it."

Nin felt her heart turn over. She took a deep breath and tried not to panic.

"The Last," she said. "Is it about the Seven Sorcerers?"

"It is indeed! You really are quite an intelligent child, aren't you?"

"I met Nemus Sturdy," she said hopefully.

"So have most Quick who travel this way," said Strood dismissively. He brushed an invisible fleck of dust from his black, silk suit.

"Did you know them?" she asked desperately.

Strood gave her a long, cool look.

"Know them," he said.

Nin shivered at the tone of his voice. "Um, I mean, being one of the Fabulous I just thought you might have met them."

Strood stared at her for a moment and then flung his head back and howled with laughter. Nin wasn't sure if this was good or bad.

"What makes you think I'm Fabulous? The fact that I have power? Oh no," he hissed, hunching forward in his chair. "The Sorcerers may have thought they would reign forever, but they didn't as it turns out. Look at them now! An old oak, a few stone walls, a desperate vampire and a body-skipping madman. And those are the ones that survived! The rest are just so much dust. They can't even rot to feed the flowers!" His voice had become a savage snarl.

Nin stared at him. Even if she could have unstuck her tongue enough to speak, she wouldn't have known what to say. She could have pointed out that Simeon Dark was supposed to be still alive, but she thought it would only make him angrier.

Strood settled back in his chair again. His voice went back to being mildly amused.

"Oh no, girl. I'm not Fabulous," he said calmly, "I'm just immortal."

23

Big Luck

Strood picked up a silver bell perched on a shelf under the table and rang it. Almost immediately the door sprang open. A figure filled the doorway. It was wearing a chainmail shirt and carrying a spear.

"Yessir!"

A shiver ran through Nin. He had sent for the guard and that could only mean one thing. She opened her mouth to say something, anything, to put off what was going to happen next, but Strood got there first.

"Take her away," he said.

The guard, whose emerald eyes showed him to be a Grimm, picked Nin up like a doll. He tucked her under one arm and tramped heavily out of the room.

"You can put me down if you like," squeaked Nin breathlessly, her ribs crushed to breaking point. "I won't try running away."

The guard chuckled. "Not a lotta point!" He dumped her on the ground, fortunately with her feet downward.

"Um, I'm Nin," she said in her friendliest voice. "What's your name?"

"Errol," said the guard cheerfully. He was about seven foot tall and nearly as wide. "Yer the one

Bogeyman Skerridge jus' brought in right? I 'eard," he glanced over his shoulder and lowered his voice, "I 'eard as ya made a Fabulous!"

"That's me," said Nin. "But how did you know?"

Errol looked at her in awe. "Yer famous. Stories like that, they get about. And BMs are terrible gossips, y'know." He sighed heavily. "'S almost a pity I gotta frow ya to Mr. Strood's Deff."

Nin was still having a problem with how anyone was going to throw her to Mr. Strood's death. Her own maybe, but someone else's?

They had been walking for ages down a wide, high-ceilinged corridor. Nin realized that the House was seriously huge, even bigger than she had thought when she saw it from the garden. Finally they reached some stairs that led down to another long hallway. As far as she could work out, Mr. Strood lived on the first floor and they were now going back down to ground level. At the foot of the stairs was a large picture of an old man strapped into a carved wooden chair. The man looked hideously crazed and the great staring eyes seemed to follow Nin as she walked past.

"Tha's Gan Mafig, that is," said Errol conversation-ally. "Used ter own the 'Ouse, long ago, afore the Seven Sorcerers 'appened and Mr. Strood did what 'e did to Mafig an' took over."

Nin didn't ask. She had a feeling that Gan Mafig's fate had been a horrible one and felt she would be better off not knowing what it was.

"Mr. Strood's Deff lives in a kennel right next to the inner garden," went on Errol. "The 'Ouse is built round the garden, like. Nobody's allowed in there, 'cept to walk the Maug round the lake. Sometimes Mr. Strood goes t' look at the roses, though."

At the end, the corridor turned at right angles to itself and kept going. About a third of the way down they arrived at a plain door with a key on a hook next to it. Errol unlocked the door and pulled it open. Somewhere, a bell began to toll, its heavy sound rolling over Nin like waves and making her skin prickle.

"It's jus' the Evebell," said Errol, raising his voice over the reverberation. "It rings every day, right at the moment the sun begins to sink."

Nin nodded to show she understood, though she didn't. The bell stopped, its last bong echoing in the still air.

"In yer go then, I'll be right behind ya." Errol nodded toward the open door.

Cautiously Nin inched round the door, closely followed by the Grimm guard. She froze.

They were in a courtyard, enclosed on all sides, but open to the sky. Ivy covered the high walls except for the one to their left, which had a window one floor up. There was one arched exit through which Nin could see a path, a tree, and some shrubs.

In the middle of the courtyard was a kennel as big as a garden shed. But it wasn't the kennel Nin was staring at, it was the dog.

It turned its great head in her direction. Nin couldn't see any eyes, although she knew they were there because she could feel them watching, and its fur wasn't fur because fur didn't drip darkness like water. It had been lying down but as soon as it saw them it got up on to its massive paws and stood waiting hungrily. It opened its mouth and let out a breath that turned instantly to frost in the warm evening air. Even its teeth were made of darkness. It bared them at her in a snarl that she couldn't hear, but that sent a bolt of freezing fear right through her.

"Yeah, tha's it. Tha's Mr. Strood's Deff. 'E calls it the Maug. Blimmin' thing. Dunno 'ow many servants we've been froo wiv that. Thank goodness it only needs walkin' once a fortnight, eh?"

Nin nodded automatically, not taking her eyes off the Maug for an instant. She was shaking.

"Now, 'ere's ow it goes. 'E's on a chain that don' stretch far, so I shove yer out inter the middle—just over that line there what we've painted on the ground at great risk t' life an' limb—an' tha's it really. It don' take long. I'll stay 'ere till yer gone, if ya like," Errol added kindly.

"Th-thanks," muttered Nin numbly. "W-what will it do?"

"Eat ya, o' course. It likes to eat life. Only Quick life, mind, and the younger the better. Well, it's been nice knowin' ya." Errol stuck out a hand.

Nin shook it politely.

"Yer so calm," Errol went on admiringly. "Not many Quick can stay calm in the face of the Maug. Mostly they jus' scream an' beg fer mercy."

"Thanks," said Nin. She didn't feel calm. She thought her body was going to shake itself apart with fear. It was all over. Jik and Jonas were in the hospital and Skerridge had gone. What she needed now was some really big luck, but even that seemed to have deserted her. There was nothing she could do, nowhere to run and no one was coming to rescue her. This was it. The End.

The Maug threw back its head and howled. The howl was made of fear, not sound. It ripped through the air like knives of ice and it was only the barest edge of pride that kept Nin from screaming helplessly and begging for mercy. Darkness rose from it like steam. Even Errol had gone pale.

"Better not keep it waitin'. 'Ere," he went on gently, "I'll come wiv yer up t' the line, 'ow's that?" He led her toward the red stripe painted across the paving stones. The line was sloppy and had lots of breaks and smudges. He stood just on the outside of it.

"D'ya wanna go by yerself or shall I give yer a shove?"

Nin thought that she would go by herself, if she could, but she took a last moment to look up at the sky. It was dusky blue and perfect and empty of everything but for a tiny black speck that might have been a bird. The Maug howled again and the shockwaves reverberated out and up making the servants shiver in their quarters, the guards stop halfway through their tea and the bird overhead drop the snail it had been carrying and swerve sharply off to the left, never to come this way again.

Errol wiped his brow. "Time ter go," he said.

Nin stared, shivering, as the snail hurtled down through the air faster and faster gathering speed until . . .

"Ouch!" Errol staggered. He was far too big and solid to be hurt by a snail, even one traveling at velocity, but he was already unnerved by the Death Dog and so the blow from above startled him. He jumped back a couple of paces and dropped his spear.

Nin looked at Errol and Errol looked at Nin. Then they both looked at the red line, which was now between them. He had one breath to try and get to the right side, but goblin-Grimm weren't known for speed and the Maug was already in the air.

"Blast," said Errol, as the Death Dog landed on him, taking him down with a crashing thud that shook the ground. His voice rose to a howl. "Run fast an' never ferget the Eyes . . ."

It had been waiting far too long for its dinner and

though it would have preferred the young one to the old half-Fabulous one, right now anything would do. There was Quick in it, the Maug would just have to eat around the Fabulous bits.

Nin hurtled backward and crouched against the wall beneath the window with her fingers in her ears to block out the tearing, sucking sound of the Maug at its dinner. There wasn't a lot of screaming from Errol, just the first howl of terror followed by a horrible gurgling sound and then nothing.

When it was all over, Nin unraveled herself, feeling numb and strangely cold. She stood up, shaking helplessly. In front of her the Maug turned its horrible eyes her way as if wondering about dessert. It licked its lips and dribbled darkness mixed with blood. Between its paws lay what remained of Errol.

All the Quick in him had been sucked away leaving only the Fabulous part. The leftovers of shriveled, beetle-like skin and bone struggled feebly where it lay before it finally dissolved into a bluish goo.

With her back to the wall for support, Nin edged toward the door on jelly-legs. The Maug watched, its body tensed ready to spring.

"Nice dog," murmured Nin pointlessly.

The edge of the doorframe was under her fingertips. She slithered over it until her back was against the wood. The Maug crouched.

Nin screamed just as the Death Dog leaped at her. She scrabbled at the door and it fell open beneath her, pitching her through into the corridor beyond. At her back the Maug, brought up short by its chain, let out a silent howl that shook the Terrible House right down to its fearsome Engine.

✳ ✳ ✳

Strood's study was a large, comfortable room with one big window that looked out over the courtyard. A minute ago, Strood had left the desk where he had been sitting, mulling over his next poem, and had gone to the window to watch the Maug feed. He had missed the incident with the snail by a split second and all he saw was his pet enjoying its dinner.

Normally he would have stayed to watch right to the very end, but today Strood was inspired and wanted to write down all the words swimming around in his head as quickly as possible. So by the time Nin moved from beneath the window where she had been safely out of his range of vision, he was back, sitting at the desk in his study staring into space with a smile playing about his horribly scarred lips.

Strood selected his favorite pen. He had thought for a while about how to tell the story and now it was time to begin. Solemnly, he dipped the nib into the ink and leaned over the waiting page to write the title of his next great work. It was:

The Ballad of Ninevah Redstone

Within moments he was so absorbed in his writing he didn't even notice his pet howling with rage and disappointment.

Nin followed Errol's advice and ran fast. She hurtled silently down the corridor and past the stairs with the horrible picture. She didn't want to go up them because Strood was that way, so she turned a corner and kept on running until she ended up in front of a door.

Everything was quiet. She pushed open the door and stared in amazement at the scene in front of her.

It was a wood. Growing right on the edge of the cliff and encased in crystal, but definitely a wood. There were trees, their branches rustling in the breeze, shedding the odd leaf on to the grassy path. There were smaller shrubs with pale flowers, glowing in the evening light that fell in splintered gold through the crystal walls, and there were even ferns and mosses that hid the ground with their soft covering. Nin crept inside. Then she half sat, half fell to the ground beside a tree and lay for a while, racked with sobs that shook her like a leaf, finally understanding how stupid she had been to hope she would see her brother again. Because if she had survived only by the wildest stroke of luck, what were the chances that Toby had made it past the Maug as well?

It was a long time before she fell asleep, worn out with fear and grief and loneliness, but fall asleep she did and peace, or what passed for it in the Terrible House of Strood, finally settled in for the night.

24

Skerridge Goes Rogue

The Lockheart Sanctuary was quiet and those of its patients who were not in too much pain had long gone to sleep. Only the sisters were still up, their thin, blue-clad shapes moving silently along the corridors going about their business of comforting and healing. And Jik. Jik was still up because mudmen did not need to sleep.

He had spent most of the night wandering Mr. Strood's moonlit gardens, looking for Nin. He had found two gazebos, an orchard, a stagnant lake, a grotto shimmering with gemstones, a peacock house, a cave full of blue spiders bigger than he was, a hothouse that had clearly gone insane and an overgrown maze. But there was no trace of Nin.

But he did find the note pinned to the sanctuary door with bloodstained splinters and now he was standing in a corridor that smelled of cool water, waiting for Jonas to be in a fit state to read it.

In front of Jik was a closed door and behind the door was Jonas, being cared for by three of the Lockheart sisters. From inside the room came the sound of singing. Listening to it made Jik's mud tingle.

Through the window next to him, the outside world was beginning to grow lighter as the first flickers of morning touched the horizon. Then dawn ignited and flames the color of blood blazed over the sky in ruby tongues, giving the Drift a distinctly doomsday look. At once the singing stopped, the door opened and the sisters came out. Jik wondered if he should go in or wait a while longer.

Inside the room, Jonas stirred, his eyes flickering, half-open. Three candles guttered around the bed. As the dawn flames burnt out, the sky grew clear and bright again, slowly filling the room with soft gold. The glow condensed into the form of a woman sitting by his bed. Her hair was shorn almost to her scalp and she wore a robe the same blue as a summer sky. She was made of light and she was so beautiful it hurt him to look.

She smiled. "Better now?"

Jonas tried to focus on her. He could feel cool air around him and soft sheets on his skin. He felt clean.

"Much," he mumbled, his voice blurring.

"We don't have long to talk," said the woman. "I'm just a memory, you see, a kind of ghost. I can only speak to people at times like this, the instant between oblivion and consciousness."

"I'm waking up?"

"Yes, but I can hold on to the moment for a little while." She smiled at him and his breath caught in his chest. "My sisters have been singing Pleads for you all night and the candles that you see there each have one drop of unicorn blood in them. They were the last drops of the last unicorn ever and we were saving them for such as you."

"For me?" Jonas watched her, transfixed. Her voice

sent fingers of silver into his heart and made him want to laugh or cry or both. "Why me? I'm not important."

The woman looked at him gravely. "No. You are not important. But you are part of something that is. It would take months to chase the Hounds entirely from your heart, but we have only this one night to do the best for you that we can. And so we used the candles. They will give you the strength you need to fight the battle when it comes, but in the end it will be down to you."

"Thank you. But why only one night?"

"That you will know soon enough." She smiled. "Always remember that the feeling of power never lasts. Those who run with the Hounds soon become desperate and unhappy, chasing across the sky, forever hunting their lost life. You have been saved from that fate in the Storm, don't let it claim you on the Land."

The woman was blurring in front of him, blending into the light.

"Don't go! I don't know your name!"

She laughed. "I am Enid Lockheart," she said. "Remember me."

Jonas sat up and the room was filled with nothing but early-morning sun. The door banged open and Jik tumbled through, clutching a scrunched-up piece of paper.

"Yik bikik?"

"I am, thanks." Jonas shook his head, trying to clear his thoughts.

A tall, fair woman dressed in blue appeared behind Jik. Her eyes were golden and her face held an echo of Enid Lockheart. But only an echo. Jonas wondered what sort of Grimm the sisters were, what kind of Fabulous ran in their blood.

She smiled at Jonas. "I am Elinor, one of those who cared for you last night."

"IK," said Jik impatiently. He held out the paper and Jonas saw that it was singed around the edges and had writing on it. He took it nervously. It said:

GOT HER AT LARST! IF YA WANT TO GET HER BACK BETTER MOVE FARST! BUT DONT GO THE FRONT WAY.

"Skerridge," groaned Jonas.

"Nice of him to send a note," said Elinor. "Even if it is written in blood. Bogeymen don't usually bother about the kids after they've delivered them."

"Blood?" said Jonas anxiously. "Whose blood?"

"There's a P.S. on the back."

Jonas turned the paper over and sighed. It said:

SKWIRREL

The kid in the bed looked insufferably cute, snuggled up under the covers with only a tuft of dark hair showing. Skerridge made a gagging face and reached for his sack.

He paused. He had been feeling edgy after the Redstone fiasco and decided on one final check to make sure he had not forgotten anything. Carefully, Skerridge ticked everything off his mental list.

He had spun the memory of the boy out of his mother's and father's heads. Tick.

He had paid a visit to both sets of grandparents and spun their heads empty too. Tick. And three of his best friends. Tick. And, just to be on the safe side, he had even done the cat. Tick.

Skerridge frowned. Maybe he had overdone it with the cat. BMs didn't normally bother with pets, but cats were tricky things and liable to remember stuff when other people forgot. He nodded firmly. Best to be sure.

Next Skerridge had erased all physical traces of the kid, from his favorite toys right through to every photograph of him that had ever been taken. Big tick.

Nope, nothing missed. Satisfied, Skerridge was just about to wake the boy when a chill ran down his spine.

He *had* forgotten something after all. Something so important, so much a part of the job, that he might as well not have bothered.

He was a bogeyman and bogeymen scared kids, it was in their bones. Normally he took at least a couple of weeks, but this time he had gone straight to the snatch. This time, and this was a ghastly fact indeed, HE DIDN'T EVEN KNOW WHAT THE KID LOOKED LIKE!

Horror brought him out in an icy sweat. He gave a strangled half-sob as the terrible truth dawned. Somehow, during the great chase across the Drift after the Redstone brat, Skerridge, Chief Bogeyman and Champion Kid-Catcher, had lost it. And then things got even worse.

All of a sudden, Skerridge realized that the thought of crouching in a closet and laughing maniacally at a kid was dreary. Hiding under the bed and tickling the backs of their ankles as they sat on the edge of the mattress? Tedious beyond belief. Skerridge moaned and hid his face in his hands.

It was earth-shattering. It was a revolution. It was like a vampire discovering that, actually, sucking blood was a bit of a bore. In an instant his world had turned upside down and he had no idea what to do about it.

After a moment, he looked at the kid again, then up

at the window. It was early morning and if he didn't hurry it would be dawn. Skerridge stared at the pale square of window, just above the humped shape of the sleeping boy. He wasn't thinking exactly he was just . . . waiting to see what came next.

A beam of sunshine broke in over the sill. It crept across the bed and on to a red-eyed, bony thing with too many mismatched teeth and a fancy vest. Skerridge blinked.

Then he reached into his pocket and took out the memory pearl that he had just made from the kid's loved ones and woke the kid up. It gave one brief squawk then shut up as Skerridge scowled at it.

"Right, kid. Know what I am?"

"B-b-bogeyman?" the kid wailed and burst into tears. When it had its mouth open for a particularly loud wail, Skerridge popped the pearl in.

The kid gulped in surprise and swallowed. Thin strands of silver light began to waft away from him. It went on for about half a minute and then faded. His parents would have trouble figuring out where the kid's things had gone to, nothing Skerridge could do about that, but they would at least remember that they had a kid in the first place.

"There ya go," said Skerridge. "Fink yerself lucky ya got me when I was 'avin' a crisis. By the way, just as a side issue like, d'you know any scary places round 'ere?"

The kid blinked.

"'Urry up or I'll eat yer ears."

"T-T-Tanglewood!" gulped the kid and went back to screaming.

Somewhere down the hall a door was thrown open and a voice called, "Mikey? Are you all right?" followed by the sound of someone hurrying to the room.

Skerridge grinned and left by the window.

All the other bogeymen would sneer at him and say he wasn't a proper bogeyman if he didn't want to hide in dark places and scare kids, but quite frankly he didn't care. There were far more interesting things to do in the world than catch kids for Mr. Strood and Skerridge intended to do them. He knew it didn't do to get curious about the Quick, but it was too late to worry about that now. So he was going to start his new life by finding out if the Redstone girl had been eaten by the Maug. Because Skerridge was ready to bet his fancy vest that she hadn't.

He found Tanglewood easily enough in a hidden stretch of wilderness, surrounded by overgrown hedges, dark trees and the distant backs of houses. Hurtling through the suspiciously rustling undergrowth, Skerridge found himself back in the Drift in a wood some miles south of the House. Miles are pretty much nothing when you can move at superspeed and in less time than it would take a Quick to walk down to the end of the road for a newspaper or some candy, Skerridge was back in the garden of the House, looking up at its uninviting face thoughtfully.

The problem was how to get inside. Normally, bogeymen just walked in through the front door, but that was when they were taking a kid to Mr. Strood. It would be so weird for a bogeyman to turn up at the House without a kid in a sack that rats might be smelled and questions might be asked.

So, Skerridge had to find another way in. He stared at the house for a few minutes, looking it over carefully. Then he grinned. It was obvious really. It wouldn't do for a Quick, but for a bogeyman it was near perfect.

He set off toward the house, approaching it from the

side rather than up the path, just in case someone was watching. When he got there he avoided the guard at the front door and scurried swiftly up the wall and onto the roof.

Nin was dreaming about darkness that came alive and ate her slowly from the feet up. It was trying to get to her heart and however hard she fought, it kept on, relentless. And then the world began to tremble and shake and come apart around her.

She woke up. It was early morning and a boy was shaking her. For a moment he looked so like her stolen brother that she gasped.

"Toby?"

The kid stopped shaking her and stared. It wasn't Toby at all. Toby was only four and this one looked like a very small eight. Although the sun made his hair shine it was really brown, and his eyes were black instead of deep blue. Nin burst into tears.

"It's okay. Really." The boy sat down next to her. "I won't tell the guards you're here."

Nin tried to get her face under control by wiping her eyes on her sleeves and sniffing a lot.

"How did you get here?"

"Oh—um—I just—a bogeyman brought me," Nin said, still sniffing.

"If a BM got you this far, he would have given you to Mr. Strood."

Nin stared at him blankly. "Um . . . he t-tried to feed me to the Maug only it w-went wrong and the guard got eaten, so I ran away," she stuttered after a moment.

The boy gaped, then reached out and touched her hand.

"Here, you look like you could do with some break-fast. I always bring mine down here to eat while I sweep. You can have it. Samfy'll give me some more later. My name's Milo," he added, pushing a hunk of bread made into a jam sandwich into her hands. "I'm one of the up-house servants. And I'm betting you're Ninevah Redstone."

Still sniffing, Nin took a bite. "You know me?"

"I know *about* you. We all do. You're the girl who gave Skerridge the slip, made a Fabulous and got away from the Hounds. Looks like you escaped the Maug too! Wait till I tell Samfy!"

"Who's she?"

"Samfy looks after me since my mum and dad died. My mum got blown up in the laboratory and my dad got eaten by the Maug."

"How . . . um . . . old are you?"

"Ten," said Milo, "but we aren't as big as normal human Quicks. We're part mouse, you see. Mr. Strood made us to be timid so we wouldn't cause any trouble." He smiled at Nin. "We're his servants and we keep his rooms clean, serve his meals, do his washing and that. We live in the attic, the one next to the pet tigers. We're called the up-house staff and we're run by the house-keeper, Mrs. Dunvice. She's a werewolf Grimm, so you have to watch out. Then there are the down-house servants to look after the servants. And the servants to look after the guards, plus the guards themselves and Mr. Strood's Eyes."

Nin coughed on a mouthful of juice. "Mr. Strood's Eyes," she repeated and shuddered, remembering Errol's last words. "And—um—what exactly are Mr. Strood's Eyes?"

"Oh he made them too," said Milo cheerfully. "He likes to distill things down to their basic elements then blend them with other things to make . . . well, creatures really. The Eyes are made from the essence of one of those big blue spiders from the garden mixed with an imp and with liquid crowsmorte for blood. Samfy says Mr. Strood can look out of their eyes any time he wants. They run round the house checking everything, but they're getting old now and they keep exploding and he can't make any more because there are no more imps." Milo smiled. "I expect he'll find a way around it though."

He glanced out of the crystal wall. The sun was well on its way up the sky by now.

"Look, I'd better get on. I sweep the Sunatorium in the morning, to get rid of the night's leaves. Then I go over it again just before Mr. Strood takes his afternoon walk. He likes it neat."

"The Sanatorium?" said Nin, puzzled.

"*Sun*atorium," corrected Milo. He stood and picked up a broom and sack that lay abandoned at his feet. "It's where Mr. Strood goes to get the sun, see. You can help if you like."

So she did. She had nothing better to do. Toby was dead, she was sure of that. She was way too late to save him.

25

The Hound in the Tunnel

E linor led Jik and Jonas through the twisting corridors of the hospital until they reached the cellar. There were a couple of lamps and some matches on a shelf by the door, so Jonas lit them both, handing one to Elinor, and they started down the stairs. Jik went first, his eyes cutting red holes in the darkness.

They came out in a cool, dry room stacked with bottles, boxes and sacks. Beyond that, two more held crates and large barrels. Finally came a fourth that held nothing but cobwebs and dank air.

"I still can't believe you have a tunnel right into his house," laughed Jonas.

"Many years before Strood took over, even before it belonged to Gan Mafig, the House and its grounds were owned by a sorcerer. This building was where his mistress lived, protected from the eyes of his wife by magical spells. One theory is that he made this tunnel so that he could get here secretly. Of course, it may have fallen in by now. No one has passed this way for decades."

At the far side of the cellar, Elinor pointed the lamp toward a flight of steps ending in a half-rotten door.

"Remember, Jonas," said Elinor. "You aren't free yet. We have loosened the Storm's hold on you, but that is all. It is still there and in the end you will have to fight it alone. Hang on to what is yours, don't let it take your heart."

Jonas reached out and touched her hand, feeling her cool and slender fingers against his palm.

"Thank you again," he said. "I'll never forget." And then, with Jik close behind and the lamp held high, he walked down the steps and through the door into the unknown.

After a while they found some steps up to a low-roofed tunnel that sloped downward.

There were several twists and turns and one very sharp dip before it rose again, but there were no forks so they had no decisions to make about which way to go. Then they ran into a roof fall. The pile of earth was thigh high, but easy enough to scramble over.

"Great," Jonas muttered, "all this effort and what's the betting it'll be blocked further up?"

The second fall they came across was bigger. Jik pushed his way through easily, but Jonas had to crawl over it, half-smothered in loose earth and bruised by stones, until he slithered out the other side and fell with a thump on the hard ground. More earth and rocks fell as he did so, blocking the way back. He had lost the lamp as well.

"Great! Brilliant!"

They paused to let Jonas calm down and get his bearings. Without the lamp they had only Jik's eyes to rely on and they did not penetrate dark as far or a brightly as the lamp had. Jonas tripped once and bumped his head on a low-hanging bulge in the roof. He snarled under his breath and Jik sent him an anxious glance.

Fueled by anger and frustration, the Hound inside Jonas began to pace. His eyes started to glow white and even though he didn't notice, he began to manage more easily in the dark than a mere Quick should have. Jik noticed though and took care to hang back, following a few feet behind so as to keep out of the way.

The third fall fell on them. So did the fourth.

Jonas pulled himself out of the last pile of earth, the white light in his eyes glowing brighter. He growled, then cocked his head. Behind him the debris heaved slightly as Jik began to push his way out, the red lights of his eyes just beginning to show through the loose rubble. There was a rumbling sound as more soil fell, then stone, then more soil until the tunnel was blocked by a wall of earth and the two red glows had been buried completely.

Jonas barely noticed. Voices echoed up the passageway from the darkness ahead. Snarling, he faced the sounds and waited.

Floyd was looking forward to a sit down with a mug of mulled cider. So was his mate, Stanley. They had been on duty all night and their shift should have been over, but Secretary Scribbins had sent them to investigate rumors of a crack in the wall of the east corridor on the graveyard level. As well as the crack, Stanley had spotted a suspicious-looking tunnel at the back of the graveyard and so they were doing more investigating as per instructions.

Stanley swapped his spear from one hand to the other. He wished he was the one holding the lantern they had borrowed from the gravedigger.

"This 'ere tunnel's goin' on a bit," said Floyd. "Reckon we should go back an' report it? We might've found that Secret Way what's s'posed to be in the down 'ouse somewhere."

"Shhh! There's somethin' up there!"

Floyd got ready with his club and Stanley pointed his spear. They crept on further, treading as silently as possible for a goblin-Grimm. Suddenly something moved in the darkness.

Stanley screamed. He would spend the rest of his life trying to live it down. Guards weren't supposed to scream.

The whatever-it-was snarled at them and Floyd waved his club menacingly at the creature. Its eyes glowed in the darkness.

"It's a Quick!"

"Quicks don' look like that," wailed Stanley. "Not yer normal sorta Quick anyway." He was pointing his spear at the whatever-it-was. The spear wobbled in his shaking hands.

"Pull yerself together, mate," said Floyd in disgust.

Stanley would have liked to pull himself together, but he had never seen anything as eerie as the thing in front of him. It wasn't the eyes filled with white lightning, or the savage snarl that unnerved him, it was the fact that both of these things were on the face of a Quick.

It paused for a moment, eyeing them up. Then it went for Floyd.

Stanley jabbed at it with his spear and missed. Floyd roared and went over backward, the thing at his throat. The dropped lantern rolled against the wall sending shadows everywhere. There was a struggle in which Floyd also dropped his club. Stanley grabbed it and whacked as hard as he could.

Floyd roared again.

"Sorry, mate," yelped Stanley.

The bundle that was Floyd and his attacker rolled on the floor to a lot of hideous snarling. Blood spattered on the wall making Stanley gulp. He judged his moment and tried again. This time he got it.

Floyd staggered to his feet, gasping. "Blimmin' thing nearly had me throat out!"

"I got it!" Stanley looked lovingly at the club. He was going to trade in his spear, he decided.

Floyd stared at the thing on the floor. Now it just looked Quick.

"Crumbs. I think ya killed 'im."

"It was goin' for yer throat," snapped Stanley. "Look at ya, covered in blood!"

"Ya didn' need to kill 'im."

"Yeah, I shoulda waited to see if it ripped ya t' pieces first!" said Stanley sarcastically. "Too late now, any'ow. Come on, we carn' leave 'im 'ere. At least it's not far t' the graveyard!"

"Dead Quick," said Floyd dumping one end of Jonas on the ground. "Nearly 'ad me throat out!"

"I saved 'im," added Stanley, looking nervously up at the gravedigger towering over them.

The gravedigger raised an eyebrow. "What, two hulking great things like you couldn't catch a Quick without bashin' its 'ead in! Want me t' bury 'im?"

"Thanks, mate," said the guard, sounding more cheerful now the problem was off his hands.

Leaning on his shovel, the gravedigger watched them tramping away into the distance. Everything went quiet. Then he leaned over and prodded the corpse in its ribs.

"You ain't dead," he said. "I know dead when I see it and you ain't it. Own up, or I'll bury you anyway."

Jonas rolled over and sat up on his elbows, turning the throb in his head into an agonizing thud. Wincing in the light, he opened his eyes and looked to see what had rumbled him.

It was horrible. It was at least nine feet tall and would have been taller if it bothered to stand up straight. It had skin as dark as granite that looked hard and shiny, like a beetle. Its eyes were yellow with cat-like pupils and it had talons. And teeth. Big talons and teeth. Its face would have looked fine as a Halloween mask and it was wearing a pair of sackcloth trousers topped by a huge T-shirt decorated with the words "Gardener of the Year."

"Fabulous," muttered Jonas.

"Too right! One of the last goblins, me. Name's Taggit Sepplekrum. And you are?"

Jonas tried to rise and bright lights flashed in front of his eyes. He flopped back again. "Jonas," he mumbled weakly.

He lay for a while, listening to Taggit digging. Eventually the pain in his head died down enough for him to drag himself into a sitting position. He thought he might be sick all over Taggit's well-kept grass, but fortunately he wasn't.

Although he was in a vast, underground graveyard— he could see the rocky ceiling above him—there seemed to be daylight. Turning his head slowly he saw huge arched windows cut into the rocky wall, looking out on to sky. Fresh air blew in through them. After a while he managed to get to his feet and wander, very, very carefully, over there.

Propped against the strip between two windows, Jonas breathed in the air and began to feel better. Now he could see that the windows were cut into the cliff face. Below, sea swirled against the rocks. He could smell the salt and hear seagulls crying.

"Better?" Taggit was standing behind him, carrying the shovel on his shoulder.

"Much, thanks. I've . . . um . . . lost a mudman though. Have you seen one about anywhere?"

"Oh we don' 'ave Land Magics 'ere. Don' need 'em, see. Got the servants."

Jonas nodded, wondering what to do. He could go back and look for Jik, but the pain in his head told him he wouldn't get far. The gravedigger hadn't given him away to the guards, but even so, Jonas wasn't sure he counted as a friend yet. Best to keep quiet about Jik. The mudman was perfectly able to look after himself and it meant that one of them was still free to search for Nin.

"I expect he'll have gone back to earth by now anyway," he said, as if it didn't matter.

"Right-oh. Come with me and we'll brew a cup of tea. Then you can explain all this glowin' eyes and goin' for the throat stuff."

"It's a long story," said Jonas, following Taggit toward a wooden hut at the edge of the graveyard. He went slowly because his head was spinning.

"We'll just 'ave t' brew a big pot, then, won't we?" The goblin pushed open a door and led the way in.

The room was a fair size, although with Taggit there it seemed small. There was a table with two chairs, a bed, a sink, a stove, a crate full of food, a crate full of china and pots, several shovels, a couple of pictures in frames, a vase of flowers (dead), a spare coffin and a lot of oversized cushions.

"You've got a garden?" said Jonas, nodding at the gravedigger's T-shirt as he sank gratefully into a chair.

"Just the graveyard," said Taggit, putting the kettle on and tracking down a couple of mugs. He tipped the old tea down the sink, gave them a rub on his T-shirt and set them on the table. "But I keep the grass nice and do a lot of plantin'."

"What? Flowers and things?"

"People mostly," said Taggit with a grin.

Jonas stared at him and then laughed. It hurt his head and shadows clouded his eyes for a moment.

"Now, you get started with the story and I'll sort out this tea, then we'll do your 'ead. Want some cake? It's sticky lemon. Not sure it's s'posed t' be sticky, but that's 'ow it came out so that's what it is."

"Um. Maybe just a small piece," said Jonas cautiously as he wondered where to start.

Deep under the pile of earth Jik stayed still and thought. He was perfectly comfortable where he was, cocooned in the mud he was born from, but he knew he had to get out if he was to help Nin. He wondered what had happened to Jonas—had he been buried too and if so was there anything Jik could do about it, or had the Quick's oxygen run out already?

He listened for signs of struggling. There was nothing to hear but the sigh of the Land, which was everywhere all the time anyway. He began to move, swimming through the mud like a fish would swim through water, curving round the bigger rocks and pushing the stones aside as he went. He soon fell out the other side, but there was no sign of Jonas.

Jik set off, running quickly down the middle of the tunnel until he came to a fork. Which was a problem as he had no idea which way to go. He scanned the ground. The earth was packed too hard and was too stony to show any footprints, but there was something dark and wet-looking on the floor to the left.

Jik hadn't had much experience of human insides. If he had, then he would have recognized the dark wetness for what it was, the blood that had dripped from Jonas as the guards carried him on down the left-hand tunnel.

As it was Jik kept out of its way in case it meant puddles further on. He chose the right-hand fork and kept going.

26

Over the Roof

Most of the Sunatorium trees grew on the left with the crystal wall on the right. At the top, the glittering surface had grown around the branches, leaving them room to poke through.

"It's alive," said Milo. "It was one of Mr. Strood's experiments. He blasted a fortune-teller's crystal ball with leftover magic from a wand and it started to grow, so he trained it over a frame to make the Sunatorium. It screams if you break it and it's poisonous."

He was sweeping the Sunatorium path, which was scattered with fallen leaves and petals from the greenery. Nin followed, holding the sack open for him. The soft rustle of the trees and the splintered sunshine was already doing her good. While they worked she told Milo about Errol. She didn't think she would be able to talk about it, but once she started it all poured out.

"So that's it," she finished sadly. "My brother has to be dead. Nothing could survive the Maug, right?"

Milo looked at her oddly. "You did."

"Yeah well, how often is a snail going to drop out of the sky and whack a guard on the head?"

"But that's not the point, is it? The point is that YOU are lucky. He doesn't have to be."

Frowning, Nin turned this over in her head. "You mean, like, *he* doesn't have to be lucky to escape the Maug, because if *I'm* lucky then I'll find my brother. And that means he'll have to have escaped the Maug somehow so that *my* luck can work. Right?"

"I think," said Milo.

Nin dropped the sack and beamed at him. "Milo, you're brilliant!"

Milo beamed back at her. "You can't go looking for him like that, you'll stick out a mile and the Eyes'll spot you. Look, when I come back at lunchtime, I'll bring you a uniform. That way you'll look like a servant."

"A disguise, you mean?" said Nin, eagerly, her hopes rising even further. "Thank you, Milo, that's perfect!"

The top of the House was a world of slanting roofs, unexpected windows and crumbling chimney pots. In the center, rising above the weathered brick and tiles, was the bell tower. Skerridge knew that the bell ringer would be somewhere about, but that was no problem. The creature wasn't a guard. If anything, it would probably look the other way as soon as it saw him.

Moving fast, though not at superspeed just in case he melted the tiles, Skerridge soon reached his destination at the far end of the Terrible House. The crystal roof of the Sunatorium.

He stared at the shiny expanse sweeping away to nothingness before him. Its uneven surface splintered the light and made the whole thing sparkle like it was studded with diamonds. It made his eyes water. Where the crystal had grown around the branches of the trees below, allowing them to burst out into the air, leaves rustled in the breeze. They looked out of place against all that glitter.

What Skerridge had to do was aim for one of those branches. What he had *not* to do was break, chip or crack the poisonous crystal.

He drew in a deep breath and let steam whistle out slowly from between his teeth. Then he picked a branch and hopped nimbly on to the top of the roof.

"Shoulda lowered meself carefully," he muttered, as his feet went from under him. "Make a note fer nex' time."

He found himself on his front slithering face-first towards a sheer drop, right past the branch he had been aiming for. Panic stirred in his insides. He was gaining speed as the roof curved away before him, a glittering slide into thin air. He could feel the coolness of sea breezes on his face, see the gulls whirling in the emptiness ahead, hear the crash of the waves hurling themselves on to the rocks below.

A splash of green appeared to the left. Skerridge reached out to make a grab at it, but it was too late. Leaves brushed his fingers and then they were gone. The only result was that now he was spinning like a Catherine wheel as well as hurtling toward certain death.

"GAAAAAH!"

In a second Skerridge plunged over the edge. Below him the waves dashed their frothy selves nonchalantly over the jagged rocks. This is it, thought Skerridge, and shut his eyes. He opened them again pretty sharply when something stabbed him in the ear.

Far below the waves and the rocks were still doing their thing, but they weren't getting any closer about it. Which was nice.

Gently, so as not to disturb anything, Skerridge turned his head. The thing sticking in his ear was now sticking in his eye. But at least that meant he could see that it was a twig. Twigs belonged on branches and branches were usually found on trees. Skerridge grinned broadly.

Somehow, by some phenomenal piece of luck, he had caught himself on one of the lower branches sticking out of the side of the Sunatorium wall. So here he was, dangling by his fancy vest, far above certain death.

There was a loud crack. Skerridge winced as his branch jerked under him. With one hand he grabbed hold of the branch where it poked out of the top of his vest above and behind his head. With the other he undid the buttons.

Reaching up awkwardly he slashed at a shoulder seam with a claw, cutting it open. Once one arm was out, the vest sprang free, flicking over the branch and dangling loosely from his other arm. This was a good thing as Skerridge was fond of that vest and didn't want to lose it entirely.

Gripping the branch he swung round so that he was facing into the crystal wall. The branch gave another crack and this time it dipped as well. Skerridge hung on grimly. He went hand over hand toward the crystal wall where the branch was wider and he was able to pull himself up. All he had to do now was squeeze in through the glass where the branch came out.

His heart sank as he looked at the gap. Bogeymen were pretty good at squeezing through tight spaces, but it added another dimension when the tight space you were squeezing through could kill you horribly. Still, he had come this far so he might as well go on. In fact the way things looked, he had no choice.

Skerridge pulled the damaged vest from his other arm and tucked it into his pocket with his sack. Then he flattened himself against the branch. Aiming his fire-breath at the twigs in his path, he let out a short, controlled blast and burned them back to the branch so that they would not get in his way. Carefully he began to inch forward.

At last, propped in the crook of the tree on the inside of the Sunatorium, Skerridge stopped to rest. The gap had been so narrow that when he squeezed through, the edge of the crystal wall had scraped gently down his back. He had felt the sting as its rim rubbed over his skin.

The crystal hadn't been broken, and that might be the saving of him, but he had a nasty feeling that even that much contact might be enough to give him a dose of Temporal Phase Fever.

Which meant that he had better stop hanging about and get himself to a place where he could be ill in comfort. Just as he was about to move, he heard voices.

When Milo came back, he had a brown cloth dress, a white full-length pinafore and a cap, all stuffed into his sack.

"They should fit," said Milo, "you're quite small and thin. I sneaked them out while nobody was around. I thought it was safest not to tell anyone about you just yet, not even Samfy."

Nin ordered Milo to look out of the crystal wall while she nipped behind a tree and changed into the dress. Then she bundled her own clothes up and stuffed them into her rucksack.

"I'll hide that in the rag box for you," said Milo. "What're you going to do now?"

"Find Toby. Find our memory pearls. Escape."

"If anyone can, you can! Look, I've been thinking about where your brother might hide. There's the great library, for a start. Nobody goes there much so it'd be quiet. Or there's the storeroom, which is one floor below that and has got plenty of supplies in it. They're the best places. After that you could see if he's wandering about on the thirteenth floor. There's nothing there but a locked room."

"Great! You wouldn't happen to know where the memory room is, I s'pose?"

Milo shrugged. "Only the BMs know that, and they wouldn't tell anyone."

"Is it a secret?"

"Nope, they just don't wanna tell. Mean-minded lot, bogeymen."

"Well, I'd better get on anyway. The storeroom sounds like a good start."

But she sat quietly with Milo for a moment longer, enjoying the sun through the trees, before starting her search.

Once they were gone, Skerridge allowed himself a huge grin. Then a chuckle. And then a roar of laughter that he choked off instantly, more to stop himself from accidentally crisping the trees than anything else.

At last he clambered nimbly down the trunk to the ground, vaporized the couple of leaves he had brought with him, and headed for the way out.

27

Fish Man

Jonas was sitting at Taggit's cramped table, poring over a map. The lightning in his eyes had faded to a white shine and he looked tired and edgy.

"So there are nineteen floors including the up-house ones, right? Four above ground, counting the attic, and fourteen below. Plus the ground floor." He rifled through the clipped-together pages.

"Back in the old days there'd've been a map on one sheet of paper that just showed exactly what you asked for." Taggit sighed. "Some of the sorcerers could do fantastic stuff!"

"Did you meet them?" Jonas looked up from the map and stared at Taggit.

"Meetin' a sorcerer ain't exactly clever," said Taggit reasonably. "There were a few of 'em about back then, it weren't 'ard to run into one occasionally. They were a snooty lot though, didn't mix well with others."

"They weren't nice to the Quick, I know that. Though Nemus was all right."

"Oh yeah," snorted Taggit. "I expect 'is attitude's improved a lot now 'e's worked out 'e needs the Quick to keep goin'!" He got up and went to the stove. "More?"

Jonas looked at his mug. Taggit's tea was like watery tar, but it tasted fantastic after the first few mouthfuls. Horrible, but fantastic.

"No, thanks. I'd love to hear about them, but I'm not going to be around that long."

"Wouldn't bet on it," said Taggit comfortably. "When you've either found the kid alive or worked out that she's copped it, you'll 'ave to think about what to do next. Gettin' out of the 'Ouse, now the Secret Way's caved in, ain't gonna be a picnic. So, you can come back t' me if you like. Good to 'ave a bit of company. Well, some that's alive anyway."

Jonas laughed, then folded up the map, tucked it into the pack that Taggit had given him and gulped down the last mouthful of tea. "Better get on. Got a busy morning, what with finding Nin, finding her memory pearl and escaping from the House. Thanks for everything, Taggit."

The goblin grinned, showing yellowed fangs that a shark would be proud of. "Good luck, kid. Yer gonna need it."

Jonas thought that if Nin had escaped Strood then she might take cover in the main storerooms. According to Taggit, you could live there, undiscovered, for months. He checked the map one more time, put it back into his coat pocket, then shouldered the bag Taggit had given him, packed with food and a bottle of water, and moved on up the narrow, shadowy stairway.

On the next floor he found the vegetable garden. He didn't know what he had expected, but not this. For a start a gentle, warm rain was falling. Jonas peered up. Copper pipes ran across the rocky ceiling and strung along them at regular intervals were metal clumps that looked like a cross between a dandelion head and a watering-can sprinkler.

Like the graveyard there were windows to the outside world, but here they were round holes plugged with crystal. Sunlight streamed through the crystal, its heat magnified and its light scattered about the cavern. The ground was rich and loamy and neat rows of cabbages, carrots, parsnips and potatoes ran from wall to wall. Further over, poles were twined with leafy peas and runner beans. There didn't seem to be anyone about.

Jonas followed a central path through the gardens to a long corridor, which opened out into a dome-like space filled with a shimmering gloom. Although there were still windows in the wall of the dome, they were small and high up and let in only thin beams of light that glanced off the walls and reflected on the ripples in the water below.

For the floor of the dome was water. It was so deep it looked like black glass beneath the surface glints of light. The room was cool too, and the faint lap of the water had a hollow, echoing sound.

On the other side, opposite where he was standing, he could see an archway like the one he had just come through. A broad strip of the wall was covered in pictures carved into the stone. The last picture looked unfinished.

He stepped out of the corridor and down on to a ledge that ran around the pond toward the second arch. Beside him, the dappled water flicked and flashed with the silver backs of fish as they surfaced and then dived again.

When he got to where the carvings began he paused to take a look. It was clear that each picture had been done with infinite care and patience. As far as he could see, every image told a story. At first Jonas did not recognize any of them, but then he realized that the first was obvious.

It showed a group of Fabulous gathered around a shape on the ground. Another figure, this time Quick, hovered outside the group anxiously, his face a mask of terror. In the background a complex pattern of wolf-like shapes milled and snarled, showing cruel teeth and narrow eyes. The figure in the center was hardly visible between the slender forms of the Fabulous so he switched his gaze to their faces. All of the figures, except one that had its back to the viewer, wore expressions of misery, horror or shock.

These were the Seven Sorcerers and this must show the Final Gathering. He took a step back to see it as a whole and as he did so his eye worked out the figure in the middle. The reason it looked so strange was because it was in pieces—nothing more than a heap of scraps.

He couldn't restrain a soft "eugh" of horror. He turned away to look at the next picture. This one he didn't know. A beautiful, young woman stood at the head of a flight of steps, looking down. In one hand she held a torch high, the other clasped a locket shaped like a thin diamond, the chain it hung from twined around her fingers.

After the woman came a picture of chaotic industry. Figures dug and hauled and built in all directions. There were carts and horses pulling away rubble or bringing materials. Ropes and pulleys and shovels and even some of the workmen's lunches were there too, recorded in tiny, exact detail. And over it all towered something familiar.

"They're building the House!" he said out loud.

"Yeth."

Jonas started so violently that his foot slipped under

him and he thought he was going in the water, but he regained his balance and straightened up.

"Thorry. I didn't mean to thtartle you."

"I—um—didn't see you there."

"People don't. It'th becauthe I'm thilver like the water."

The creature was right. It was silver because it was covered in fine scales. Sitting on the ledge in the wavering light, it looked like part of the water.

"My nameth Gorgle, what'th yourth?"

"Jonas. Are you, sort of, part fish?"

"That'th me. Part fith, part man. I'm one of Thtrood'th ecthperiments."

"I'm sorry."

"Tho am I," said Gorgle. "But thomeone hath to be."

Jonas walked past the arch to where Gorgle was sitting. As he got closer he could see that Gorgle had webbed fingers and feet like fish tails. He had no hair, but fine tendrils ran down his skull to the back of his neck and along his spine. He was wearing nothing but a pair of cut-off trousers in something thin and gray.

Jonas crouched down next to Gorgle, who watched him from eyes like silver discs.

The fish man pointed toward the picture on the wall. "What they're building ith the down-houthe. The Houthe wath already there. It uthed to belong to Gan Mafig, the apothecary that helped the Theven make the Deathweave."

Jonas nodded. "I know that bit. It was their magic that went into the weave, but without Gan Mafig to distil the seven spells and mix them together it would never have happened."

"He wath the betht apothecary ever. He even thought up the mortal dithtillathion proceth."

"The what? Oh, mortal distillation process. What's that? Is it different to distilling spells?"

Gorgle nodded. "It'th about how to dithtil a living thing. Mr. Thtrood utheth it a lot in hith ecthperimentth. Like me. I wath a fith and Mr. Thtrood infected me with dithtillathion of man."

"I wondered how he did the things he does." Jonas looked back at the picture thoughtfully. "I never knew this was Mafig's house!"

"Hith and hith daughterth. That'th her in the thecond picture. Her name wath Theraphine and the ran away during the Final Gathering. Not becauthe the wath thcared, but becauthe the wanted to be with her lover. He wath jutht a woodthman and her father thought the daughter of thomeone ath important ath he wath thould marry a thortherer."

"How do you know all this stuff?"

Gorgle shrugged. "People tell me thtorieth and I put them in pictureth, that'th all."

"You did this?" Jonas stared at him in amazement.

"Yeth. The one I'm doing now ith about the girl who made a Fabulouth."

"She's the one I'm looking for."

"Ninevah Redthtone ith your friend?" asked Gorgle, his voice filled with awe. He tugged Jonas's arm. "Come and thee."

Gorgle led Jonas to the carving furthest along, the one that was unfinished. It showed a girl standing on a hillside, with another figure beside and just behind her.

"She'll love that!" laughed Jonas. He looked closer. "But I have to tell you, Jik isn't that big."

Gorgle shrugged. "He'th a Fabulouth. He mutht be."

The image of Jik was striking. Gorgle had made him a lot taller and somehow more powerful-looking. It also looked as if he were rising straight out of the earth, joined to it somehow.

"You will want to go on and look for her now, I think," sighed Gorgle. "And it'th about time I filled the pool too." Seeing Jonas's puzzled glance, he went on, "the water thinkth into the ground at the bottom of the pond and leakth away. Tho, every day I have to top it up with thea water."

"How do you do that?" asked Jonas. "Is there a way out of here?"

Gorgle shook his head. "I go down on the winch in a pail, you thee." He pointed to the ropes next to the slit in the wall. "I take the bucket and lower mythelf down to the water, I fill the bucket with thea and then I pull mythelf up again. But there ith no way out. The thea ith violent here."

Clambering up to the gash in the wall, Jonas leaned into it and peered out. The wind hit him, dashing a faint trace of spray into his face even this high up. Below, the waves crashed against rocks like jagged teeth. There was nothing but angry sea and empty sky.

"Okay," said Jonas with a sigh. "You're right." He went to sit back down again. "What a shame. The tunnel I came in through is collapsed, the Secret Way, Taggit called it. So when I find Nin we'll need another exit."

"There mutht be one," said Gorgle. He nodded at the second carving. "No one knew how Theraphine uthed to get out of the Houthe without her father knowing. Everyone thayth her Thecret Way ith the tunnel you uthed to get in, but I don't think tho. Remember, the down-houthe didn't exthitht in her day. I think Theraphine's Thecret Way wath here before the down-houthe wath built. I think it thtarted in the up-houthe thomewhere."

"But when they were digging to build the down-house, wouldn't they have found it?"

"No. Thtrood forbade them to dig under the thentre of the Houthe. He didn't want to rithk anything collapthing. I've thought about it a lot and I think the Thecret Way thtartth in the inner garden, the one the Houthe ith built around, nexht to the Maug'th court-yard. Theraphine loved the garden."

Jonas stared at the fish-man. "Gorgle, you're brilliant. I am very glad I met you!"

Gorgle smiled shyly and blinked his silvery eyes.

"A top-notch artist too. These carvings are wonderful."

"Thankth!" Gorgle hung his head bashfully. "I like carving. It taketh my mind off thingth. Ethpethially on Fridayth."

"What happens on Friday?"

"Mithter Thtrood hath fith for dinner on a Friday." Gorgle's face twisted in misery. "Every Friday after-noon, the girl cometh from hith kitchen and taketh a fith."

Jonas looked at Gorgle and then he looked at the pond, where the silver-backed fish swirled beneath the surface.

"They are my brotherth and thithterth," said Gorgle. Tears were welling in the corners of his eyes. "I have to give him one of my family to eat. But if I don't he will kill me and if he killth me then who will fill the pond? And if no one fillth the pond then they will *all* die."

"That's terrible!"

By now the tears were on Gorgle's cheeks. "They underthtand, my brotherth and thithterth. Every Friday I athk them who will go and one of them, one of the older oneth, thwims to the thurface. Every Friday."

Jonas reached out and put an arm round the fish-man's thin shoulders.

"It breakth my heart," said Gorgle and then fell silent, staring empty-eyed at the pool as it glimmered in the fractured light.

28

Evebell

If Milo hadn't been hanging on to her, Nin would have frozen on the spot.

"Eyes," he hissed, dragging her along with him.

It was thin and spindly and covered in spiky hair, with arms and legs that looked out of proportion. Its face was mostly eyes. Huge, bulging, black, glossy eyes. Underneath them was a tiny mouth like a slash. Nin felt a dart of fear as it ran past, but the creature ignored her.

"It's the uniform," said Milo comfortingly. "Makes you as good as invisible, but only as long as you're where a servant ought to be."

As they went past Gan Mafig's picture, Nin glanced nervously up the stairs to where Mr. Strood had his rooms.

"Doesn't he have a bodyguard?"

"What's the point? No one can hurt him. He's immortal. As in never going to die."

Nin remembered Strood telling her that he had been thrown to the wolves once. She also remembered how scarred he was.

"So even if someone, say, chopped him to pieces he'd just heal up again?"

"Yep."

"Ugh! I always thought being immortal would be nice."

Milo shook his head vigorously. "Nobody'd want to be like he is!"

They kept going down the corridor. Here, the walls were lined with pink-and-burgundy-striped paper, not silk, although the carpet on the floor was still deep and soft. When she had seen the House from the outside, Nin had noticed the bricked-in windows. Here on the inside, all traces had been papered over and the walls were flawless. Light came from lamps on metal brackets in the wall that burned steadily with a yellow-white light. Nin thought the house had a strange feel, as if it were its own world, far apart from the Drift or the Widdern. They passed a couple of servants, who shot them timid smiles and said nothing, but no more Eyes. Once they were past the kitchens, where the clean scent of soap and hot water mingled with rich smells of lunch, Milo pushed open a door.

"Here you are. The stairs to the down-house. It's two flights to the storerooms. Then if Toby's not there, go all the way along the storerooms corridor and up the stairs at the other end, all right? And BE CAREFUL."

Nin leaned over and kissed him on the cheek. He smiled at her. The door swung shut and she was alone. Nervously, she followed the stairs down into the part of the House that was built inside the cliff until she reached the stores. Here, the occasional wall lamp pitted its glow bravely against the shadows, and in the dim light, doors marched two by two into the distance. It looked like they went on for miles. She had a lot of rooms to look in and it would take her some time, but with no one around, at least she would be able to call his name.

✳ ✳ ✳

The tunnel had been sneakily curving back on itself for a while, and now it had narrowed down to a thin slit in the rock. Irritably, Jik stared at the gap. It was too small even for him. If the wall had been earth and not rock he might have been able to . . .

He stopped mid-thought and turned, hurrying back to a point just before the tunnel had started shrinking. Here the walls were not rock but densely packed earth. Putting his hands out in front of him he stepped slowly forward, his stumpy arms burrowing easily into the earth. Though it wasn't really burrowing but blending.

Inside the Land he paused to get his bearings and then moved on, swimming through the earth, part of it and yet not. From listening to the way it sounded, he knew that toward the cliff face and right down at the lowest parts of the House the Land was mostly rock. Underneath the House, the Land was soil and he would be able to travel through it easily, as long as he avoided the wooden struts built in to support the walls and floors of the many rooms.

After a while Jik decided to step outside the walls for a look around to see where he was. He found himself in a corridor that led to a bathroom containing a bathtub big enough to take a whole Grimm guard. There was a scrabbling noise coming from the bath, so he climbed on to the chair next to it to look in. It was a spider.

It was dark blue, its eyes were purple—all eight of them—and it sat in a knock-kneed jumble of legs up at the plug end, watching him nervously. Jik had seen something like it before in the House gardens, so he wasn't surprised by its size.

"Jik?"

"Hss." The spider looked sulky and bunched her legs up even closer. She had been stuck in the bath for a long time and was obviously fed up with it. The edge was just too high for her to reach and every time she tried she slithered back on the enamel surface.

"Jik gik yik ik? Yik hik mik fik mik frik?"

Hss brightened up. "Yss pss! Yss."

Jik nodded and was about to lean over to give her a legs up when the door burst open and one of the servants darted in clutching a bundle of towels.

She spotted Hss straight away and screamed. There was the sound of footsteps running along the corridor. Jik, who was on the other side to the maid, did a neat back flip into the next bathtub along, where he crouched out of sight. He had a moment of sick horror when it dawned on him what would have happened if the bathtub had been full instead of empty. When the dizziness cleared and he could think again he realized that help had arrived.

"What is it? What's happened?"

"Oh Susan," wailed the first maid, "there's a s-spider!"

"Goodness, is that all! Get me a glass and some card." Jik heard Susan edge forward to look. "Oh lor!" She staggered back, having changed her mind about the glass and the card. "It's one of those bigguns from the garden. Hurry up, girl. Go and fetch a guard!"

Feeling very down, Nin traipsed up the stairs at the far end of the storeroom corridor. There had been no sign of Toby and now she was heading toward the great library where all the books that Mr. Strood didn't take a personal interest in were kept. The first thing she saw when she reached the landing was a sobbing maid.

"It's B-Bogeyman P-Polpp," the girl wailed as soon as she saw Nin. "I-I've got to s-sweep the library and he th-threw me out."

"Did he hurt you?"

"I hit my head," babbled the girl. "He called me a stupid moo and said he'd fry my apron if I didn't get out."

Nin took the girl's broom. "I'll do it," she said firmly. "You get on with whatever else you've got to do." An idea was forming in her head. What had Errol told her? Terrible gossips, bogeymen.

The girl stared at her out of eyes so brown they were black and then she turned and ran like a frightened mouse. Taking a deep breath, Nin pushed open the door of the library.

"Excuse me, Bogeyman Polpp," she said politely.

The creature curled up on an old sofa between two bookcases raised its head and glared at her with irritable red eyes. Polpp looked something like Skerridge only less tidy. He was also hairier and bigger and wore a pair of tartan trousers tied up with someone's old school tie.

"What?" he snarled, "make it quick, kid, or yer toast."

"I can't do toast," said Nin, "but I do have some bread and honey tea." Out of the big pocket in her pinafore, she pulled a flask and a half-loaf that Milo had given her.

The bogeyman gave her a long look. And then a longer one. Something about her got its curiosity going.

"I don' know yer name," Polpp said. "An' the only names a bogeymen don' know are them what's been stolen."

Nin smiled. "I'm Ninevah Redstone, but mostly people call me Nin." She hoped she wasn't making a huge mistake, after all he could report her escape to

Mr. Strood. But somehow she didn't think he would, and besides, the reward would be worth it. She might not have found Toby yet, but maybe her luck was handing her an opportunity not to be missed.

The BM's mouth twitched. Something horribly like a grin struggled across it, revealing a set of teeth like broken tombstones.

"'Er what made a Fabulous? 'Er what escaped from the Storm 'Ounds?" The grin broadened. "'Er what got away from Bogeyman Skerridge?"

Polpp burst into laughter. Nin ducked as a spurt of flame flickered over her head and burnt a sooty patch on the wall behind her.

"To be fair . . ." Nin began.

The bogeyman waved his hand dismissively. "So what if 'e gotcha in the end. Troof is, tha's the closest any kid's ever come to it." Red eyes looked her over thoughtfully. "Awright, 'and over the grub and tell me all about it."

It took a while because Polpp found some of it so funny that he made her tell it twice.

"Why are you so interested?" asked Nin when she had finished.

"Finks too much of 'imself does Bogeyman Skerridge," Polpp snorted. "All that 'Never lost a kid' stuff. 'Ooo cares. Kid gets lost. Yer goes and gets anovver one. Plenny of 'em out there."

Nin clamped her mouth shut. Now was not the time to lay into him about the fate of the children he stole, not if she wanted to find out anything useful.

"An' the stoopid part is, there's one fing that just AIN'T DONE fer a bogeyman an' tha's goin' out in the daylight." Polpp made a disgusted face. "Blimmin' Skerridge makes a big song an' dance outta not losin' a kid, then does somefin' like goin' out in the daylight what goes right against a bogeyman's grain! There's somefin' wrong in 'is 'ead if yer arsk me." Polpp yawned. "Anyway, better get on, I guess. Been fun meetin' y—'Ang on . . ." He stopped mid-stretch and stared at her. "'E got yer in the end? 'Anded yer over t' Mr. Strood?"

"Yep. Tipped me out right on the rug."

"So . . ." Polpp's voice took on a tone of awe, "so 'ow come yer 'ere?"

Nin smiled. "I got away from Mr. Strood," she said quietly. "And if you like, you can be the first to tell the other BMs how. Only there's a price."

"I'm list'ning," said Polpp. And he did.

When she was done, he chuckled. "They're right about yew bein' a lucky sort then. Snails outa the blue, eh?"

While Nin waited patiently, the hollow boom of the Evebell echoed through the down-house. She was hungry and her throat was dry with talking, but any minute now it would all be worth it.

"Well," said Polpp cheerfully, "yer'll be wantin' me t' keep my part o' the bargain, eh?" Reaching out he grabbed a book from the shelves and ripped out a page. Then he ripped off a splinter of book shelf, burned it into charcoal and began to draw. When he had finished he wrote two words above it and underlined them heavily.

They were:

Memory Room

Then he handed it over to Nin.

* * *

Samfy was in the laboratory feeding the kid in the cage when two guards struggled in carrying something between them in a net. Outside, the Evebell began to toll as the sun slipped low in the sky.

"Watchit, the blimmin' thing jus' bit me again!"

They headed toward the second cage and yanked the door open, throwing the struggling thing inside. Then they left, sounding a lot more cheerful and talking about a nice cup of tea.

The kid in the cage, a small blond boy with blue eyes that seemed to grow larger and darker every day, went pale. He shivered inside the loose shirt and trousers that Samfy had given him to wear instead of his pajamas. Mr. Strood had been keeping the boy caged up, waiting for the time when one of the garden spiders wandered into the House and got caught. Samfy hadn't told Milo anything about it because she thought he would be upset, she had just done her best to make the captured kid's last days bearable.

She reached in through the bars with her small hand and stroked his head to comfort him.

"They don't hurt people," she said. "It's only so big because Mr. Strood experimented on its great-grand-spider, that's all."

The kid in the cage looked at her with his violet eyes and Samfy tried not to cry for him. She knew what the captured spider meant. The experiment to make new Eyes could begin and she had better hurry out of the way before Mr. Strood turned up to start preparing some of his special Fusion.

But she stayed a moment longer to hold the boy's hand.

Jonas strode on up the stairs. He felt torn inside. Part of him was elated at having found another escape route so easily, the rest was angry and afraid.

Sitting with Gorgle while he cried over his brothers and sisters, Jonas had finally understood that Strood was both insane and evil.

Somewhere a bell began to toll, its deep boom echoing down the corridors, filling his head. He was beginning to hate the terrible House of Strood. The things that were done here filled him with rage, and the fear of what might happen to Nin was growing with every step. And inside him, the hound began to pace.

At last he made it to the storerooms. Staring down the long, dimly lit corridor, Jonas rubbed a hand over his face and was surprised to find that he was crying.

Some time later he ground to a halt. He had been from one end of the storerooms to the other and although he had found a great many things, he had found no trace of Nin. He was tired, afraid and angry and the hound inside him was close enough to bring a weird light to his eyes. Once or twice he caught himself snarling under his breath. He began to pace, going back over the corridors even though he knew that Nin wasn't there.

An inner lurch brought him to a halt, a moment of confusion while he worked out where he was. Jonas gazed around, trying to hold back the tide of panic growing inside him. A moment ago he had been near the stairs, wondering whether to go on up or sleep where he was. Now, somehow, he was halfway down the corridor again. The lamps had been turned off and only a couple of night lights lifted the darkness.

There was a blank in his memory. Time was missing.

Jonas looked down. His hands were bloody, the nails ripped and broken. He looked up. The earth walls around him were scored and marked in a hundred places, as if some hound had been clawing at them, trying to get out.

Jonas flung back his head and howled.

Then, overcome by a wave of sickness, he sank to the floor. His head was spinning and he could feel darkness lurking behind his eyes. Darkness and something else.

The battle with the hound had begun.

29

The Ballads of Arafin Strood

Most of Skerridge was curled up in the rag box in the cupboard next to the servants' quarters. It was quiet and comfortable there, apart from something knobbly hidden amid the rags and wedged up against his left shoulder.

The tiny grains of Sunatorium crystal rubbed into his skin had been multiplying all through the afternoon and evening, each new particle fastening itself to a cell in his body and starting to twang it to and fro between yesterday, tomorrow and some completely random time in the past. So, while some of him was reliving the morning's elation at getting in over the roof, other parts of him were feeling the pain and regret that tomorrow would bring. On top of that, more bits of him were locked into memories of so long ago that he couldn't even begin to remember what they were about.

He was feeling worse than he had ever felt in his life. Everything was blurry and his head hurt. He couldn't remember what day it was and once or twice had found himself holding conversations with people he hadn't seen for years. One of them was actually dead and had been for nearly three decades.

The small part of his brain that was hanging fiercely on to reality was aware that this was just the beginning. Once the Temporal Phase Fever really got going, conversations with dead people would be the least of his worries.

The disease reached its peak not long after the lights dimmed and the House began to settle down for the night. The molecules of crystal began to work in harmony and Skerridge's jumbled dreams of the past became clear and focused. Once TPF had fixed on a memory, it dragged its victim there and locked them up, making them live in the event until the fever passed, killed its victim or turned them permanently insane. By now, the conscious part of Skerridge had lost contact with the rag box and was watching in a disembodied way as the most significant event of his past played out before him.

Skerridge had been there at the Final Gathering, had been part of the fateful event that marked the last days of the Seven Sorcerers, the rise of Mr. Strood and the dreadful end of the apothecary, Gan Mafig. The memories were scored into his brain like images carved on a monument and right now, fired by the TPF, they were becoming as sharp and vivid as life.

In the real-time House something howled, the sound echoing up from the nighttime corridors far below. The servants shifted in their beds or paused at their late suppers, and the guards glanced uneasily over their shoulders, but the Terrible House was used to horrible howlings from the Maug and on the whole took no notice. If he had heard it, Skerridge might have realized that this time it wasn't the Maug, but he was too far in the past by now, whimpering nervously as he realized what he was about to live through all over again.

In front of him the scenes of the Final Gathering began to unfold.

Nin closed the library door quietly behind her. She was feeling a lot more positive about things. Polpp had gone about his business leaving her free to search the library, so she knew for sure that Toby wasn't there. She just had to hope she would find him on the empty floor. And then she would have him *and* the map to the memory room and all she would have left to do was find the tunnel in the graveyard.

She paused, thinking about her next move. It was growing late and she knew that she should go back to the Sunatorium. A maid creeping about the House at night would be worthy of notice.

Something howled, its chill sound sweeping over her and making her skin prickle. She couldn't tell exactly where it came from, but it didn't sound like it was far away. Nin shuddered, remembering what Milo had said about the housekeeper being part werewolf.

With something like that around, she didn't fancy going back through the dark storerooms. Head down and clutching her broom like a talisman, she flew along the corridor and up the stairs at the other end, the stairs that led to Mr. Strood's laboratory and the hallway to the Sunatorium. No one passed, not even an Eyes. It was some time since the Evebell had sounded and the House lamps, bright during the day, were now turned low.

When, at last, she reached the Sunatorium, some-thing made her pause, she didn't know what. It was a good thing too, because there was somebody there—a woman, tall and angular, a bunch of keys hanging from a chain around her severe, brown dress. She was staring out of the crystal wall, gazing at the fat, nearly full moon that stared back at her, turning the trees to ink silhouettes and gilding the floor with silver. Nin had no doubt at all that this was the half-wolf housekeeper. And if that was the case then what was it that had howled so horribly in the down-house? It couldn't have been the Maug because the Death Dog lived up here and the sound had definitely come from below.

Jonas, she thought. Jonas followed me. She turned at once to go back. She would have to find him, help him fight the Hound inside him and then together they could look for Toby. She had barely started down the corridor when she heard the heavy tread of one of the guards coming toward her. She had no choice but to run the other way, up the hall toward the picture of Gan Mafig. In the dim light it looked even more horrible and the old man's eyes seemed full of unspeakable torment.

This was the point where the corridor branched, left toward the Maug and right toward the kitchens. Now she could hear something else, a soft padding that might be an Eyes. Frozen she stared left and right into the gloom, but whatever it was had not yet turned the corner. Behind her, the door to the Sunatorium swished open. Panic gripped her. The werewolf Grimm would see her. She was going to be caught.

Quickly, Nin ran up the stairs. There was a half-open door so she hurried in and pulled it shut behind her. She looked around at the solid slab of a desk in the middle of the room. Her heart began to thump as she realized that she was hiding in Mr. Strood's study.

After a moment she calmed down and began to think. It was unlikely that Mr. Strood would come in here at this time of night. Perhaps she should give it half an hour or so before she moved. Hopefully any end-of-the-day activity would have finished by then and everyone would be in bed, leaving her free to make it to the Sunatorium in safety, as long as she managed to avoid the Eyes.

While she waited, Nin took a look around. The study was furnished pretty much like everywhere else, except for a large window behind the desk. Unlike the others in the House this one was not blocked up, just covered with a heavy velvet curtain. She peered behind it, but backed off quickly when she realized that it overlooked the Maug's courtyard.

The other walls were lined with bookcases and Nin wondered if some of the books might hold useful information. She began to browse along the shelves.

Her first discovery was a row of large volumes bound in faded silk that must have once been vivid scarlets and blues. They were titled *The Deeds of King Galig of Beorht Eardgeard*, and he had to be a Fabulous because no mere Quick life could fill that many volumes. Nin found herself longing to read the stories, but she did not have time and so she moved on to a smaller bookcase where the books were thinner and mostly seemed to be Mr. Strood's poetry. She wondered if they would be like a diary, a record of the House and things that happened in it, so she took one down and dipped in.

To her surprise they were fascinating. They told the story of Celidon, giving her a taste of life in a dying world where desperation walked the streets and even the strongest lived in fear. Then she found the last ballad of the book.

It had originally been called "The Ballad of the Final Gathering," but Strood had obviously changed his mind, and had scored through that page and then started again with the title "Gan Mafig's Servant." The poem was different from the rest and had been written directly into the book instead of being drafted on scrap and copied in when it was finished. The writing was larger and more sprawled, perhaps done in a hurry or with anger. Further down Strood had given up on poetry altogether and had just written words so furiously that in one place the nib of his pen had torn the page. Nin began to read:

Gan Mafig's Servant

T'was on the ~~day~~ eve of **Candlesong**
When all the sky was dark,
Sorcerers came they seven strong
And EVIL ~~it did~~ made its mark.

For evil cruel deeds they did that night
Under the cloud-filled skies.
They used their Fabulous magic might
To cast the **Spell of Lies**.

And with them went the ~~apoth~~ chemist,
His servant at his side,
To ~~mix~~ twine their cast with soul-mist
And death from life divide.

Cowards! Cowards! Stinking cowards may their innards rot forever. And history dares to call them Great!

Do you know what they did? These GREAT sorcerers.

They were dying and knew it and they wanted a way out, a way to extend life. AT ANY COST.

Cowards. Bone deep, jelly-livered COWARDS. Call them Fabulous!

And Mafig. The GREAT apothecary. Miserable, treacherous son of a sewer rat. Nothing fabulous about him. He was just a chemist. Just a pitiful, groveling, whinging chemist.

He ran away, yellow-hearted gutter dog. RAN AWAY. After all the years i served him. All the years of faithful service. May his brain fill with pus and his heart burst!

But then, i saw to him, didn't i? I made him pay for what he did to me. I couldn't get them, but i got him all right.

I got HIM.

And then suddenly the evening lamps went out and night took hold of the Terrible House. With the door closed and even the hall lights gone, Nin found herself in a darkness so thick that all she could do was crawl into a corner and shiver until exhaustion plunged her into a sleep full of confused dreams and the painted image of Gan Mafig's tortured face.

30

One Burns, the Other Grows

Taggit Sepplekrum had long since finished his last grave of the day. As usual at the end of a lot of hard digging, he had thrown his spade to the ground, wiped his clammy forehead with the bottom of his T-shirt, and reached for his flask of soured milk. After a long swig he had settled back on the grass, staring at the distant ceiling with the flask balanced on his middle while late evening crept into deep night.

A fly buzzed past. Absentmindedly, Taggit flicked out a long black tongue and snapped it up.

He had been talking to Jonas for less than half of his morning, but however brief it had been, the contact with someone from outside the House had brought back memories of a time when his world had not been confined to the graveyard. Inevitably, that led him to the event that had changed his life beyond recognition. Like many other Fabulous, Taggit Sepplekrum had witnessed the Final Gathering.

Back in those days, when Celidon was a living world, the House was called Sea View and it belonged to Gan Mafig, the evil genius behind the Mortal Distillation Process and the greatest Quick apothecary that Celidon had ever known. So, when the Sorcerers came together to cheat the plague, they gathered at Sea View with Gan Mafig present to distill and weave the spells, and Gan Mafig's servant on hand to hold the cloaks.

And it was after the Final Gathering, when the world was picking up the pieces and trying to get on with life not knowing yet that life would never be the same again, that Taggit Sepplekrum made the worst decision of his life.

Celidon was dying. The Final Gathering of the Seven Sorcerers had failed and soon even they would be gone. Although the goblins, bogeymen and tombfolk might hang on for a century or so, eventually they would join the rest of the Fabulous in extinction. But, after the events of the day, Taggit knew in his bones that when Celidon was dead the power that ruled the remains would be living here at Sea View. And if Dread had anything to do with it, Sea View would be the last part of the Land to die.

A few weeks later, Arafin Strood took a horrible revenge on Gan Mafig for his part in it all and the apothecary vanished without trace. Some said he was still imprisoned within the House, but Taggit knew that story couldn't be true. The Final Gathering had taken place too many decades ago when Mafig was already in his sixties. Even if Strood hadn't finished him, Mafig would have died of old age long ago.

After Mafig had disappeared, Strood had claimed ownership of the House and had begun to draw a web of power around him. So Taggit had decided to stay and help with the excavations, overseeing the Quick and the Grimm whose hard work built the down-house. And after that he had taken the job of gravedigger. Since then, all he had done was dig graves. Taggit blinked thoughtfully. After a life packed with event and adventure he had spent the last few decades digging graves. Nothing else. Not a thing.

He had stayed at the Terrible House because he wanted to live longer, but as it turned out he hadn't been living at all.

As Jik swam through the walls toward the center of the Terrible House, he heard something howl. It was muffled by the layers of earth around him, but it was unmistakable. Jonas was still alive. Jik also guessed from the horribleness of the howl that its owner would not be in a fit state to do any rescuing. It was all down to one mudman, and time was ticking by.

Jik paused, listening to the Land. He could sense its disturbance, as if something bad was nearby. He knew that he was passing close to a small room on the thirteenth floor and so he stepped out of the walls to take a look.

The room was dimly lit, and in it, strapped into a large wooden chair with leather belts, was an old man. Beside the chair, on a tall rod of ornate silver, a yellow candle burned with a red flame. Tallow dripped like oil on to the floor to join a spreading pool. There was a second, unlit candle on the other side of the chair.

The figure stirred and Jik could see that it was human, but only just. The old man was little more than a skeleton covered in yellowed flesh with a few wisps of hair clinging to his withered skull. His eyes, set deeply in their sockets, were a pale, milky blue and huge as marbles. They focused on Jik.

The mudman stepped forward. "Mik Jik. Yik?"

There was a long silence while Jik waited patiently. The Quick had long outlived its natural span by some means or other and was finding it hard to operate the desiccated body it was trapped in. A ghastly smile stretched its lips.

"Mafig," it said in a voice like dead leaves rustling. "Gan Mafig." It gave a short, bitter laugh. "Once, I was the owner of this House."

Jik made a massive effort. "Likik fik Nikikik Rikstik. Shik wik Strik. Escik."

Mafig began to laugh again. It shook his frail body like a leaf clinging to a branch in a high wind. Then he began to cough, which shook him even more.

"Nothing escapes Strood," he whispered. "I should know. See those candles?" He turned his milky eyes to the one at his side. "They keep me alive. One burns, the other grows. When the burnt one is done he lights the other, and while that burns the first remakes itself. Endless life so long as I am within their light." He cackled, like it was a huge joke, his head bobbing madly. "A present to Strood from Ava Vispilio."

"Jik pik ik ik?"

"Only a sorcerer can put it out!" Now he howled with crazy laughter. "And you don't see many of *those* about nowadays!" He stopped suddenly, alert and listening. His eyes rolled upward and he shuddered. "The shadows," he hissed. "The SHADOWS! The shadows are coming. See them?" His voice became urgent and foam flecked his mouth and chin.

Glancing around nervously, Jik backed away.

Mafig leaned forward again. "He made them especially for me, the shadows. Do you know what they are? DO YOU KNOW WHAT THEY DO?"

Jik backed away so much that he ended up in the walls. Hurriedly, he moved onward and upward, wondering as he went what it was that the man had done to offend Strood so badly. Or Vispilio for that matter.

As he rose steadily through the earth foundations of the House, the image of the old man, horribly tortured in some nameless way, stayed with him, making his eyes glow like scarlet bonfires with fear and rage. It had never occurred to him to doubt that Nin had survived so far. She was his creator and he would know when she died. But this was the Terrible House of Strood where a poor Quick's life could be lost in a heartbeat and even if she was alive NOW, every hour, every minute, could bring her closer to a horrible end. If Jik was to save her, he had to move fast. There was no time to lose.

He tore on through the walls until at last he rose from the earth into a dark, cool cellar. Shaking himself to throw off any loose soil, he noticed that some of the mud clung to him like a thin topcoat. The new earth was darker than his old, reddish mud giving him a dappled look. He could do with a baking, but that would have to wait. At least his core was still nice and hard.

It took him no time at all to get out of the cellar, through the silent kitchen and into the hall. From here he could turn either left or right. He chose to head toward the back of the House, because he knew the front was full of guards.

Around him, the lamps went out, even in the hall-ways. Only a few dim night lights burned in the main corridor. Everything was still, with that waiting quality that places have at night.

Except that there was life in the corridors after all.

Jik hopped seamlessly into a doorway and flattened himself against the wall. He watched the odd thing as it went past, its eyes reflecting the night lights in their bulging, shiny surfaces.

When it had gone he waited for few seconds then moved on, head up, sensing the air. It wasn't much further before he caught an echo of Nin's presence somewhere up ahead. He was close, very close, so he got moving. He was concentrating so hard on getting to Nin that he didn't hear something coming up behind him.

Before he knew it, Jik was seized and lifted from the ground. As he whirled through the air he caught a glimpse of a large Grimm, a push-along trolley and a metal bin. He was so shocked he hadn't got around to objecting before the Grimm threw him into the bin, the lid thumped shut over his head, the latch clicked and he was trapped inside.

And then the trolley was on its way again, carting the day's rubbish to the incinerator, down at the bottom of the Terrible House.

31

The Final Gathering

There were nine people in the scene before Skerridge, seven in a cluster and two just outside it. Shapes watched from the sidelines. A handful of bogeymen lurked in the deep recesses of an archway, keeping well out of the light. A goblin, its inky-blue skin almost part of the shadows, watched silently from the shelter of the nearby trees. There were other watchers too, many of them. Witnessing.

Of the central group, the clustered seven were Fabulous and the other two were Quick. One of the Quick hovered edgily, close to the Fabulous but not with them. The other stood apart, listening. The edgy one was clad in rich robes, embroidered with gold and scarlet thread. The other wore black.

Skerridge recognized both Quick and six of the seven Fabulous. The seventh looked unfamiliar, but Skerridge knew who it was anyway.

"We are all resolved, then?" asked a woman with a face that would not only launch a thousand ships but send them round the world as well. Her voice made Skerridge shiver because each note was so clear and sweet. She was robed in a cloth woven from moonlight.

"I see no other way, Senta," answered a man with a long white beard. Nemus Sturdy spoke quietly and in spite of his age there was no sign of weariness or frailty in his body.

"As you say, Nemus." The sorcerer who spoke this time had a mane of dark hair that flowed down his back and Skerridge recognized him as Morgan Crow. His tone was cheerful and he got a sharp look from Nemus Sturdy and a kind one from the second of the two women, the one who wasn't Senta Melana.

"This is no light task," Nemus Sturdy said quietly, "but an event that may change the face of the world. We must undertake it seriously and with caution."

Morgan Crow went on smiling brightly as if he did not see that Nemus meant the comment for him.

"We know that, old man," snapped the tallest of the Fabulous. Azork's silver eyes glinted with impatience and he looked as if he were trying not to shake them all into action.

Senta Melana frowned at him. "This is hard enough as it is without you . . ."

"Yes, yes! And that's why we should get on with it. We're all agreed, right?"

The Seven Sorcerers looked at each other.

"We are," said one of the three who had not spoken yet. He was pale and fair and unlike the others he wore no jewelry save for an ancient ring on the middle finger of his left hand. Of the seven only this one, Ava Vispilio, looked calm.

Skerridge hunched his insubstantial shoulders.

A slight movement above the group and its watchers caught his eye and he turned to look. Someone was gazing down on the scene from a window in the house. It was a girl, wrapped in a cloak and holding an unlit lamp. Her face was pale and serious, her eyes dark and her hair a wreath of silky shadow. With his excellent bogeyman vision, Skerridge could see her clearly enough to know that she had the fragile beauty of a Quick, and that her face was touched with sadness and warmed by love. This was Seraphine. The apothecary's daughter.

"Then let the casting begin," said Nemus firmly, as if finally reaching a hard decision.

Vispilio smiled.

There was a ripple of anticipation in the circle of sorcerers, tension radiated out from them, alerting the watchers. The time for debate was past. Now was the time for action.

Skerridge felt that the focus of the whole world was here, on *this* stretch of lawn, in front of *this* elegant mansion. Because what was about to happen here was going to change everything.

He glanced up. The girl at the window had gone. Overhead, clouds were gathering like dark-winged eagles.

The seven stood in a ring with their faces to the center. In the middle of them stood the more richly dressed of the two Quick.

"Mafig," muttered Skerridge, his voice nothing on the empty air.

The apothecary had stopped being edgy now and his manner had changed from anxious hanger-on to commander. Even though he was concentrating on his work, part of him was conscious that he, a mere Quick, was orchestrating this group of Fabulous sorcerers. This was the proudest moment of his short Quick life, the pinnacle of his career, and it showed on his face and in the way he stood.

The other Quick, Gan Mafig's servant, was standing

outside the circle, holding his master's cloak and looking on. His name was loud in Skerridge's mind and the bogeyman couldn't stop himself bobbing his insubstantial head in deference.

Because the name of Gan Mafig's servant was Arafin Strood.

All the Fabulous, except for Azork, who gave several loud sighs, waited patiently while Gan Mafig set up his distillation apparatus on a small table in the center of the circle. It was a complicated arrangement of tubes running from a tulip-shaped funnel made of spider silk and archaic crystal into seven small flasks. Mafig used a crystal spindle to catch and channel the spells so that they gathered in liquid form in the flasks, ready for him to weave into one mighty spell. When the apothecary was ready he bowed his head to Nemus Sturdy and the casting of the Deathweave began.

The sorcerers had a strict pecking order when it came to casting and it was not the level of their power. Nemus Sturdy went first because he was the oldest. The fact that he was also the most powerful was just accident.

Each sorcerer had their own way of casting. Nemus used a staff carved of ancient oak that shone with a golden glow. He held it at arm's length, with both hands grasped around its bole, and bowed his head. He said no words, but the ground trembled. In the center of the circle Gan Mafig was working, frowning with concentration as he channelled the spell into its glass beaker where it pooled like liquid gold. He glanced up and bowed his head to Ava Vispilio.

Skerridge winced. The bow had been a little curt, Mafig would pay for that later. Vispilio wouldn't let anything he saw as a lack of respect pass unpunished.

Vispilio cupped his hands around a crystal globe that he held out in front of him. As he began to speak, the globe crackled with green sparks that filled his hands and overflowed. His voice hissed too and the sound of the sparks blended with his words, filling the air with sibilance that stung the flesh of those who heard it. Gan Mafig went on working, even though he winced with discomfort, and Vispilio's part of the spell soon glittered in livid green at the bottom of the second flask.

After Vispilio came the second of the two women, the one who had not spoken yet but who had looked so gently at Morgan Crow. She neither raised her hands nor used a staff or wand. She simply spoke. Enid Lockheart's voice would have broken Skerridge's tough old heart, if he had really been there. Apart from Vispilio, all those who listened had tears on their cheeks by the time she finished.

Next it was the turn of the dark-skinned, silver-eyed Azork. He held his staff high and his words filled the sky with forked fire. After him, the only one of the Seven Sorcerers that Skerridge had not immediately recognized made ready to cast. Simeon Dark raised his slim and graceful hands. Gan Mafig sent him a nervous look.

The watching Skerridge chuckled. Simeon Dark had a reputation for being mysterious, secretive even. It meant that he was hard to pin down on practically anything, including his casting. He might not be the most powerful sorcerer there, but Gan Mafig would certainly find his spell the hardest to capture.

Like Enid Lockheart, Simeon did not use a wand, staff, orb, or any other device. Nor did he speak. Instead he made three simple gestures with his hands. At least, three was all that anyone saw. After the second movement a mantle of shadows began to settle quickly around him. After the third, nothing could be seen of the sorcerer but a pool of darkness. Gan Mafig was white with effort. Sweat beaded his brow and his forehead was scored with a frown of concentration as he caught and channeled a spell the color of midnight.

And then Simeon Dark was visible again and Senta Melana stepped forward, raising her wand of blackened silver, carved with ancient sigils. From it poured a white light that illuminated her, bathing her in a lake of brilliance. The watchers gasped, riveted by her beauty. Gan Mafig almost, but only almost, forgot to work.

Last came Morgan Crow. As with Nemus Sturdy, his position was determined by the fact that he was the youngest of all of them. Had they been acting in order of strength he would have been second. Smiling cheerfully, as usual, he fished a slender wand from his belt, raised it and began to chant. His wand flicked this way and that in time to his words and spilled out a soft light that lit up the grass and the circle of waiting Sorcerers. People nodded in time to the sound of his voice and the movement of his wand and Gan Mafig's face relaxed as he worked. Overhead the clouds began to disperse.

And then, as Gan Mafig distilled the final drop of Morgan Crow's spell, the Sorcerers stepped back to let him work alone. He turned each flask on its head. Drop by drop the distilled spells ran into a large beaker until at last, woven together by Mafig's crystal spindle, they united to form a thick, purple-black fluid.

The Deathweave was complete.

32

Gan Mafig's Servant

By now it was late afternoon and some of the watchers had disappeared. Skerridge, or at least the dreaming part of Skerridge, cowered in the shadows offered by a clump of bushes.

The Sorcerers were arguing about who was to try the Deathweave first. Gan Mafig stood looking at them with an air of suppressed irritation. He was holding the beaker of purple-black fluid. It didn't bubble or steam, but a sighing sound came from it that was making the apothecary nervous. He wished they would just get on with it and take the wretched potion away from him.

"Just give it to me," snapped Vispilio.

"What? And let you pour the rest away before we can get to it?" sneered Azork. "I think not!"

"Now why," said Vispilio softly, "would I ever want to do that?"

Nemus Sturdy raised a hand. "Let's not quarrel over it. There is enough in the beaker for all of us. As the oldest I should go first, this is the way of things."

"Hang on," grumbled Morgan Crow. "It's not fair! I'm the second strongest, but I always get to be last. This time, I object. You say there's enough, but there might not be. There might be none left by the time I get there. This time we should go in order of strength."

"Never!" hissed Vispilio. His eyes flashed angrily.

Simeon Dark smiled at him. If they went in order of strength, then either Vispilio or Dark would be last. As it was difficult to be exact about how much power Dark had, no one was sure which of the two it was. Vispilio always insisted that he was sixth and Dark seventh. His anger betrayed the fact that he feared he might be wrong.

"We could draw lots for it," said Enid Lockheart. "That way it would be down to chance."

There were nods from the others.

"That's settled then, is it?" asked Senta. She was looking nervous.

There was silence for a few moments. When it came down to it, the Sorcerers began to realize that they weren't as worried as they thought they were about there being enough potion for everyone. What they were really worried about was something more serious.

"Thing is," said Azork cautiously, "this has never been done before and it could be dangerous."

"Someone just make a decision!" snapped Senta. Her tension was beginning to show.

"I think . . . ," began Vispilio slowly.

Many pairs of eyes fixed on him. The watching Skerridge hunched his shoulders nervously.

"Go on," said Azork eagerly.

"I think we should try it out on a Quick first. I know it means wasting a sip, but I am sure there is more than enough here."

Nemus frowned. Enid closed her eyes.

"Excellent!" said Azork hurriedly. "Who shall we use?"

Nemus raised a hand again, but before he could speak Azork carried on.

"It's perfect. Either it works or it doesn't, and if it works it will give some short-lived Quick the kind of lifespan they only dream of!"

Senta was looking thoughtful. "We would be offering a great opportunity, I suppose."

Dark smiled. "Thing is," he said, "if it's as simple as Azork says then why are *we* afraid to take it?"

Silence fell. Vispilio sent Dark an evil look.

After a while, Senta spoke. "Just supposing it were to backfire. If, instead of removing death, the potion summoned it. Then it would not only fail to work, but would kill the drinker."

"So what," snapped Vispilio. "We'd hasten a Quick's death by . . . Oh . . . All of few years. Big deal."

"Die at the drop of a hat, Quick," said Morgan Crow cheerfully.

Nemus frowned. "That's no reason to . . ."

"Oh for Galig's sake," grumbled Azork, "must you object to everything, Nemus? Where's the harm in it. As Ava says, even if it does go wrong they don't live long anyway."

"And there are hundreds more Quick out there. *We* are a dying breed remember?" This was Vispilio's trump card and he knew it. "This isn't just about saving ourselves, this is about saving Magic."

"The survival of Celidon depends on us," nodded Azork.

Enid shook her head. "It's not right to make them take risks we are too frightened of ourselves."

"Why don't we just vote on it," put in Vispilio smoothly. "Even Enid can't object to a vote. All those in favor of trying the Deathweave out on a Quick first, raise their hands."

Vispilio's hand shot up, followed by Azork and Crow. Senta raised hers more slowly. Dark shrugged then put up his as well. And then, finally, so did Nemus. They all looked at Enid.

"It's wrong," she said.

Vispilio rolled his eyes. Azork groaned.

"Is that all? Look, what's one Quick death?"

"There's another possibility for error," she said quietly. "One we are all thinking of, but no one has mentioned."

Vispilio ignored her. "Six for, one against. Right, who do we use?"

Gan Mafig swallowed nervously.

"Not Mafig, he's useful. Hey you, come here."

In the watching silence, Gan Mafig's servant stepped forward.

"What is your name?" asked Nemus kindly.

"Arafin Strood," said Strood and smiled. It was a friendly smile, affable almost.

"Well, Arafin Stood, would you like . . ."

"Don't ask him," sneered Azork, "just give him the stuff."

"Have you been listening?" asked Dark.

Gan Mafig's servant nodded.

"So what would you say to trying out the Deathweave?" put in Vispilio with a warm smile. "We made it to extend life for a while. If you try the potion for us, it could do nothing at all, but it will probably give you another hundred years of life at least."

"Or it could do something else," added Dark quietly.

"Look at it this way," said Vispilio, "we are the seven

most powerful sorcerers in the world. We are good at what we do and we made this potion to save our own lives. So how likely are we to have made a mistake?"

Arafin Strood looked at him thoughtfully. "And how is it supposed to do this?"

The sorcerers looked blank.

"How should we know?" shrugged Crow. "It's just magic. We do it. We don't need to know how it works. Do you know how whatever it is that powers you works?"

"Just do it, Strood," barked Gan Mafig suddenly. The potion in his hands was winding his nerves up to breaking point. It wasn't only the weird sound, it was also the fact that he had been holding the beaker in his hands for ages and the thing was still ice cold. "Look on it as an experiment."

The servant's eyes brightened almost imperceptibly.

Vispilio smiled. Skerridge wondered if maybe Gan Mafig had earned a reprieve for his curtness earlier. But no, that wasn't Vispilio's style.

"Just a sip, mind," said Crow, as Gan Mafig held out the potion eagerly. "That's all you need and we don't want to run out."

Arafin Strood took the beaker and lifted it to his lips. He sipped. The tension in the atmosphere was almost painful. Nothing happened except that the air around Strood darkened briefly.

"How do you feel?" asked Enid anxiously.

Strood was looking at his free hand in a puzzled way. It was curled around something. "Fine, just fine," he said absently. He opened his hand. On his palm was something small and dark that moved, coiling in on itself like oily smoke. It reminded the watching Skerridge of ink dropped into water.

Behind Strood, green light flickered for a second,

then Ava Vispilio put his orb back into the folds of his robe. In answer to the call came a tide of ragged creatures, all gray fur, yellow eyes and teeth, spilling out from the trees beyond.

"You can't!" cried Enid.

Dark raised a hand wearily to his face and Nemus cast his eyes down. Azork looked unbothered by the whole thing and Crow's smile was even more vague than usual.

Senta paled and swallowed hard. "What are you doing, Ava?"

Vispilio's wolves came to a halt, milling a short distance away from the group, just behind Arafin Strood. On the horizon, the sun began its descent in the sky, slipping down into a sea of golden light. Skerridge shuddered. He had forgotten that Mr. Strood had the Evebell rung every day at exactly this time for a reason. It was a reminder.

"Right," said Vispilio. "As Enid so kindly pointed out, there is another possibility. Something that I think would make us all hesitate. Our aim is to control Death, put it off for a while, not banish it. No one wants to live forever. So, time for part two of the experiment."

Gan Mafig backed away. Skerridge wished he could wake up.

Vispilio raised a hand, pointed at Strood with his forefinger and let loose a short bolt of power. Enough to knock the apothecary's servant off his feet and send him flying backward, right into the middle of the wolf pack.

"After all," said Vispilio, "we need to know the full story before we drink it, don't you think?"

Skerridge covered his ears to block the screams and the horrible wet sounds. Gan Mafig ran to hide. Of the sorcerers, even Azork had to look away.

Only Vispilio watched to the end.

* * *

Skerridge opened one eye and unplugged his ears. Sadly he had not woken up yet, but the scene had moved on because day, like the wolves, had gone. Now the scene was lit by a ring of bright sun-globes cast into the night sky by Vispilio. The end of the Final Gathering was in sight.

Enid was sobbing bitterly in Senta's arms. Nemus was pale and strained, age suddenly showing in the lines of his face. Crow looked sick and wandered about nervously, while Dark stood still and silent, apart from the rest. Azork was trying not to show his fear and Vispilio was scowling.

Skerridge, like the other watchers, had his view blocked by the bodies of the seven, but he didn't need to see to know what they were looking at.

In the center of the circle was Arafin Strood, naked and scarred like a road map from top to toe.

He smiled.

He flexed his fingers.

"So," he said, "who's next for the potion?"

The sorcerers backed away.

"Enough," Vispilio turned his back. "It seems we made a mistake, after all. He's immortal."

Azork nodded. He swallowed, avoiding Strood's eye and then followed Vispilio as he left.

Crow coughed. "Perhaps we'd better rethink this." He smiled apologetically at Strood. "Thank you for your time."

Dark gave Crow a cold glance, then turned and left without a word. Nemus, his head bowed, walked away with Senta at his side. Enid was the last to go.

"I'm sorry," she said to Strood. "Forgive us."

"Never," said Strood. He grinned. "Not so long as I live."

33

Another Day Begins

Jonas was howling with grief and with rage. Grief at all that he *thought* he had lost when Nin had rescued him from the Hounds and rage because he should not have lost them at all. He should have stayed with the Hounds, because being rescued from them was impossible.

But slipping in under the memory of all those things that he *thought* he had lost came other memories, memories of things that he *had* lost. Really lost.

Lost, perhaps, forever.

The howling stopped and Jonas sank to the ground, his head buried in his bloodied hands. He could barely keep up with the images flooding into his head.

There was a house. It seemed huge, with great, bright rooms full of light and color. There were trees in the garden. There were summer holidays and Christmas and birthdays. There were lessons and school friends and a white terrier with bright black eyes that he called Snowy after the one in *Tintin*.

There was a woman with warm eyes and short, honey-colored hair who was sometimes stern, but usually smiling. A gray-eyed man with slender hands and a mobile, intelligent face. And a baby sister who handed him half-sucked sweets and got in his way all the time; who seemed to grow while he watched, turning from a toddler into a kid in school uniform with a satchel on her shoulder and her eyes all scrunched up because she was trying to understand something.

All this he had had and it was so much better than anything the Hounds had to offer that the pain of having lost it knocked the pain of losing the Hounds into a cocked hat.

Wearily, his face by now stained with tears as well as blood, Jonas raised his head to see a huge, horrible shape heading down the corridor toward him, hurrying anxiously past the blood-smeared walls. As he watched, the lamps began to pop back on and another day began. Dawn was breaking outside and the House was waking up.

"Galig's Sword, boy! Been fightin' the 'Ounds, I take it?"

Jonas nodded weakly, as relief surged through him.

"Did yer win? Yeah, yeah. Daft question. If not, you'd 'ave been at my throat by now, right?" Taggit dumped a bulging pack on the ground next to Jonas.

"I think that if I had lost, even if you had been Nin I would have tried to kill you," croaked Jonas, "but I won."

"Per'aps we'd better do somethin' about the state you're in. We can start with a drink of water and then a look at those bloody stumps you're usin' for fingers."

Taggit pulled a flask out of the pack, whipped the cap off and helped Jonas take a few mouthfuls. It was just water, but it was cold and clean and wonderful for a raw throat.

Next the goblin pulled out a battered tin containing

a pot of Honey Healing Balm, a wad of gauze and some bandages. Jonas watched as Taggit began to bathe his torn fingers. He was tired and dazed, but his head felt oddly clear. Clean, almost. Taggit smeared ointment on the wounds. It felt to Jonas's fingers like the water had to his throat.

"I'm glad you came," said Jonas.

Taggit peered down at him, his look unfathomable. Then he smiled. "Thought I needed a change o' scene," he said. "Good thing too, eh. Looks like you could do with some rest and somethin' to eat. But don't be too long about it, eh? If yer wanna find that friend of yours, we'd better get on. Dunno about you, but I've got a nasty feelin' that time is runnin' out."

Skerridge woke up just as the lamps flicked back on, feeling a whole lot better. The TPF had gone, leaving him firmly in the present and very hungry.

His first task was to steal some thread and a needle to sort out the torn shoulder seam of his vest, and his second was to raid the servants' larder and take the booty back to the rag box. He quickly polished off three chicken sandwiches, two cake-sized slices of jam sponge and some lemonade, then wiped his mouth and fingers on the rags, burped hugely and settled back to think. It was a mistake, because thinking took him straight back to the scenes he had just relived.

The fact that such a terrible act had been committed by the Fabulous was enough to make him go cold all over. The guilt belonged, not just to Ava Vispilio who had thrown Strood to the wolves, or to the Seven who had cast the Deathweave, let him drink it and then failed to stop Vispilio, but to the whole of the Fabulous for the carelessness with which they treated the Quick. The carelessness that had made the whole thing possible.

He closed his eyes and winced. Because didn't that include him too? All the kids over all the years, just to carry on the fear so that bogeymen could go on living, could become so steeped in dread that they would be among the last of the Fabulous to die.

In the darkness of the cupboard, scrunched up in the box, Skerridge experienced something that felt horribly like remorse.

He was drowning in the knowledge that Ninevah Redstone had every reason to hate and despise him. The entire Quick species had every reason to hate and despise him too, but somehow the fact that Nin did was the bit that hurt the most. After a while he reached for something to blow his nose on. His groping hand came back with the knobbly thing that had been sticking into his shoulder all night. He stared blankly at the pink rucksack, then wiped his nose on it anyway.

While Skerridge sat huddled up amid the rags, clutching Ninevah Redstone's backpack and feeling sorry for himself, Skerridge's brain got on with the process of thinking. He was pretty sure that any time soon Ninevah Redstone would be making a break for it. The only escape route that wouldn't get her caught or killed was Seraphine's Secret Way, which he was also pretty sure meant the tunnel in the down-house graveyard. But something wasn't right.

Most likely, the Secret Way was an old escape route, built into the house right at the start for its owner to use if there was ever any trouble. And that meant there had to be a door of some kind, because what escape route wouldn't have a way to cut off pursuers?

And *that* meant there had to be a key. Only thing was, what had happened to it?

Skerridge blinked as an idea thundered into his brain. He brightened up, blew his nose again and hurried out of the rag box, heading through the servants' dining room to the next door along, the one marked "Here be Tygers."

He had better move fast. Somehow he couldn't get rid of the feeling that time was running out.

In Mr. Strood's study the lamps popped on, filling the room with morning. Curled up by the bookcases, Nin awoke with a start. Remembering the night before, a wave of panic swept over her that she hadn't been able to reach Jonas and help him. She felt tears spring into her eyes and rubbed them away firmly. He would have survived the night somehow, she was sure of it.

Stiffly, she clambered to her feet and crept quietly to the door. Outside she could hear feet pattering up and down as the servants took Mr. Strood his breakfast and got things ready for the day ahead. She would have to wait a little longer.

The book she had been reading when the lamps went out was still lying open on Mr. Strood's desk. Reluctantly Nin moved toward it, not wanting to know anymore but still drawn to the end of the story. The words caught her eyes and she found herself reading anyway, horrified but unable to stop.

The ballad, flipping between poetry and prose, went on to describe the Final Gathering. Toward the end, Strood's writing became so frenzied it was barely legible and Nin struggled to make sense of it. When she finally understood that she was reading a description of what it felt like to be torn apart for hours before the

Seven finally gave up trying to see if he could be killed, she stopped and covered her face with her hands.

Which was when an Eyes trotted around the desk, took a long look at her and then trundled off, unnoticed.

Having finished his early breakfast, Mr. Strood was eager to get on. Following the capture of the spider yesterday afternoon, he had put a batch of Mafig's Fusion on to brew and now it was ready and waiting to be used.

Mafig's Fusion was the most important part of the mortal distillation process. Until Mafig, nobody had been able to distill a living being without several weeks, even months, of hard work. To distill a living being you had to crush its spirit completely and then drain out its essence. Even the darkest of sorcerers found it heavy going. But Gan Mafig worked out a way to distill a living being in a matter of hours by injecting it with a Fusion designed to plunge the victim deep into the heart of its worst nightmares, many times concentrated, until its spirit collapsed from the sheer weight of terror. This Fusion was the discovery that made him famous. Gan Mafig wanted to be thought brilliant, he hadn't meant to be evil and having invented the mortal distillation process he used it only once, just to make sure it worked.

The process itself was simple. Take a living being. Seal it into a confined space so that the essence didn't evaporate. Drip Fusion into one arm. Watch the victim scream a lot. Collect the essence with a collection funnel and drain it into a suitable container. Throw away the leftovers.

Mr. Strood's laboratory was large and clinical with

its walls, shelves, cabinets and work surfaces all painted white. The floor was covered with small tiles of white porcelain that could be washed if they got covered in, say, blood or anything nasty. The room was not completely lacking in color, though. The shelves were lined with jars and bottles, each filled with liquid, powder or objects in a variety of hues. Some of them were vivid greens, blues, reds and yellows. Some were darker purples and crimsons.

There were a lot of glass beakers and test tubes on the work surface, all sparkling clean, and a strange contraption like a glass cage along one wall. Right now Secretary Scribbins was herding the spider into the contraption, which happened to be Mr. Strood's Mortal Distillation Machine.

Scribbins yelped. The spider didn't want to go and he was having trouble keeping it from running up the walls in an attempt to escape. Fortunately the net was holding fast and the stunning wand was useful to numb it and stop it scuttling off. Even so, it managed to scratch him with one hook-ended leg.

Once it was in the machine and the glass door was closed, Strood took over and began to hook it up to the system of tubes going in and out of the glass walls. One lot to feed the Fusion into the spider's helpless body, the other lot running from the collection funnel to a suitable container. This time, rather than simply collecting the essence of the spider in a bottle, he wanted it to drain straight into the boy that would soon become Eyes. So he ordered Scribbins to push the kid's cage closer to the machine and added an extra run to the collection tubing so that he could stick the collection needle straight into the boy's arm.

The kid whimpered, but that was all and in no time everything was all set to go.

Strood stood poised, ready to open the valve that would start the Fusion on its deadly path into the core of the creature at his mercy.

Which was when the Eyes sent him a mental image of something that made him turn pale with rage.

34

The Kid in the Cage

After a while Nin put her hands down from her face and looked back at the page. There was something she wanted to find out, one last thing she didn't get. She read on quickly. Once they had sent the wolves away and Strood's body had been allowed to heal fully, the Sorcerers left. Gan Mafig was, according to Strood, cowering in his study. Those who had witnessed the Final Gathering and its terrible consequences had slunk away. Only Strood was left. Strood and something else. Something small and dark, like a marble of inky cloud.

The thing Strood had found clutched in his hand after he'd drunk the potion was . . .

"The Maug!" murmured Nin. "Mr. Strood's death!"

What the Deathweave had done was exactly what Strood had written in his ballad. It had separated Strood's death from Strood's life. Which was why Mr. Strood couldn't die.

"I used to keep it in a jar on the mantelpiece until it got too big," said a soft voice behind her. Nin spun around.

"It didn't *need* to eat, of course. But I gave it flies and wasps and small things and it enjoyed taking the lives so much I gave it more." Strood spoke affectionately. "Mice and rats first, then cats. And the more it fed, the more it grew." He smiled at her. "And now I give it children. It will eat any Quick, but it likes the young ones best."

Strood wandered over to the large chair in the corner and sat down.

"I . . . um . . . was just dusting . . ."

"Don't even bother to try," said Strood softly. "I know you, Ninevah Redstone."

Nin shut her eyes. For a moment there, just one moment, she had thought she might get away with it, but it seemed her luck had run out after all.

"Um," Nin croaked nervously to the vast guard who had tucked her under one arm and was carrying her down the corridor, "I kind of noticed, we're going to Mr. Strood's laboratory, aren't we?"

"Tha's it," said the guard. "Though I dunno why, cos 'e's already got a kiddie fer the Eyes experiment. Perhaps 'e's jus' gonna distill ya. Ours not to reason why, eh? Tha's what my mate Stanley always says." Floyd pushed open a plain white door and marched her up to a cage standing against the wall. In it was a kid.

"'Ere we are then," said Floyd as kindly as he could. He held her still with one hand—Nin could no more move than if she had been wrapped in steel—and pulled out a key with the other.

Inside the cage the kid stopped being a scrunched-up bundle in the corner and uncurled to look at Nin.

Who felt as if her heart had stopped.

When Floyd shoved her in and locked the door again, she didn't resist at all. Because the kid in the cage was Toby.

* * *

Skerridge shooed away one of Mr. Strood's pet tigers that had come to have a look at him. It gave a short, barking growl, so Skerridge treated it to a blast of fire-breath that singed its paws, but didn't do any real harm. The tiger bounded away, its gold-and-black blending into the dappled darkness of the attic.

This part of the loft was scattered with earth and had many small, unglazed windows through which beams of light shafted down. To make the tigers feel at home, trees and exotic plants grew in giant pots placed close together, their fallen leaves carpeting the floor and partly burying the skeletal remains of those unfortunates who had annoyed Mr. Strood. Through the center of the vast space, water ran along a narrow trough, its gentle trickling filling the air. And everywhere, piled against the walls, in between the trees and scattered at random along the banks of the trough river, were packing cases and old trunks.

When Strood had taken over the House from Gan Mafig, all of the apothecary's personal belongings had been crated up and shoved here in the attic—the tigers had been added later.

Skerridge was ready to bet that Seraphine's things were here too.

The day after the Final Gathering, when Gan Mafig finally came out of his study to discover that Seraphine had gone, he searched Sea View from top to bottom, but all he found was his daughter's favorite pendant. He never told anyone where he found it exactly and the general view was that she had dropped it somehow in her haste to get away.

But the more Skerridge thought about it the odder it seemed. Like the way Seraphine always wore the pendant, even though it wasn't very pretty. So his big idea was this. Maybe Seraphine hadn't dropped it. Maybe she had left it behind, like she didn't need it anymore. Or like somebody else might. In fact, maybe Seraphine's pendant was more than just a necklace.

So, hidden in all of this stored bric-a-brac was the thing that Nin would need to get out of the Terrible House of Strood. She didn't know she needed it yet, but she would soon enough. And when she found out, Skerridge would be there. It might make up, in some tiny, infinitesimal way, for the harm he had done in the past.

He was just ripping open his fourth crate when the attic door slammed open. A guard appeared, carrying a thick club and blinking in the dim light. He peered at the scene before him, turned pale when he spotted the culprit, and then tried desperately to look stern.

"Oy," he yelled, only it was more of a croak, "Bogeyman Skerridge, whadda ya think yore . . ."

Toby scrabbled over the floor of the cage and bundled up against Nin. She put her arms around him and hugged, rubbing her chin against his head. His blond hair was longer and he was thinner, but he was still the same Toby. He smelled the same and felt the same and sounded the same when he said, "I knew it was you! I pushed Monkey out so's you'd see him and come to find me."

He stuck his arm out to show her a bruise in the crook of his elbow. "Mr. Strood stuck a pin in me then he went all quiet and said, 'That girl is still alive,' then he went away and I *knew* it was you."

Nin kissed his head, hardly able to believe that when she thought her luck had run out it had really been better than ever. She had been so close to Toby all this time, but she would never have thought of the laboratory. And if she hadn't been caught at exactly that moment, then by now Toby wouldn't be Toby anymore.

Nervously, she looked around the room. Floyd was still watching over them, but there was no sign of Mr. Strood. In a second cage was the most amazing spider she had ever seen, sitting in a knock-kneed jumble of legs up against the bars, watching her nervously.

The laboratory door slammed open and Strood stalked in. He was angry, Nin could see that at once. Behind him hurried a man who looked like a walking ruler. Or at least half a ruler because he was not tall enough to be a whole one. He had a pinched face, which was mostly nose, and gray eyes. He was wearing pinstripe trousers, a frock coat with a spotless white shirt and a large bow tie.

"Go on, Scribbins," snapped Mr. Strood.

"Then he . . . um . . . nailed the guard into a packing case, sir," gasped Scribbins. "Only we can't get Guard Stanley out again because one of the tigers has fallen asleep on top of it. The other BMs won't come out to help because it's daylight . . ."

Mr. Strood froze. "But you said it was a bogeyman that was in the tiger's attic?"

Scribbins closed his eyes. He was twitching all over with nerves.

"W-we th-think . . . it's B-Bogeyman Skerridge, Mr. Strood, sir."

Strood hissed.

Scribbins flinched and whimpered.

"But he's my BEST bogeyman. My champion kid-catcher!" Mr. Strood fell silent for a moment and then snarled. His eyes settled on Nin.

"It's all to do with you, isn't it? You've turned him rogue!"

Nin shrugged. "You can't blame me," she said. "He's his own bogeyman, you know."

Strood ignored her. He walked over to a bottle of cloudy pink fluid sitting on the work surface. Something about it made Nin nervous.

"Excuse me," she said loudly. "What's that?"

Strood turned and looked at her. He smiled.

"That," he said warmly, "is Gan Mafig's Fusion. It's an interesting concoction of crowsmorte, powdered goat intestines and neat vodka. Of course, Mafig had to use holipine, but crowsmorte gives a far more . . . interesting result. It's slower and more agonizing, and you get a purer end product too."

"And that is?"

"In this case, about half a beaker of liquid essence of Ninevah Redstone. Oh, and some physical leftovers." He waved a hand airily.

"You're going to kill me?"

"Naturally, though it will take a little while for you to die. After all, I can't have people just escaping, you know. Undermining me. Giving people hope. There has to be consequences."

He selected a beaker from the shelf and began looking along his collection of bottles and jars for the right ingredients, humming contentedly.

"What are you doing?"

"Making up another batch of Fusion. It has to be left to ferment for a while, you see. So it can be brewing while you are distilling, then as soon as you're done I can get on with the Eyes experiment."

"Efficient."

"Naturally."

"Um—what exactly is the Eyes experiment?"

Strood smiled at her. It was almost friendly.

"My Eyes are dying," he said, "and unfortunately there are no imps left so I cannot make anymore. But I do have," he waved a hand at the shelves of bottles, "some essence of imp. My plan is to use the small child here," he waved a hand at Toby, "as a base. I picked him because he is a nice size and reasonably bright. I will distill the spider into him to give him speed and night-vision, then add some essence of imp to provide the element of magic. Finally I will replace his blood with crowsmorte, which, along with the essence of imp and a drop of my own blood, will allow me to see through his eyes. No guarantees of course, but I think it will work." Strood beamed. "I do like a good experiment, don't you?"

Nin stared at him in horror and held Toby all the more tightly. While Strood got on with measuring and mixing, she looked hopefully at the door. From the howl that she had heard last night she knew that Jonas—and probably Jik too—had followed her. Which meant that any minute now, someone would be here to rescue them. She knew it. Any minute now.

"I . . . um . . . really enjoyed your ballads."

Strood ignored her and went on measuring out the powdered goat's intestines and adding it to the mixture. He was humming to himself as he worked.

"It must be rewarding, writing stories like that."

He selected a thin crystal rod from a drawer and began to stir the Fusion carefully. Nin frowned. She could feel eight purple eyes and two deep-blue ones watching her. She needed to buy time, just in case Jonas and Jik got delayed. Which they wouldn't. Trouble was, Mr. Strood wasn't playing. She took a deep breath and tried something else.

"It was awful, what they did to you."

Strood stiffened. The rod chinked in the beaker. He set it down on the work surface and came over toward her. Crouching, he brought his face close to hers. Nin noticed that even his eyeballs had scars.

"And it'll be worse," he said softly, "what I do to you." He stood up and went back to work.

35

Any Second Now . . .

Nin gave up trying to get him talking. If any part of Arafin Strood had ever been a normal person, it had long since gone completely and utterly insane. She looked at the laboratory door again. Any *second* now, she thought anxiously. She didn't have any minutes left.

"Put the girl in the machine," ordered Strood, without looking up from his mixing.

Floyd sighed and moved toward the cage, feeling sad that the story of Ninevah Redstone had to end like this. Toby tightened his grip on Nin, who was still watching the door. Any second . . . right . . . now? Please?

Opening the cage, the guard reached in. By now Toby was sobbing.

"Shut him up," snarled Strood.

"Toby, be quiet now," Nin told him firmly. "Everything will be okay."

Toby looked at her and went quiet. She hated the way he trusted her so much. She thought it would upset him more if she struggled, so she went quietly.

Once she was safely in the Distillation Machine, Floyd secured her arm in a kind of sling. She was trying to keep one eye fixed on the door. Jik and Jonas had better get a move on.

Strood took hold of the needle at the end of the tube attached to the bottle and stuck it in her arm.

"OW!"

"Believe me, as soon as the first drop of Fusion reaches your blood, you won't notice the physical pain."

For the second time that morning, Strood undid the clip that stopped the fluid from the bottle running down the tube. The first drop set out on its way.

The spider was scrabbling madly in its cage. Toby was still silent, watching. Suddenly he piped up, "When's it going to be all right?"

Nin shut her eyes. "Any . . ."

Many floors below, surrounded by the ashes of yesterday's rubbish, Jik was hammering on the furnace door. He had been hammering for hours, and had made some good dents in the hatch, but couldn't get it open.

He paused. There was movement outside. Maybe the boilerman had come to stoke up the furnace? There was a grinding of metal bolts being drawn. The hatch swung open.

Jik had no time to say thank you, but he took care not to knock the man over as he flew out of the furnace and dived into the walls. He tore through the earth like a shark might tear through water and the Land drew back to let him go. He swam on, speeding up past the cemetery and the floor with the empty room and its tortured captive. Past the gardens and living quarters and storerooms toward the center of the House.

". . . second . . ."

✳ ✳ ✳

He was in the untouched ground now, the foundations of the House where Strood's servants had been forbidden to dig. Pushing aside stones and smashing through layers of shale and rock, Jik moved on with increasing ease, until . . .

". . . NOW!" she finished, and opened her eyes again. She looked at the door and her heart sank as it stayed shut. She barely noticed the rumbling that came from beneath their feet.

Strood had moved to stand next to the work surface. As the rumbling began, he switched his gaze from Nin to the ground, a puzzled frown gathering on his face. Floyd, positioned between Toby's cage and Nin so as to block the poor kid's view of what was about to happen to his sister, shuffled backward as the floor began to tremble. Perched on a stool at one end of the work surface, Scribbins turned pale. The rumbling grew fast to a sound that shook the room.

Toby yelled as the floor erupted sending tiles and mud flying through the air. Something rose up through it. Something angry with eyes that glowed like beacons.

Safe behind the glass door of the Distillation Machine, a shocked Nin watched as fragments of tile rained down everywhere. In their cages by the wall, Toby and Hss got the least of it. On the lower shelves, bottles and jars exploded as tiles smashed into them, scattering their contents everywhere. A stone ricocheted off a sealed bottle marked "LETHAL" high on a shelf above the work surface. The bottle didn't break, but there was a cracking sound that nobody heard amid all the yelling. A chunk of broken tile got Mr. Strood in the face, cutting a line from cheek to chin. Blood spattered onto his white coat.

"Jik!" screamed Nin and the mudman charged through the debris toward her. Floyd could have stopped him, but had just breathed in a lungful of powdered goat intestines and was too busy coughing horribly. Red in the face, eyes bulging, he collapsed to his knees just as Jik reached Nin and pulled the tube from her arm. The first drop of Mafig's fusion dripped harmlessly to the floor to be followed by the rest, leaving Nin giggling with relief.

Rigid with fury, Strood pointed a finger that trembled with rage in Jik's direction. Already the slash on his face was healing, the edges pulling themselves together, the scar blending in with the others.

"Rip it apart," he snarled.

The guard and the secretary leapt to obey. At least, Floyd staggered to his feet, still struggling to breathe, and Scribbins tumbled off his stool to run on wobbling legs toward the target. Floyd launched himself into a rugby tackle intended to crush the mudman to dust, but Jik did a neat somersault out of the guard's grip, landed in front of the glass door and yanked it open. Scribbins got there a second later, but Jik had already gone, leaping at the wall, bouncing off it and grabbing the key ring from its hook as he went. Trying to follow, Floyd spun dizzily, lurched to a halt, bent over and made a loud whooping noise followed by a horrible retching one.

"I said rip it apart not puke it to death, you pea-brained moron!" howled Strood. He was white with fury and the scars on his face stood out in livid red. "If you can't manage that lump of earth, at least GET THE GIRL!"

White with terror, Scribbins turned to grab Nin as she pulled her arm free of the sling and tumbled out of the machine. She shrieked and pushed him hard in the chest. He staggered, slipped in the puddle of sick and fell, bashing his head on the half-open glass door.

As she ran, Nin caught a glance from the doubled-up Floyd. He was pale and sweaty, but his eyes were focused and she was sure, really sure, that if he had tried he could have got her.

"Thank you," she breathed and kept moving.

Strood had given up on his underlings. By now, Jik had unlocked the cages, pulled out Toby and the spider and the three of them, followed by Nin, were headed for the way out. Over the other side of the room, Strood was too far away to grab Nin before she reached the door. Instead, he spun toward the cabinet behind him, throwing it open to reveal rows of neatly labeled drawers. As the door slammed back on its hinges, hitting the shelves next to it, the already damaged bottle high above Strood's head exploded sending perfumed, green liquid spattering over half the laboratory.

A splash skated across the top of Floyd's massive leather boots as he leaned against the work surface. Another splash sailed over Nin's head, hit the wall and slithered down it leaving a melted groove in the tiles. Barely back on his feet, Scribbins began to scream and pull off his clothes as a dollop of the stuff ate rapidly through them.

But most of the fluid went over Mr. Strood, who had just found the drawer he wanted and pulled it open. The stuff ran down the left side of his face and body. The perfume was replaced by a horrible smell of barbecue. Strood froze.

"That," he hissed, "was the last ever bottle of distilled faerie venom. The LAST EVER, do you understand!"

He spun around, clutching something in one hand that looked like a metal star

"Nik tik wik KIK!" Jik threw open the door and Hss headed through it.

Toby looked back for Nin who had paused to throw a horrified stare at Strood as a thick dribble of venom ran down his face. Or maybe it was his eye. The sleeve of his white coat had burned away and his skin was beginning to smoke.

Strood raised the thing in his hand, the razor-sharp teeth glinting as he aimed for Nin's heart. He had a clear shot and his arm was in motion, his fingers uncurling to release the star.

Floyd lurched into Strood's line of fire, cold sweat breaking out on his corrugated forehead and his ruined boots flapping about his feet as he threw himself toward the escaping captives. Strood howled, for a split second he faltered. Then he let the star go, spitting fire as it blazed through the air.

Jik shoved Toby through the door, grabbed Nin and towed her out of the laboratory.

The door slammed shut in Floyd's face.

The star slammed into the door where it stuck, burning a deep gash and showering sparks everywhere. There was a smell of scorched guard.

Mr. Strood went mad.

"RELEASE THE MAUG!"

Floyd gulped. "Do ya mean . . . let it loose?"

Strood turned a look on him that made him flinch.

"Do it," he hissed, "and do it NOW! Or I'll feed you to the tigers piece by piece and MAKE YOU WATCH."

* * *

Having made it to the up-house, Jonas and Taggit were wondering which way to go next when they heard the thunder of many feet running at speed up the corridor. Jonas grabbed Taggit and pulled him out of sight under the stairs.

When they were past, Jonas peered round the corner, too late to see who it was. Then he heard someone yelling from somewhere down the hallway.

"What was that?"

"Sounded like 'release the Maug' t' me."

"It's got something to do with Nin, hasn't it?"

"Wouldn't put it past 'er to 'ave got up Strood's nose some'ow."

"Come on, then. Follow me."

"Right y'are," said Taggit, grimly.

With Toby hanging on to her free hand and Jik and Hss at her heels, Nin ran as fast as she could, trying to remember the layout of Polpp's map. She reached the door to the Maug's courtyard and yanked it open.

The Death Dog turned its heavy head to look at them. Toby gasped, clinging on to Nin, and Hss bunched up nervously as it galloped toward them, only stopping when it reached the end of its chain. They ran past it, across to the arch and through into the gardens beyond with the Maug's icy howl at their backs.

"Now . . ." Nin stared around her. Polpp's sketch had shown something that looked like a big, blurred cabbage. "Gotta be!" she said, and headed across the grass toward Mr. Strood's rose garden.

A second later, Floyd staggered through the door. He gazed at the Maug with horror as it howled after the escaping Quick, its unseeable eyes, darkness in darkness, fixed on the retreating shapes in the distance. It howled again, turning the air to frost.

Already pale, Floyd went the color of cottage cheese. He lurched a few steps toward it, then a few more, not wanting to do what he had to do. Muttering to himself, he unclipped the chain from the collar around the Maug's neck.

It took off through the archway at a horrible speed.

As he watched it go, the door behind him burst open on a Quick with eyes that glowed and a Fabulous goblin several sizes larger than Floyd. The guard raised his fists, ready to fight, but they had already gone, thundering past him, hot on the tail of the Death Dog.

They ran, but Toby was only small and he was weak from his long stay in the cage. Nin couldn't carry him without slowing down, so they could only go as fast as he could.

Behind them the Maug was gaining. It loped over the grass like a bundle of nighttime that had got loose in the day, leaving a ripple of darkness in its wake that swirled like ink in water until it dissolved in the light. Nin ran on, towing Toby behind her, across the neatly cut lawn, through a gap in the dividing hedge and into the rose garden.

In front of her, row upon row of dark red rose-bushes all led straight to a marble-pillared temple in the center. She headed for that. Toby was white with effort, tears leaking from the corners of his eyes, but he struggled after Nin, trying to go just a little faster. Jik dropped back behind them.

The Maug came on. It might look like a dog, but that was all. It could not see or smell in the normal sense, but it could detect the glow of a living soul from a hundred yards. It liked the bright ones best, the ones that glowed with years of glorious life to come. The young ones.

Ahead it could see three glowing forms and one dusky one. The dusky one it wasn't interested in, Fabulous life was no use to a Quick Death. Of the three glowing shapes, the nearest shone with a silvery radiance, and the furthest with a clear, golden light. But the Maug ignored both of them, because trailing just behind the golden one was another little life, one so bright it was dazzling.

And that was the one it wanted.

It took the ground in vast leaps, roses withering and dying as it passed, dropping their silky petals like crimson snow. Ahead, Jik turned, ready to face it.

It reached him and went to leap over his head. He jumped, grabbing for its darkness-dripping underbelly. For a moment everything went black and cold and then it was gone and Jik was left gripping nothing. The Maug, to the Fabulous at least, was as insubstantial as the darkness it was made of.

Bewildered, Jik spun around, feeling his inner fires chill with fear as the Maug headed for Nin and Toby. Hss dropped back and reared up, poised to attack. But the Maug leaped again, sailing over her upraised legs.

Nin and Toby had nearly reached the marble temple at the center of the rose garden, but Toby couldn't run anymore and Nin knew it. She could hear his breath rasping in his throat and when she picked him up, he was shaking. With his weight slowing her down she knew it was hopeless, but she ran anyway. She didn't look back, except at the end.

* * *

Even if he had conquered the Hound inside him, it would never be gone entirely and Jonas flew over the petal-covered ground, his eyes lightning white. Taggit charged after him, even his long legs barely keeping pace. Jonas sped past Jik and kept going, close enough now to see Nin's eyes as she turned to look Death in the face.

As the Maug gathered itself for a final spring it looked less like a dog and more like what it was. Darkness incarnate. Before it could leap, Jonas covered the last few yards, throwing himself at the creature and hitting its side. The force of his body colliding with it, knocked it off course, rolling it onto the ground with Jonas underneath.

The Maug sprang back onto its feet in a strangely fluid movement, but it was too late. Taggit had already grabbed Nin and Toby and run with them up the temple steps and in through the marble columns. Two strides in he found that the temple had no floor and all three of them vanished, plunging out of sight into the vaults below.

With its target vanished, the Maug turned on Jonas, still on the ground, half-frozen from his contact with the Death Dog. Hss launched herself at it from behind, scrabbling up onto its back and digging in with her hook-ended feet. As the Maug tossed and twisted, trying to reach her, Jonas rolled to safety and staggered to his feet. He heard Jik yelling "thik wik!" and saw the mudman charging toward them across the grass.

Hss could feel Death creeping into her blood, but she held on, too terrified to let go, while the Maug tried to shake her off, scattering darkness around it like rain. Jik reached them, running straight through the Maug and out the other side. When he got there he was carrying Hss on his shoulders, her legs wrapped around him. He looked like he was wearing some weird kind of cloak.

Before the Death Dog had time to realize that Hss had gone, the three of them had charged into the temple and vanished from sight through the missing floor, leaving the Maug bewildered and cheated. It gave a howl that made ice flakes fall from the air, then it turned back to the House.

36

Seraphine's Secret Way

Nin scrambled to her feet and turned to face whatever it was that had grabbed her and Toby.

It was horrible. It was at least nine foot tall, had a face like a nightmare and was wearing baggy trousers and a T-shirt which said: "Looks Ain't Everythin'."

A second later, Hss and Jik tumbled in, closely followed by Jonas. Fortunately, Taggit was quick enough to catch them.

Toby was staring around him.

"Bubbles," he whispered.

They were standing at the foot of a well. From about halfway down, the circular walls of the well gave way to pillars that made a tight circle of arches. Beyond them was a huge vault, filled with the radiance from thousands of marble-sized spheres, hanging suspended in the air.

"Not bubbles," said Nin, also whispering, "memory-pearls."

Toby held out his hand, reaching toward them. His movement made the pearls closest to him drift away, but then, from deeper within the vault, a single pearl spun down through the air to land in his palm.

"That one must be yours, Toby," said Jonas. "Keep it safe."

Toby clutched the pearl nervously. Taggit bobbed down until he was on a level with the boy.

"Why don't you pop it in your pocket 'ere what buttons up."

While the goblin helped Toby tuck his pearl away, Jonas stepped forward.

"I always said I wouldn't do this, but . . ." He held out his hand. There was a pause while the pearls skimmed aside, leaving a space around his hand. The pause lengthened.

Hss raised a leg, pointing to a disturbance in the pearl-filled air above and to the left. A pearl spun through the horde, dropping neatly into Jonas's hand.

Nin stuck her hand out. Five minutes later, while they all stared with dismay at the undisturbed air, she put it down again.

"It's not here," she said blankly. "Skerridge lied."

"We carn' 'ang about with Strood on our 'eels," said Taggit firmly a short while later, when Nin had stopped crying into Jonas's shoulder. "We'll 'ave to deal with the lyin' bogeyman problem when we're out of danger. The good thing is, it'll take all the guards 'e's got to get the Maug under control when it's in that mood. Which'll give us some time, like."

"It's no use." Nin sniffed hard, rubbing her wet face on her pinafore. She felt so disappointed it was eating at her spirits. "Jonas said the tunnel to the sanctuary is gone, the roof's fallen in . . ."

"What about Seraphine's Secret Way?" Jonas gave her a reassuring hug. "According to Gorgle it's beneath the main house. He thinks it might run from the garden."

"It figures." Taggit looked thoughtful. "Apart from the roses, everythin' 'ere's the way she left it, more or less. 'Cept the temple we're in. Gan Mafig put that up just after Seraphine ran away, an' just before Strood took over. It 'ad a statue of Seraphine in it, but Strood must 'ave got rid of it when 'e took away the floor an' started usin' the vault to store memory pearls."

"A statue," said Nin, pointing. "You mean like that one?"

It was behind them, framed in the curve of the arches and almost hidden by the memory pearls. The marble figure wore a hooded robe over a long dress and was holding a lamp high in one hand. Around her neck hung a diamond-shaped pendant.

"She was one lovely lady," sighed Taggit. "The sort o' person who always made you feel better about things."

Nin had to agree. And if the statue of Seraphine was anything like the original then she had been beautiful, and strong too. It must have taken strength to leave wealth and security behind for the sake of love. Feeling slightly better about things, Nin squeezed Toby's hand and smiled down at him.

"It says something!" Jonas read the inscription around the base aloud. "Let . . . love . . . light the way."

"Sounds like a clue t' me," said Taggit firmly. "The Way. Must be the Secret Way, right? So the statue 'as somethin' to do with the Way."

"It was in the temple, over this vault. So maybe the Secret Way is down here."

They stared around. Jik frowned at the marble floor, trying to feel the Land behind it. There was definitely something there. Or rather nothing there. Hollowness.

"Yik!"

"Right, so where's the way in?"

"What're you lookin' at, kid?" asked Nin.

Toby was staring at the ground underneath the statue. He pointed. At the back, the base of the statue was not level with the floor, tipping her slightly forward.

"There's something making her crooked."

Taggit was already putting his arms around the statue, shifting it easily over to the left to uncover the metal ring of a trapdoor. He pulled up the marble slab and peered into the darkness below.

"Looks like we found our way out! Well spotted, kid."

Jonas was already digging into his pack, looking for his tinderbox and a candle.

"I'll go first. Nin, you and Toby stay right behind me. Everyone else can see in the dark, right?"

There was a chorus of grunts, yiks and yssses. Nin watched anxiously as Jonas lit the candle, then went ahead, stepping down into the darkness. She had a nasty feeling it was all a bit too easy.

Strood paced the laboratory, walking round and round the hole left by the mudman's unexpected arrival. He had retrieved the throwing star that had missed Ninevah Redstone and was clutching it as if waiting for another chance. Bits of him lay scattered about the floor. Other bits of him, the ones that were still roughly in the right place, were trying to heal in spite of the venom eating at his flesh. His face was half gone and he still only had one eye. Scribbins had been sick already and even Mrs. Dunvice was wishing she hadn't had breakfast.

"Sho," slurred Mr. Strood coolly. "Let me get thish

right. My chief bogeyman and my gravedigger have turned traitor. All my guardsh have had to leave their poshts to deal with the eshcaped tigersh and the Maug, caushing a riot in the Engine."

He paused as the lights flickered, just to demonstrate the point.

"One guard ish trapped in a packing cashe, two have been mauled by the tigersh and one hash been eaten by the Maug, which you have only jusht managed to get under control."

The Housekeeper's yellow eyes watched her master warily as another chunk of flesh dropped off to join the mess on the floor. There seemed to be so much of it, but then it would keep trying to grow back.

"Sssho, tell me, WHAT HAPPENED TO THE GIRL?"

Mrs. Dunvice swallowed hard. "It's possible, sir, that she and her friends have found Seraphine's Secret Way."

Strood turned a look on her that would have sent her to her knees begging for mercy, except that werewolf Grimm did not beg from anybody. Cowering behind her, Scribbins whimpered, shivering in the remains of his long johns.

"How posshible?" Strood asked icily. He raised one hand to stop his jaw from falling off.

"Very possible," said Mrs. Dunvice reluctantly.

Strood snarled and turned sharply. It was a mistake. His leg, already half eaten through, snapped and sent him reeling toward the hole in the ground. His arms windmilled as he teetered on the brink, one hand flying off at the wrist and hitting the wall with a dull thwack. Staggering, he lurched the wrong way, stepping into the hole instead of away from it. There was a crack as his head connected with the remaining edges of tile and then he was gone.

For a few moments they could hear his smothered howls of rage as he plummeted downward, until finally the sounds were swallowed up in the depths.

There was a soft sound, like heavy rain only more earthy and then silence.

Mrs. Dunvice stepped carefully toward the edge of the hole, but there was no hole left. Strood must have clawed at the earth as he fell, disturbing the loose soil. At any rate, it had caved in refilling the shaft completely.

"W-what do we do now?" wailed Scribbins, wringing his hands.

The Housekeeper shrugged. "Start digging?" she said.

Skerridge was halfway down the tunnel in the grave-yard, staring thoughtfully at the wall of earth in front of him. Rumor had it that the tunnel had been here even before the down-house had been built, that it was Seraphine's Secret Way and had once led all the way from the up-house to the secret love-nest built in the grounds of the house, the building that had since become the sanctuary. But there were things that didn't fit. For a start, where was the door? You wouldn't find a door in a mud-walled tunnel like this. And Skerridge was certain that he wasn't wrong about the door. He looked at the diamond-shaped key in his hand and grinned.

If Ninevah Redstone's luck was in, then this *wasn't* Seraphine's Secret Way. Which was a good thing, because the roof had fallen in and there was no exit here.

Skerridge got moving. Finding Nin might be a problem, but he knew where to start. He burned air all the way to the memory room.

From there it was easy. Taggit had pulled the trap-door into place behind them, but he couldn't put the statue back. Skerridge grinned broadly.

"Right y'are." He chuckled as he set off down the stairs, raising sparks from the stone as he went.

The stairs spiraled down through walls of old and crumbling brick for a very long time. They walked in single file, with Jonas and his candle in the lead, followed by Nin and Toby, then Jik in the middle because his eyes gave a little more light. Hss came after Jik, with Taggit last. At the bottom was a small landing and a door. It was made of thick oak, barred with iron and set in a stone arch, and it was locked. Taggit squashed past them down to the front and put all his weight into shoving, but it didn't give an inch.

"I don't believe it!" Nin groaned, sinking against the wall.

"We carn' go back," muttered Taggit. "Once the Maug's under control Strood'll be after us an' . . . well, it doesn't bear thinkin' about."

"Maybe it's magic. Maybe it opens to a word," suggested Jonas hopefully.

"There's a keyhole," said Taggit dryly.

"Oh? Oh yeah. What are we gonna to do then?"

They stared at one another blankly. No one had any suggestions. There was a sizzle in the air, some sparks and then a pop.

"Ya could always go frew it," said Skerridge, holding out something shaped like a diamond and etched with symbols.

There was a stunned silence and then Nin burst out. "You lied to me!"

Skerridge looked crestfallen. "I was goin' t' drop yer pearl off after I gave ya t' Strood, but in the end I fought I'd keep it. As a memento of our adventures across the Drift, like."

Nin glared.

"An' I didn' lie as such. I said the pearls were in the 'Ouse, I didn' say that yer pearl was wiv 'em is all. I 'ad it on me all the time. Funny really. Ya was chasing off t' the House t' get the pearl, but it was wiv me an' I was chasin' . . . Ya don' fink it's funny, do ya?"

He sighed, then rummaged in a pocket inside his waistcoat. He pulled out a small bag tied with a drawstring, opened it and tipped the contents into his palm. In the dim light, Nin's pearl glowed with bright colors.

Nin held out her hand and the pearl drifted through the air toward her. She held it for a moment and then tucked it in the pocket of her dress.

"Thanks." She gave him a watery smile.

"No problem. I found yer bag an' all. It were in the rag box, see?" He held out a battered and no longer very pink rucksack. "Blimmin' uncomfy t' sleep on an' all."

"Right," cut in Taggit. "Give us that key. No time for reminiscin'."

"Awright!" grumbled Skerridge, handing it over. "Took a lotta trouble over that, I did."

Taggit slotted it carefully in the lock. There was a screech of metal as the bolts and bars began to draw back of their own accord, one after the other, releasing the door. Taggit pushed and it swung open silently, even after all this time. They stood on the threshold and stared.

They were looking into earth, only it wasn't earth, it was the ghost of earth.

"Fink of it like the soil 'as been shifted over a bit, dimenshunally speakin'," said Skerridge, seeing Nin's baffled look. "What we're seein' is like an echo, the real stuff is jus' slightly somewhere else, geddit?"

"So, while the magic is still working, we can just walk through it like it was a tunnel? But where's the magic coming from?"

"Dunno, but see that sorta golden light? Tha's the bit where the magic's workin'. Where it ends, the soil is still there."

"Um . . . what happens when the magic runs out?"

"S'easy. The soil pops back inter it's proper place and the tunnel's gone."

There was a moment of silence, then Taggit cleared his throat.

"Better get movin'. I'll go first. Bogeyman at the back, right?"

Skerridge grinned. "In yer goes. Door'll bolt up again as soon as we pull it shut, and I'll 'ang on t' the key. Don' wan' anybody follerin' us, do we?"

Strood hissed irritably as he tried to bend his arm to raise it up past his chest to shoulder height. In a space barely big enough for him to draw breath it wasn't easy. He had finally slithered to a stop at a point where the tunnel bent sharply, blocking his downward plunge. On the plus side, he was no longer falling. On the minus side, he was wedged tight, deep in the foundations of the House with no obvious way of getting out. Except that his one remaining hand was still clasped around the throwing star.

At last he got the star to about shoulder height. He paused to check that he was facing the right way. He had worked out roughly where he was in relation to the down-house by mentally calculating his angle and speed of descent. Next he had inched painfully around so that he was pointing in the direction of the indoor garden, far below where his roses should be.

Because, many years ago when he was pleading for his life, Gan Mafig had told Strood a secret or two. Like where he had found his daughter's pendant, lying on the ground before a closed and locked door. She had left it, Gan Mafig said, by way of a farewell to her father. Something to remember her by. So naturally Strood had taken it away from him and thrown it into the attic with all his other belongings.

As to the Secret Way, Strood had ordered one of the workmen to put the statue of Mafig's daughter over the trapdoor (it was the last thing the workman had ever done), and the Way had stayed hidden ever since. After all, it wasn't like anyone could use it since the key had gone along with Seraphine. Unfortunately, Strood had a bad feeling that Ninevah Redstone would manage somehow.

Strood gripped the star firmly. There was no room to throw it, but if he could just get up a little forward motion . . .

He shoved his hand hard into the earth, hoping the movement would ignite the star. Nothing happened, but then the earth was only about an inch in front of him. Irritably he tried again and again, the action slowly burrowing out a hole into which he could thrust his hand. And then finally, it worked.

The star came alive.

Magical devices like staffs or wands relied on their sorcerer owners to keep them filled with power, but the throwing star was designed like a small generator. Once it was in action, it created its own power. It would never run dry and could never be earthed. Which was a good thing under the circumstances.

Spitting like a firework, the star began to spin. In the air it would have been white hot in seconds, but here there was resistance and it could only move slowly. It did move though, the sparks burning the soil as it turned, leaving behind a dry black grit that Strood could push through easily.

The star was meant to be thrown, not held on to, so it burned Strood's fingers as well. Not that it mattered. He was already growing some more.

37

Earthed

They set off down the steeply sloping tunnel. The air was thick and heavy and even though the golden light was all around them, Nin could feel the soil that should have been there.

"The magic is coming from those, look." Jonas pointed to a cone of tarnished copper on the right of their path, set on a stone plinth about knee-high. The golden light sprayed from its point like fire from a volcano. There was one every few yards, each decorated with the sign of the long-gone sorcerer who made them.

"They're prob'bly all connected," said Skerridge from the back, "linked like. If one goes out, the others'll follow. Light musta been brighter once, kep' the air clearer, like a proper passage. Been dimmin' over the years, no doubt. But don' worry, it'll be a few more decades afore they go out altogevver. What've yer stopped for?"

By now the tunnel had levelled out and the floor had changed from earth to uneven rock, though it was still soil all around them.

"We're right at the bottom, near the front of the

cliff," said Jonas. "Those," he nodded at two cones on the ground in front of them, "are the last."

The passage ended in an open space, the soil held at bay by two of the light-cones. But beyond those the golden light ended and there was only rock.

"The sea is just there, behind the cliff face, but how do we get out? The rock could be feet thick."

Taggit was studying the cones. In between them was a hole in the ground, full of gold-lit water.

"My guess? Beneath 'ere is an underwater cave that leads out through the cliff face into the sea. This 'ole goes through the floor inter the cave, see? The 'ole is 'eld open by a cone, like the passage, but I'm bettin' the tunnel underneath is natural."

Peering into the hole, Nin saw shadowy traces of the rocky floor, its echo still there, occupying the same space as the sea water lapping at her feet. There was a single light-cone keeping the rock at bay, set into a niche in the walls of the hole.

"Can yer all swim?" Skerridge asked.

"You've got to be kidding!"

"Nope. The Way goes on under water, right? So tha's where we gotta go too. We'll come out by the beach jus' below the cliffs."

"She was a good swimmer, Seraphine," said Taggit reflectively. "Everyone knew that."

"NO!" said Nin. "Jik can't go, so I won't."

Jik went to the edge of the hole and looked at it thoughtfully. He shrugged. "Wik kik gik bik."

"Ya looks kinda harder t' me," said Skerridge. "Gravelly like, specially wiv the new top layer. If we wraps yer in everyfin' we got, ya might jus' make it."

There was a long silence while Nin struggled with

the knowledge that to save Toby and Jonas she might have to lose Jik.

"Okay," said Jonas at last, "here's the plan. We wrap Jik up tight then strap him to Skerridge's back. Skerridge can move fast so he can get Jik out as quick as possible. Then Taggit can take Nin and Toby and I'll take Hss. I'm guessing you can't swim?"

"Nss."

Jonas took off his coat. "We can use this."

"This first, then the coat." Taggit dragged off his T-shirt. It was huge. Jonas laid it on the floor and Jik settled in the middle of it. It went round him three times.

"Okay?"

"Yik," said Jik, his voice muffled by the layers.

Nin pulled off her pinafore and turned her back on the others to fumble under her long skirt and drag off her petticoat. When they had added those to the T-shirt they wrapped the whole bundle in Jonas's coat. Then Hss webbed the lot into a silvery package.

"Looks like one o' them chrysalis things," said Skerridge. "Strap 'im on then." He stood still while they fastened Jik on with some more webbing.

As soon as they were done, Skerridge said. "See yer on the ovver side," and jumped.

"Look kid," said Taggit to Jonas. "You go next. That way, if you get into trouble I can pick you up on my way through."

Jonas nodded and Hss clambered on to his shoulders. A splash and they were gone.

Nin glanced uneasily over her shoulder. She could hear something weird, like a muffled hissing or spitting sound. Crackling perhaps, like a buried firework.

Taggit paused in the middle of settling Toby on his hip with the boy's arms around his chest. He looked at Nin. She looked at him.

"Better move it, kid," he said evenly, just as the earth behind her began to boil and crumble.

Something bright shot out of the soil, followed by a hand that grabbed it, dulling its brilliance, turning it back into a metal star even as it burned the flesh that held it. Strood tumbled into the hollow. For a moment Nin barely recognized him. He was in tatters. His clothes were rags and his skin not much better. The venom had seen to that. On his left side, some ribs were visible, he was missing an eye and one leg was doing its best to grow back, but it couldn't quite manage because the venom was still at work. It was mostly bone.

There was a moment of stunned silence.

Strood's remaining eye fixed Nin with a glittering stare she would never forget. He grinned with a mouth that was barely there anymore. Slowly he raised the throwing star.

"Got you," he said, and threw.

The star curved through the air toward Nin, its light fierce again, sending out sparks like hot knives. She screamed and leapt at Taggit who grabbed her around the waist with his free arm and swung her out of the way. She felt the star's heat as it flew past, sparks ripping her thick servant's skirt to rags and burning her legs.

It circled them, arching high, then swooping down again, burning a line in the air as it came for her.

I've killed us all, thought Nin, I should have run the other way, drawn the fire so that Taggit could get Toby to freedom.

With a roar, Taggit spun around. On his other side, Toby hung on grimly, arms and legs wound tight around the goblin's massive chest. The star swerved behind them, missing Nin again, its jagged sparks slashing the air and cutting a bloody rift across Taggit's back and Toby's wrist.

"Kill her! KILL HER," yelled Strood crazily. He was almost dancing on the spot, his eye bright with excitement.

Skimming the floor, the star swung upward. As it went, the rim of sparks brushed one of the light cones, knocking it from its plinth and sending it flying point first toward the earthy walls.

"Breathe!" yelled Taggit and jumped.

In that single moment, hanging half upside down, fingers knotted into Taggit's belt, Nin felt as if she could see every grain of soil in the walls, hear each separate breath as they all filled their lungs. The air in her chest was like hot fog and her blood hurtled through her veins like fire. She heard Strood howling with triumph, felt the star burning toward her back, and the air swirling past her face as they plunged toward the only way out.

But what filled her with terror was the sight of the cone flying through the air to bed itself in the wall, its tip digging into the soil.

The cone earthed. And Skerridge had been right, they were all linked. Power streamed down the passage draining from cone to cone, running out of the earthed tip like bathwater down a drain. Golden light drenched the air as the magic poured back into the Land.

Nin sent a last look at Strood before the water closed over them. She saw his face change, his glittering eye go cold and hard as it fixed on hers. And as they passed through the hole into the cavern below, she felt the last of the power drain out of the cones and the golden light switch off.

* * *

With the magic gone, the soil snapped back into its rightful place, suddenly very there and most definitely earthy. The star, caught halfway through the hole just as the rocky floor refilled it, came to a sudden halt. Silence descended. And darkness. Lots of darkness.

Buried alive, deep in the foundations of the House and packed so tightly in earth that he couldn't even blink, Arafin Strood pondered his next move.

There didn't seem to be many options.

The sea was shockingly cold. Taggit paused just long enough to rearrange Nin so that she was hanging on around his neck, leaving his arms free. As they swam away, Nin took one look up to see that the roof of the cave was unbroken, the hole gone as if it had never been. All she could feel was relief that the rock had only been a layer. Any thicker and they would have been encased in it the moment the magic earthed. Fossils forever locked in stone.

To reach the cavern entrance, deep below the sea, Taggit had to swim down before he could swim up. Holding her breath was beginning to be a struggle. As well as Jik, Nin was worried about Toby because he was so small and surely wouldn't be able to last as long. If he got panicky and struggled he'd slow them down and if he breathed in water, he'd drown. She couldn't bear to lose him all over again.

And what about Jonas? He wasn't a Fabulous, he couldn't swim as fast as Taggit and Skerridge. And he had been carrying Hss. What if they came across him now? Floating here, drowned in the cave?

Her lungs were at bursting point when Taggit curved steeply up, the darkness around them grew lighter, and a moment later they broke into the air and she could breathe again.

The first thing she heard was Toby coughing.

Taggit waded up to the beach, one arm around Nin and the other holding Toby. Just beyond the water's edge, he dropped them gently on to the sand. Jonas and Hss were already there, gathered around Skerridge. Jonas looked up as they arrived, a smile wiping the fear from his face. He came over.

Nin hugged him hard, then hurried to Toby. He seemed all right and gave her a smile, so she rumpled his wet hair and went to Skerridge. The bogeyman was breathing flames on to a mess of burnt cloth and silken thread on the ground. Another burst of firebreath and the wrappings were gone.

They stared in horror at what was left of Jik.

As tightly as they had wrapped him, water had found its way in. He had no arms and no legs and his body was eaten away on the surface as if by acid. His face and head were damaged, with half the back of his mud skull melted away.

"His eyes are still lit," said Taggit.

He was right, but Nin had never seen them so low, barely glowing at all. She dropped on to one knee and looked into the dull coal eyes.

"We can fix it." She looked up. "Everybody get mud. Don't be fussy about where from, we just need to be fast."

Overhead the sun shone and a warm breeze blew in waves topped by frothy horses. The clouds raced on white wings and over them towered the great cliff, silent and dark against the sky. They worked in silence, mixing sandy earth with seawater. Hss and Jonas prepared the mud, while Skerridge and Taggit pressed it into arms and legs. Toby handed scoops of it to Nin, who covered Jik's body and head with a fresh coat and filled out the missing part of his skull. As they gave him shape and form, she was sure the lights of his eyes grew brighter. When they were done they stood back and looked.

"I think we made him a bit bigger."

"Uh-huh. His legs are longer. And his arms. Still, won't do any harm."

Next they collected as much dead wood and twigs as they could. There wasn't much on the beach and Skerridge had to superspeed inland a couple of times. They built it all in a pyre around Jik and Skerridge set it alight.

Then they watched him burn.

"Well, Ninevah Redstone," said the bogeyman edging closer to the roaring fire, "it's been fun, what wiv everyfin'. Even the scary bits, an' there've been plenny enuff o' those. But yer got what yer was after in the end." Skerridge sniggered. "An' yer gave Mr. Strood a knockin' while yer was about it too! So what's next, huh?"

Nin looked at him and smiled. "We all go home," she said.

SHADOW SPELL

By Caro King

PART
1

THE NATURE
OF SPELLS

The Bellringer

Perched on the very edge of a ragged cliff, the Terrible House of Strood towered against the summer sky in a mass of dark stone walls and pointed roofs. Far below, waves crashed over the rocks at the foot of the cliff, surging into every crevice and filling the air with spray that hung like salty mist.

The roof of the Terrible House, with its jumble of chimney pots and towers, was familiar territory to Bogeyman Skerridge since his unauthorized entry into the building a couple of days ago, shortly after he had gone rogue and left Mr. Strood's service forever.

And now he was back again, scanning the rooftops with his sharp, red eyes until he spotted the creature he had come to find—the bellringer, whose job it was to keep watch for the exact moment when the edge of the sun slipped below the horizon, and then to ring the Evebell.

Skerridge grinned. It wasn't a nice grin. In a recent fit of remorse he had promised himself never to harm another living Quick, but this creature wasn't exactly living and was only slightly Quick so it didn't count. And anyway, he was only going to torture it a little.

The creature was not at its post in the weathered stone bell tower that rose high above the rooftops. Sundown was still an hour away, so instead it was perched on an outcrop of roof enjoying the view out to sea. Treading as quietly as only a bogeyman could, Skerridge headed that way. When he was right behind the unsuspecting bellringer he leaned close and said, "'Ullo."

The creature hooted through its beak and did a twisting leap that brought it around to face Skerridge, who grinned, taking care to show a lot of jagged teeth.

"Halloo," said the bellringer, quickly working out that there was no harm in being polite. He had been sitting with his knobbly back to the beach, looking out over the waves as they dashed themselves on the rocks below and trying to forget about the handful of Quick cluttering up the sea shore away in the distance behind him. The sudden arrival of a horrible, hairy, bony figure in tattered trousers and a fancy vest wasn't an improvement on his day.

Skerridge settled down on the roof next to the gargoyle. "I'm Bogeyman Skerridge," he said cheerfully. "Wha's yore name then?"

"Jibbit," said Jibbit nervously. Being the only gargoyle in the Terrible House, he had the roof all to himself apart from the pigeons. He wasn't used to people— Quick, Grimm, or Fabulous—and found them untidy and difficult. This one had a definite air of untidy and positively radiated difficult. With extras.

"Bet it's nice an' quiet up 'ere."

"Yes."

"Lotsa time to listen to all the goin's on, eh? Bet it's been an excitin' afternoon, what wiv all the escapin' and everyfin'! Ninevah Redstone breakin' outa the 'Ouse like that, givin' Mr. Strood the runaround jus' when 'e fort e'd won. Not t' mention rescuin' 'er bruvver an' gettin' 'er mem'ry pearl back."

"Y-yes."

"So, what I wanna know is what 'appened next? Fink you can tell me that?"

Jibbit swapped nervously from foot to foot and hunched his stubby wings. He had a bad feeling about what he was going to do, but his duty was clear.

"If you're Bogeyman Skerridge, then yoo've gone rogue," he said trying not to hoot too much. "And if yoo've gone rogue then I mustn't say anything . . ."

Skerridge shot out a hand and grabbed the bellringer so fast that Jibbit barely saw it happen. One second he was sitting on the roof, next he was dangling upside down over nothing.

"Fort ya might say that. Now, if ya wan' my advice I fink ya should tell me everyfin' ya know, cos if ya don' then I'll drop ya."

Jibbit glared at the bogeyman from underneath his own feet.

"I know," went on Skerridge cheerfully, "yer finkin' that no self-respectin' gargoyle is gonna be scared o' heights. And if ya gets broke ya can be stuck back t'gevver again, right?"

"Yes," snapped Jibbit.

"But isn't there somefin' yer fergettin'?" Skerridge leaned over to bring his head closer to the dangling gargoyle. "Look. Down," he whispered.

Jibbit glared for a second longer then turned his gaze downwards. It had a long way to go. The wall plunged away from him. Jibbit followed it with his eyes until he saw where it led. The ground—in this case rather rocky and involving a lot of breaking waves, but still the ground. Jibbit hooted in panic.

"Didn' fink o' that did ya?" Skerridge chuckled. "By my understandin' gargoyles don' like places what aren' 'igh, right? An' ya don' get much more not 'igh than the ground! So, 'ave we gotta deal?"

Jibbit squeaked pitifully.

Skerridge grinned. "Righto." He pulled his arm back and dropped Jibbit on the tiles, wrong side up.

"Thanks." Jibbit scuffled on to his paws.

"Fink nuffin' of it. Off ya go then."

Staring thoughtfully into space while he got his scattered nerves together, Jibbit settled back on the tiles, making sure he had a firm grip.

"That chimney pot at the back there," he said at last, "is the one to the furnace in Mister Strood's laboratory. I . . . um . . . happened to be sitting next to it just as Ninevah Redstone got away, so I climbed down the flue too see what all the racket was about. The furnace has got a glass door, so I could see right into the laboratory. Mister Strood wasn't pleased." Jibbit warmed to his story. "In fact he was so angry he tripped down a hole . . ."

"Eh?"

"A hole. In the ground. Left by the new Fabulous when he came up through the floor to rescue Ninevah Redstone. Yoo know, the mudman?"

"Yeah, Jik, I know 'im. Go on."

"Mr. Strood was already coming apart on account of the Faerie poison getting over him, and his leg broke off and he went down the hole, see?"

"I'm gettin' the picture," said Skerridge grimly.

"And then the earth fell in on top of him and he was buried, deep in the heart of the house, far below the foundations."

"So tha's what they've been doin' then," the bogeyman murmured, "diggin' 'im up. I wondered why they weren' pourin' outta the door looking fer us."

"The servants, the guards, everybody had to dig. It was taking a long time, so the Housekeeper sent for the bogeymen. There's no daylight in the House, so three of them came to dig even though it wasn't night." Jibbit looked at Skerridge thoughtfully. "They can do super-speed yoo know."

"Course I know, I am one! Still, superspeed diggin' ain't like superspeed runnin'. My guess is it'd still take 'em all afternoon." Skerridge blew out his cheeks feeling oddly anxious. "Carn' 'ave been fun, bein' stuck down there, buried alive in the earf fer 'ours. Bet 'e'll be in a good mood after that!"

Jibbit considered. "I wouldn't call it good," he said carefully.

"They've found 'im then?"

"Yes. He must have been digging upwards too, because suddenly the Housekeeper said . . . "

"STOP!" Strood's housekeeper, Mrs. Dunvice, held up a hand. Everyone stopped. "There," she said after a moment. "Can you hear that?"

Down in the earth, some way below the bottom of the deep well that used to be the laboratory floor, something stirred. It did it with a lot of cursing and unpleasant squashing sounds, but it definitely stirred. The cursing was garbled, as if it came from a mouth that was half missing and choked with dirt into the bargain. Most of the cursing involved unpleasant things happening to somebody called Ninevah Redstone.

Secretary Scribbins gulped. "It's him," he whispered hoarsely.

A murmur ran around the gathered workers. Some of them edged away. Even the bogeymen.

"Right," said Mrs. Dunvice decisively. "Everyone out, except for the bogeymen and guards Stanley and Floyd. NOW!"

Bodies tumbled towards the complicated scaffolding running up the sides of the well. The servants got there first, scampering up and out as quickly as they could. The goblin-Grimm guards followed.

When the others had gone, the werewolf-Grimm Housekeeper pointed at the three bogeymen who had been doing the tunnelling.

"Dig some more, but do it carefully, okay?"

One of the BMs, the one wearing a pair of sacking trousers and a bow tie, blew out a slow breath. None of them fancied having to dig out a furious Mr. Strood. But then on the other hand they would be HELPING him, so maybe he wouldn't want to have them fired. The BM straightened his bow tie and stepped forward, crouching down just about where the muttered curses were coming from. The others joined him.

Now they could hear scraping, scuffling noises, like a giant mole digging its way up towards the light. One of the BMs snarled and jumped back as a hand shot out of the earth. It was a slender hand half covered in scars that made it look like a bad patchwork glove. The other half was still mostly skinned.

"We found 'im!" yelled the one with the bow tie, unnecessarily.

The hand felt around and its owner hissed.

"Ged be oud you worthlesh bunch of idiotsh!"

Mrs. Dunvice leaned forward and held out a hand, then realized that Mr. Strood couldn't see it as his head was still below the surface, so she grabbed his wrist instead and pulled. The earth heaved like a small volcano as slowly his head rose from the ground to be followed by the rest of him. Or at least, what was left of the rest of him.

Mrs. Dunvice cleared her throat. "Welcome back, sir. We found your ear. You must have lost it on the way down."

Scribbins bobbed forward, holding out the ear wrapped in a napkin. Someone had cleaned the mud out of it.

"Don'd bother," hissed Strood, "I'b growd a dew one."

"And the arm, sir? And what about . . . "

"The leg? Yesh, yesh, id'sh growd back. Sho has by jaw. Almosht."

At last, Arafin Strood stood before them, wobbling badly and holding on to the rung of a nearby ladder for balance. Mrs. Dunvice thanked her lucky stars that she had sent all the others away. They could do without all the screaming and throwing up. Scribbins was bad enough.

Several hours had passed since the accident in the laboratory, in which a shattered bottle of faerie venom had showered Mr. Strood with flesh-dissolving poison. Even so, the venom was still at work eating him away and Strood was less than whole. His clothing had suffered too and he was left with only half a ragged pair of trousers and a badly crumpled shirt collar. Most of his ribs were exposed, giving an interesting view of the workings of a heart and lungs for anyone who liked biology. His lower jaw was trying hard to grow back in spite of the persistent venom, and one hand had just about managed to reform completely. Because it was new, it was free of the scars that covered the remaining parts of Strood like an insane road map. One leg was mostly bone. One eye socket was busily refilling itself. The other was full of a horribly gleaming eye. It was a good thing he was immortal, or he'd have been well past dead by now.

Mrs. Dunvice licked her lips nervously. Behind her, Scribbins whimpered, a pathetic sound that made the werewolf in Mrs. Dunvice want to bite him. The BMs gazed on, silent and wary.

Slowly, Mr. Strood raised his head. His eye was a pool of darkness in his horribly mangled face.

"Guard Shtanley and Guard Floyd," he said in a voice like cracked ice, "brig be one of by ped digersh and a human Quick. Any Quick will do. Then ged the bordal dishtillation bachine ready. There'sh work to be done."

"Yesh . . . I mean yes, sir!" Stanley turned smartly and hurried towards the scaffolding, half falling over himself in his eagerness to get away. Floyd followed hard on his heels.

Mr. Stood switched his attention to Scribbins. "A bath. Clothesh. Coffee. Five binutes or you're doast."

Scribbins gave a strangled squawk and ran for it. Finally Strood turned to the BMs and Mrs. Dunvice.

"Only three?"

"They were the only ones we could find, sir."

Strood considered for a moment. Then he leaned forward and smiled a smile that made even the werewolf part of her nervous.

"Id will do for now, we can always ged bore later. The girl may think she'sh shafe for the moment," he said his voice strengthening as his jaw finally achieved wholeness, "but nightfall ish on its way." His chilling one-eyed stare swivelled to the bogeymen, who bunched up together nervously. "So one of you is to bring me Ninevah Redshtone, EVEN IF THERE ARE WITNESSESS, understand?"

The BMs swapped a look. Snatching kids in front of witnesses was against the Bogeyman code, but then again . . .

"DO YOU UNDERSTAND?" Strood's eye gleamed feverishly. "I need bogeymen who can be adaptable . . . " He didn't need to finish the sentence. They knew what he meant. Adapt or be fired.

"Yessir!" One of them even saluted. "I'll do it, sir!'

Strood's eye fixed on him, the gleam incandescent. "Remember I want her alive. I've got plans for Ninevah Redstone and they don't involve an easy end."

He switched back to the other BMs. "And as for you two, well . . . "

There was a long pause while some old emotion struggled to show on Strood's ravaged face. Mrs. Dunvice shuddered. She could feel something coming and it was making her blood tingle.

"I've let their pathetic leftovers linger on all these years," Strood hissed at last, "but I know they'll try to help her. So now the time has come to deal with the last remains of the Seven Sorcerers. These are your orders . . . "

Jibbit stopped. "That's when I left."

Skerridge groaned. "Gimme a break! Couldn' yer 'ang on five more minutes!"

"There was a pigeon" said Jibbit coldly, "and I was hungry."

"Sheesh! Which bogeymen were they? D'ya know that?"

"They were just bogeymen. How should I know?"

"What were they wearin'?" said Skerridge patiently. "Ya can always tell a BM by what 'e's wearin', even when 'e's in anovver shape."

Jibbit huffed. "Erm. Torn red trousers and a rope belt. Ordinary trousers like yoo and a bow tie. And . . . and . . . a pair of blue dungarees with paint on."

"Bogeymen Rope, Pigwit and Bale, then. Fanks."

"No problem." Jibbit glanced anxiously over Skerridge's shoulder. Skerridge turned to look. Out across the sea the sun was drowning in a pool of light, sinking lower and lower towards the blue rim of the horizon. The bellringer began to fidget.

"I got tooo ring the bell in a moment," he said, hooting nervously. "It's my job and I got tooo dooo it. Every sundown I ring the Evebell so people know that the day is turning into night."

Although Skerridge chose to be different, as a general rule bad things didn't like the light and that included bogeymen. So even though the BMs would not leave the House straight away, he knew that Mr. Strood's instructions would be put into action the moment the sun dipped below the horizon. Which gave him little more than a few minutes to act.

Sending a glance back over the top of the House to where Ninevah Redstone was still sitting on the beach far below, unaware of what was about to happen to her, Skerridge did some fast thinking. He couldn't superspeed over the roof because superspeed generated a lot of heat and he would simply turn the tiles into blobs of molten lead, which would fall into the attic and do some fairly serious damage to the servants who lived there. But the bogeyman that Mr. Strood had sent to get Nin would be able to superspeed all right.

On the plus side, the girl wouldn't be alone. Taggit was still there, along with Jonas of course. Toby didn't count because he was too small to do anything anyway. And although it was taking a while because he'd been so badly damaged, hopefully the mudman would be done baking soon.

While the bogeyman worked things out, Jibbit was inching towards the bell tower. Just as the edge of the sun touched the dark curve of the horizon he made a break for it, skittering away over the tiles. Skerridge jumped, landing just in front of the fleeing gargoyle, who darted left to go around him.

"No ya don't," said Skerridge. He picked the bell-ringer up and held him by his back legs, upside down and thrashing wildly.

"I got tooo! I got tooo! IT'S MY JOB!" hooted Jibbit.

"Not today it ain't," said Skerridge. "See, I need to send a message and I'm bettin' that the goblin or the boy will be bright enough, even if the kid don' work it out."

As the sun began to slip below the edge of the world, the darkening sky was filled with the bellringer's howl of anguish.